THINGS SAID ABOUT
I HATE THE INTERNET

The brilliant author of *ATTA* returns with his most audacious and stunning project, a novel purposely "anti-literary," with no more pretensions to quality than your typical Wikipedia article or Facebook update. It is a novel of San Francisco, once a vibrant city, a cauldron for social change, but now a sugarcoated sepulcher that, though beautiful still, has been hollowed out from within by the intersticed forces of technology, oligarchy, and a greed protected from failure by the Internet-induced vapidity of those who used to read, before we all started talking about Miley and Beyoncé. As one by one everyone of moral value gets evicted from their homes—like clay pigeons exploding at a carnival sideshow—the city attains the Satanic emptiness forecast by Fritz Leiber in his 1977 chiller *Our Lady of Darkness*. Jarett Kobek is profane, hilarious, biting, inventive, outrageous; he's not afraid to mine the dumbest Buzzfeed compilation of "35 hilarious facts," the better to cast a grim spotlight on the end of culture and nature as we used to think we knew them.

> Kevin Killian, LAMBA Literary Award Winner, author of
> *Shy*, *Impossible Princess* and over 2,500 reviews on Amazon.com

I HATE THE INTERNET is thought provoking—and so funny! I can't remember the last book I read that made me laugh this much. Kobek has a gift for seeing things from a different angle and for uncovering lies and invisible structures of society, and he does it in a playful, anarchistic and quirky way. The rows of association in this book—Kobek's deconstructing voice—will keep you entertained and baffled throughout the reading.

> Dorthe Nors, author of *Karate Chop*

A riproaring, biting, form-follows-function burlesque of the digital age that click-meanders its way like the ADHD freaks we're all becoming while offering up compelling narrative lines that kept me clicking faster and faster. Read this book. Now.

Dodie Bellamy, author of *The Letters of Mina Harker*, *Cunt Norton*, and *When the Sick Rule the World*

If this book sells more than eleven and half copies, I will be shocked. Inshallah, book will sell 50,000 copies at least. Sometimes a hungry chicken dreams herself in a barley barn. What can I do?

The Author's Father

THINGS SAID ABOUT THE AUTHOR'S EARLIER WORK

"Kobek's writing continues to impress."

Chris Kraus, author of *I Love Dick*

"Until recently, I would have said that the best novel of 9/11 that no one was writing about was Jess Walter's *The Zero* (2006). However, in light of some recent work... I believe this dubious distinction now falls to Jarett Kobek's *ATTA*."

John N. Duvall, "Representing the Enemy Other" in *Narrating 9/11: Fantasies of State, Security, and Terrorism*

"Highly Absorbing."

Keith Miller, *Times Literary Supplement*

i hate the internet.

PUBLISHED BY WE HEARD YOU LIKE BOOKS
A Division of U2603 LLC
5419 Hollywood Blvd, Ste C-231 Los Angeles CA 90027

http://weheardyoulikebooks.com/

Joshua Mast
Publisher

Brandon Creighton
Co-Publisher

Distributed by SCB Distributors

ISBN: 978-0-9964218-0-5
Copyright © 2016 by Jarett Kobek

Illustration "Time Magazine" courtesy of Sarina Rahman

February 2016

First Edition

10 9 8 7 6 5 4 3 2 1

I HATE THE INTERNET

A USEFUL NOVEL

JARETT KOBEK

trigger warning:

Capitalism, the awful stench of men, historical anach-
ronisms, death threats, violence, human bondage, faddish
popular culture, despair, unrestrained mockery of the rich,
threats of sexual violation, weak iterations of Epicurean
thought, the comic book industry, the death of intellectual-
ism, being a woman in a society that hates women, populism,
an appalling double entedre, the sex life of Thomas Jefferson, genocide, celebrity, the Objectivist philosophy of Ayn
Rand, discussions of race, Science Fiction, anarchism with
a weakness for democracy, the people who go to California
to die, millennial posturing, 276 pages of mansplaining,
Neo-Hellenic Paganism, interracial marriage, elaborately
named hippies practicing animal cruelty on goats, unjust
wars in the Middle East, 9/11, seeing the Facebook profile
of someone you knew when you were young and believed
that everyone would lead rewarding lives.

chapter one

Long after she had committed the only unforgivable sin of the Twenty-First Century, someone on the Internet sent Adeline a message.

The message read: "Dear slut, I hope that you are gang-raped by syphilis infected illegal aliens."

The Internet was a wonderful invention. It was a computer network which people used to remind other people that they were awful pieces of shit.

ADELINE RECEIVED THIS MESSAGE because she had committed the only unforgivable sin of the early Twenty-First Century. But before she could arrive at that really big mistake, she had to make several smaller ones.

Some of her other mistakes: (1) She was a woman in a culture that hated women. (2) She'd become kind of famous. (3) She'd expressed unpopular opinions.

Being a kind of famous woman who expressed unpopular opinions in a culture that hated women was in itself a serious mistake, but neither it nor its constituent parts were the big one.

The big one was something else.

THE ABOVE OFFERS only one possible interpretation of the message, with both spelling and grammar adjusted for clarity. The original read: "Drp slut... hope u get gang rape.... bi bunch, uv siphilis elegial alines..........."

It is possible that "elegial alines" was not referencing the citizens of foreign countries who arrive in America by methods other than state-approved visas and green cards.

It is also possible that "drp slut" was something other than a general salutation followed by one of the hundreds of derogatory English terms for women. A "drp slut" could be any number of things.

"Drp" itself is somewhat tricky, as it lacks vowels. It might be short for *derp,* a common Internet neologism denoting stupidity. And while "drp" is rendered as *dear* it could as easily be *deep.*

"Slut" is one of the hundreds of derogatory English terms for women. These terms attach importance to the number of a woman's sexual partners. There are no equivalent terms for men, which is some straight up bullshit.

"SLUT" IS ALSO the Danish word for *end.*

When stores in Denmark approached the final days of a merchandise sale, the proprietors of these stores tended to put up signs announcing a *slutspurt.*

Slutspurt was a colloquialism which meant *end of the sale. Slutspurts* were often embarrassing for Danes who hosted native English speakers.

It was possible that whoever sent Adeline the message was fluent in both English and Danish. It was possible their conjunction of the Danish word for *end* and "drp" was an erudite multilingual gambit, referencing the deep end of something. Perhaps a swimming pool.

On the other hand, the message was sent by someone on the Internet. They were probably just another dumb asshole who hated women.

chapter two

In the 1990s, when Adeline was in her early twenties and just out of college, she and her friend Jeremy Winterbloss started working together on a comic book called *Trill*. It was published in 32 page monthly pamphlets, with the art in black-and-white.

Adeline drew the pictures. Jeremy Winterbloss wrote the words.

Trill followed the story of an anthropomorphic cat named Felix Trill as he moved his way through a quasi-medieval world, discovering haunting vistas while battling other anthropomorphic animals.

Most of *Trill* was about a series of wars between anthropomorphic cats and anthropomorphic dogs. This changed with issue #50, when both sides put aside their differences and realized that they had a mutual enemy: hairless apes with a tendency towards fervent monotheism.

This shift in focus followed several months of Jeremy ingesting a prodigious number of psychedelic drugs.

During one acid trip, Jeremy had a vision of Felix Trill. The creation talked to its creator. Due to Jeremy's misfiring neurochemistry, Felix Trill spoke with the voice of an old burnout.

"Hey man," said Felix Trill to Jeremy, "You got it all mixed-up. The way you write me. It's a real bummer. Because me and the dogs and all the other animals, we're only fingers dipping below the surface of the ocean, and you're a fish, deep in the hazy water, and you know the thing about fish, man, fish are full of hang-ups. You're so uptight that all you see is the divided fingers. That's your hassle, not ours. None of us can get with that trip. Your limited perception, man, is making you see five separate entities. You can't see that me and the dogs and the other animals are all connected, we're all part of the same hand. Five fingers, one hand. The hand is the important thing, brother. You gotta get more cosmic. Don't be so heavy on the details. Keep it cool, friend."

Adeline and Jeremy published seventy-five issues of *Trill* before changes in the market made the project unprofitable.

Issue #75 appeared in 1999.

JEREMY EARNED A DECENT LIVING off *Trill*. Adeline lived off the money too, but she didn't have the same needs as Jeremy. Adeline's family was rich.

She was from Pasadena, California. She grew up there during the 1970s and 1980s.

Her father had been an oral surgeon who performed a wide range of dental procedures on some very famous people.

The heart of Adeline's father had exploded a few hours after he put a cap on the lower left incisor of two-time Academy Award winner Jason Robards.

Jason Robards was one of those character actors who earns respect and accolades during his working life and is forgotten as soon as he dies. He won his Academy Awards in 1977 and 1978.

The first Academy Award was for playing Ben Bradlee, the editor of the *Washington Post,* in a film called *All the President's Men.* The second Academy Award was for playing Dashiell Hammett, author of *The Glass Key* and *The Maltese Falcon,* in a film called *Julia.*

Both movies were based on books in which the respective authors presented self-aggrandized visions of themselves confronting the systemic evil of governments.

Both movies were better than the books on which they were based. Almost all movies are better than books. Most books are quite bad.

Like this one.

This is a bad novel.

ADELINE'S FATHER LEFT HIS MONEY to Adeline's mother, who turned out to be better at business than Adeline's father.

Adeline's mother was named Suzanne. Suzanne made sure that both Adeline and Adeline's sister, Dahlia, would never want for nothing.

Suzanne was a failed actress who met Adeline's father while waiting tables at a coffee shop on Wilshire Boulevard. She'd been an extra in several episodes of *Gidget,* a television show about a teenaged girl who enjoys surfing.

Suzanne was an alcoholic.

chapter three

Back in the early 1990s, when they decided to publish *Trill*, both Adeline and Jeremy Winterbloss recognized that their project suffered from two structural disadvantages.

STRUCTURAL DISADVANTAGE #1: the principle products of the comic book industry were 32-page monthly pamphlets containing drawings of gargantuan breasted women. These breasts resembled over-inflated volleyballs, much like the ones spiked and served by the cast of *Gidget*.

This focus on gargantuan breasts meant that most of the industry's output was subtle pornography for the mentally backwards.

There'd been a few successful books that featured talking animals, but Jeremy could think of only one semi-successful comic book about an anthropomorphic cat. That book was *"Omaha" The Cat Dancer*.

Omaha was created by Reed Waller and Kate Worley. Omaha was a stripper in an urban milieu. Being a cat dancer got Omaha into all kinds of trouble.

The pornography in *"Omaha"* was not subtle. Most issues depicted Omaha having sex with other anthropomorphic animals of many species and genders.

Jeremy showed Adeline a few issues of *"Omaha" The Cat Dancer*. Adeline thought it strange that Omaha, a cat, had a dense patch of hair on her mons pubis. But that was comics.

STRUCTURAL DISADVANTAGE #2: as with any business, the comics industry had its own culture, and that culture was soaked in sexism and racism like a Christmas ham marinating in syrup and ginger.

Jeremy had experienced the sexism and racism first hand, having worked for several years in the late 1980s as an intern at Marvel Comics.

JEREMY WINTERBLOSS was an African-American man, which meant that some of his ancestors were brought to the United States in bondage and put to work in the service of his other ancestors. This second group of ancestors owned the first group.

Many of Jeremy's ancestors were part of the social construct called the White race, and they raped many of Jeremy's other ancestors, the ones who were owned and were part of the social construct called the Black Race, whose members were also known as Coloreds or Negroes or Nigras or any of hundreds of other derogatory words.

There were not many derogatory words for members of the social construct called the White race. The ones that did exist were sort of useless and packed almost no offensive punch.

These were: *honkey, cracker, hillbilly, redneck, peckerwood.*

Peckerwood had some possibilities. The others were pathetic.

SOMETIMES WHEN JEREMY'S MALE ANCESTORS raped Jeremy's female ancestors, the underlying biology would produce babies. When these babies were born, they were owned by their fathers or their fathers' families.

You could rape your property and make new property and that new property would earn you more money. It was a nice time to own people. It was a bad time to be owned.

THE SOCIAL CONSTRUCTION of the White race was pseudoscience revolving around the misapprehension that inessential physical features represented biological distinctions amongst members of the human species.

Of all the inessential features that led to the social construction of the White race, differences in skin pigmentation were the most prominent.

There was a widely held belief amongst members of the White race that their skin was uncolored and thus *White*. In fact, members of the White race were an unfortunate pink somewhere around the shade of a newborn piglet.

According to certain people who self-described as *People of Color*, which was a remarkably offensive and unexamined phrase, and members of the White Race, *Colored* skin was the visual byproduct of eumelanin's presence in the stratum basale layer of the epidermis.

Eumelanin was the product of melanocytes, which are cells located alongside the basal cells in the stratum basale layer of the epidermis. Under histopathologic examination, eumelanin looked a little like a dried mustard stain.

Most members of the White race were so accustomed to their piglet pink that they couldn't see their own pink. To them, their piglet pink was invisible as the genocides committed by their forefathers.

An entire social order was built around the inability to see what was right in front of, and on, their faces. An entire social hierarchy was built around mustards stains in the epidermis.

This is one of several reasons why many people considered the human species to be a bunch of dumb assholes.

OF COURSE, the social hierarchy's racial component was a generalized dodge to avoid talking about the only real factor in establishing order. Which is to say *money*.

According to many first year graduate students in economics, *money* was a general agreement amongst a group of people that certain tangibles or intangibles represent the ordering of value.

In fact, *money* was the unit by which people measured humiliation.

What would you do for a dollar?

What would you do for ten dollars?

What would you do for a million dollars?

What would you do for a billion dollars?

ADELINE DIDN'T HAVE EUMELANIN in the basal cell layer of her epidermis and was thus a member of the White race.

This offered her a great deal of social prestige, particularly as she was from a rich family. But she was a woman. Being a woman detracted from that social prestige.

All women in America, even the rich White women, took a ton of shit. They were doomed if they did and doomed if they didn't.

Men had spent millennia treating women like crap. One theory as to the origins of this social ordering suggested that women's lack of upper body strength made them worse at ploughing fields and swinging swords.

Ploughed fields produced food.

Swung swords produced dead humans.

Most societies, being dominated by men, put premium value on eating and killing. This emphasis on strength over intelligence neatly avoided the fact that women are smarter than men.

Women's lack of upper body strength was only one explanation of the social ordering. There were hundreds of ideas for why women were treated like crap but very few practical solutions.

A LITTLE BIT before Adeline made her unforgivable mistake, a billionaire named Sheryl Sandberg wrote a book called *Lean In: Women, Work, and the Will to Lead*. Sheryl Sandberg didn't have much eumelanin in the basale stratum of her epidermis.

In her book, Sheryl Sandberg proposed that women who weren't billionaires could stop being treated like crap by men in the workplace if only they smiled more and worked harder and acted more like the men who treated them like crap.

Billionaires were always giving advice to people who weren't billionaires about how to become billionaires.

It was almost always intolerable bullshit.

SANDBERG BECAME A BILLIONAIRE by working for a company named Facebook.

Facebook made its money through an Internet web and mobile platform which advertised cellphones, feminine hygiene products and breakfast cereals.

This web and mobile platform was also a place where hundreds of millions of people offered up too much information about their personal lives.

Facebook was invented by Mark Zuckerberg, who didn't have much eumelanin in the basale stratum of his epidermis.

What is your gender? asked Facebook.
What is your relationship status? asked Facebook.
What is your current city? asked Facebook.
What is your name? asked Facebook.
What are your favorite movies? asked Facebook.
What is your favorite music? asked Facebook.
What are your favorite books? asked Facebook.

ADELINE'S FRIEND, the writer J. Karacehennem, whose last name was Turkish for *Black Hell,* had read an essay called "Generation Why?" by Zadie Smith, a British writer with a lot of eumelanin in the basale stratum of her epidermis. Zadie Smith's essay pointed out that the questions Facebook asked of its users appeared to have been written by a twelve year old.

But these questions weren't written by a twelve year old. They were written by Mark Zuckerberg.

Mark Zuckerberg was a billionaire. Mark Zuckerberg was such a billionaire that he was the boss of other billionaires. He was Sheryl Sandberg's boss.

J. Karacehennem thought that he knew something about Facebook that Zadie Smith, in her decency, hadn't imagined.

"The thing is," said J. Karacehennem, whose last name was Turkish for *Black Hell,* "that we've spent like, what, two or three hundred years wrestling with existentialism, which really is just a way of asking, *Why are we on this planet? Why are people here? Why do we lead our pointless lives?* All the best philosophical and novelistic minds have tried to answer these questions and all the best philosophical and novelistic minds have failed to produce a working answer. Facebook is amazing because finally we understand why we have hometowns and why we get into relationships and why we eat our stupid dinners and why we have names and why we own idiotic cars and why we try to impress our friends. Why are we here, why do we do all of these things? At last we can offer a solution. We are on Earth to make Mark Zuckerberg and Sheryl Sandberg richer. There is an actual, measurable point to our striving. I guess what I'm saying, really, is that there's always hope."

chapter four

Having worked in the belly of the beast, Jeremy Winterbloss understood the comic industry's traditions of racism and sexism.

Any product not delivered by White men would receive less orders than products offered by White men. Which meant less sales, which meant a smaller audience, which meant less money.

Many people in the comics industry remembered Jeremy. He stood out. Many people in the comic industry remembered the eumelanin in his basal cell layer.

Back in the early 1990s, Jeremy worried that if he and Adeline published *Trill* under their own names, then it would be seen as a Black book drawn by a White woman.

Which meant less sales, which meant a smaller audience, which meant less money.

Jeremy wanted to be recognized for his contribution but Jeremy also wanted to make money. He wanted to do meaningful work and be paid for it.

In this, he was different than Sheryl Sandberg. He had no interest in advertising baby powder and asking people about their favorite music.

JEREMY DEVISED AN IMPERFECT SOLUTION to the issues of racism and sexism in the comic book industry. He suggested that both he and Adeline adopt pseudonyms.

The adoption of pseudonyms was another of the comic industry's time honored traditions. Jack Kirby, who had no eumelanin in the basale stratum of his epidermis and pretty much created the comic book industry, was born Jacob Kurtzberg. He chose his pseudonym to sound less Jewish.

Adeline, who was then suffering from many strange habits including an affected Transatlantic accent and a terminal disinterest in making a statement, agreed with Jeremy's suggestion.

"Darling," she asked, "won't it be simply frightful to pretend that we're other people?"

Jeremy went with J.W. Bloss. Adeline picked the somewhat more baroque M. Abrahamovic Petrovitch.

MONTHLY PUBLICATION of *Trill* ceased in 1999. A series of unforeseen events, including the collapse of several distributors, made it very difficult for comics creators to self-publish their own work. The money just wasn't there.

TRILL CEASED PUBLICATION at the exact moment when the greater English speaking world became interested in trade paperback collections of comic books.

Sometimes these collections were called *graphic novels*.

This was a misnomer. The trade paperbacks were not novels and very rarely contained any graphic material.

An example of an actual graphic novel was *Les 120 journées de Sodome*, an Eighteenth Century book written in prison by an obese French nobleman without any eumelanin in the basale stratum of his epidermis.

Like most actual graphic novels, it succeeded wonderfully at being graphic but failed miserably as a novel. It was a book about people in a castle who fuck each other to death while throwing their own shit around like a bunch of caged monkeys.

By contrast, the *graphic novels* of the comic book industry were mostly Marvel or DC getting new money for old rope by binding together reprints of ancient material.

Typically these *graphic novels* contained nothing more than images of volleyball sized breasts and Spider-Man smashing Doctor Octopus through a brick wall while saying, "Ol' sourpus sure made a mistake messing with his friendly neighborhood webhead!"

THE TRADE PAPERBACK EDITIONS of *Trill* continued to sell after the final monthly pamphlet was printed. Each year, the trade paperbacks sold a little more than the year before.

Then two things happened in the mid-2000s: (1) On the basis of their success with *Bone*, a book by a guy named Jeff Smith who didn't have any eumelanin in the basale strata of his epidermis, Scholastic offered to print color trade paperbacks of *Trill*, granting access to the voracious children's and education markets. (2) Don Murphy, a quarrelsome producer of Hollywood films without any eumelanin in the basale stratum of his epidermis, optioned the cinematic rights to *Trill*.

UNLIKE MANY INTELLECTUAL PROPERTIES that are optioned by Hollywood producers, *Trill* was actually financed and turned into a film.

Half of the money came from a Hollywood studio. The rest was raised from private investors, including a very sizeable chunk of change via the Saudi media group Fear and Respect Holdings Ltd.

Fear and Respect was run by His Royal Highness Mamduh bin Fatih bin Muhammad bin Abdulaziz al Saud, who had a small amount of eumelanin in the basale stratum of his epidermis. The principle purpose of Fear and Respect was to invest in new media companies and old media opportunities.

HRH Mamduh bin Fatih bin Muhammad bin Abdulaziz al Saud liked film, and he could see the future. He could see that intellectual properties derived from the comic book industry were on the verge of providing very lucrative revenue streams.

Trill was his first foray into the world of cinema.

He had high hopes.

ADELINE AND JEREMY were not involved in the filmmaking process, but gave their tacit support by saying nothing against the project. They did not attend the film's premiere.

The film was computer animated, which meant scores of underpaid technicians in Asian countries spent countless hours working on devices assembled by even lower paid workers in other Asian countries to produce crude replicas of artwork that had cost Adeline about $54 a month in materials.

When the film was released in 2007, it did what Adeline considered a ridiculous amount of business: about $25,000,000.

This was $25,000,000 less than its production budget, which did not include the tens of millions more dollars spent on marketing.

Trill was a flop.

HRH Mamduh bin Fatih bin Muhammad bin Abdulaziz al Saud was sad.

But the publicity was great for sales of the trade paperbacks.

NEITHER ADELINE NOR JEREMY had wanted their identities revealed, but another producer of *Trill,* a man named Joel Silver, let the truth slip during a press conference.

Joel Silver, who didn't have any eumelanin in the basale stratum of his epidermis, later said it was a mistake.

Adeline assumed it was intentional.

She'd spent most of her early life in Los Angeles. She always assumed the worst about Hollywood people. Anything to increase tracking.

THE REVEAL OF M. ABRAHAMOVIC PETROVITCH as a woman belonging to the social construct of the White race was treated as the more interesting story than that of Jeremy Winterbloss as a man belonging to the social construct of the Black race.

Nearly ten years after finishing the last issue of *Trill,* Adeline was in demand. For her self, as her self. The details of her life became fodder for public discourse.

People were fascinated that she had lived through the grimy old East Village. People were interested that her best friend, Baby, was a gay writer of Science Fiction and the author of *Annie Zero*. People wanted to know how Adeline had kept the secret for so many years. People were fascinated by a woman working in genre comics and doing it so well. People were interested that she lived in San Francisco and wanted her opinions about the tech industry and the dotcom boom of the late 1990s.

Basically, she got kind of famous.

chapter five

Despite never appearing as a character within its pages, Jack Kirby is the central personage of this novel. He died in 1994. He was born in 1917.

Jack Kirby is the central personage of this novel because he was the individual most screwed by the American comic book industry, and the American comic book industry is the perfect distillation of all the corrupt and venal behavior inherent in unregulated capitalism.

The business practices of the American comic book industry have colonized Twenty-First Century life. They are the tune to which we all dance.

The Internet, and the multinational conglomerates which rule it, have reduced everyone to the worst possible fate. We have become nothing more than comic book artists, churning out content for enormous monoliths that refuse to pay us the value of our work.

So we might as well revere the man who was screwed first and screwed hardest.

JACK KIRBY WAS BORN Jacob Kurtzberg in 1917 at 147 Essex Street on the Lower East Side of Manhattan. He was a New York Jew at a time when being a Jew in America was a ticket to suspicion and abuse.

He was a creative genius working in a medium that disrespected the intelligence of its readers. He was a creative genius working in a medium that hid objectionable words behind strings of symbols like $#!+ and @$$.

He smoked cigars and he spoke in a Noo Yawk accent. He never graduated high school. He fought in World War Two. He was a Jew who wrote and drew comics about kicking the shit out of Nazis and then went to Germany and kicked the shit out of Nazis.

WHENEVER THERE WAS AN IMPORTANT MOMENT in American comic books, Jack Kirby was present. Always creating, always making new things, always with the new ideas.

He was one of the *lamed vavniks,* one of the thirty-six righteous who kept the world running.

Here is a list of some characters that he either created or co-created: Captain America, the Fantastic Four, the original X-Men, the Avengers, Thor, Loki, Iron Man, the Incredible Hulk, Doctor Doom, Galactus, Ant-Man, the Black Panther, Nick Fury, The Demon, Kamandi, Klarion the Witch Boy, OMAC, the New Gods, M.O.D.O.K, the Eternals, the Inhumans, the Forever People, the Newsboy Legion.

Here is a list of the above characters that he owned:

BY THE TIME that Adeline made her unforgivable mistake, Marvel Comics had transformed itself into Marvel Entertainment, which was a film production company. The films that Marvel produced were based on the comic books which it had published in earlier decades.

Marvel had released the following films: *Iron Man, The Incredible Hulk, Iron Man 2, Captain America: The First Avenger, Thor, The Avengers, Iron Man 3.* All of these films were based on intellectual property created by Jack Kirby.

Marvel had done $5,289,863,327 worth of box office business with films based on intellectual properties created by Jack Kirby. This does not include merchandizing or DVD/Blu-Ray sales.

This was more money than the respective annual GDPs of fifty countries.

BEFORE MARVEL TRANSFORMED itself into a producer of films, the company was run by individuals of dubious business acumen.

These individuals had licensed away the media exploitation rights to many of Marvel's best known intellectual properties, including the Fantastic Four and the X-Men, both of which were co-created by Jack Kirby.

The creation of the X-Men was complicated, but Kirby was there with the original concept. He did everything on the Fantastic Four.

By the time that Adeline committed the only unforgivable sin of the Twenty-First Century, the Fantastic Four and X-Men had been exploited in the production of eight films, seven of which were based on the work of Jack Kirby. These seven films had taken in $2,136,662,237 at the box office.

Combined with Marvel's take of $5,289,863,327, this totaled out to $7,426,525,564 of business derived from media properties that Jack Kirby had either created or co-created.

JACK KIRBY had worked-for-hire, when the prospect of billion dollar films of any kind, let alone those starring superheroes, was inconceivable.

Work-for-hire was one of the many bad deals that businesses offered to creative people. The terms of work-for-hire were: we pay you enough to eat and we keep everything you create.

So Jack Kirby had worked-for-hire and created a plethora of intellectual property which developed immense value while he himself held no legal ownership over that property.

He spent the last years of his life fighting with Marvel over his intellectual property and the return of his physical artwork. He went to his grave with no stake in his life's work.

He got screwed.

JACK KIRBY is also the central personage of this novel because this is not a *good novel*. This is a seriously mixed-up book with a central personage who never appears. The plot, like life, resolves into nothing and features emotional suffering without meaning.

The writer of this novel gave up trying to write *good novels* when he realized that the *good novel*, as an idea, was created by the Central Intelligence Agency.

This is not a joke. This is true. This is church.

The CIA funded the *Paris Review*. The CIA funded the Iowa Writer's Workshop. The CIA engineered the 1958 Nobel Prize in Literature.

A person would be hard pressed to find three other institutions with more influence over the development of the *good novel* and *literary fiction.*

Literary fiction was a term used by the upper classes to suggest books which paired pointless sex with ruminations on the nature of mortgages were of greater merit than books which paired pointless sex with guns and violence.

The CIA funded *literary fiction* because people at the CIA believed that American literature was excellent propaganda and would help fight the Russians. People at the CIA believed that *literary fiction* would celebrate the delights of a middle class existence produced by American dynamism.

The people who took the CIA's money were happy to help out.

The result was sixty years of *good novels* about the upper middle class and their sexual affairs.

Generally speaking, these *good novels* didn't involve characters with much eumelanin in the basale strata of their epidermises.

A SIDE EFFECT of the CIA's funding of the *good novel* was to ensure that American literature was hopeless at addressing the pace of technological innovation. This is because the defining quality of any *good novel* was the limit of its author's imagination.

And the authors of *good novels* were terminal bores. The writers of *literary fiction* were the people who'd come to your party and pass out in your bathtub and then spend years dining out on the tale.

For more than half of a century, American writers of *good novels* had missed the only important story in American life. They had missed the evolving world, the world of hidden persuaders, of the developing communications landscape, of mass tourism, of the vast conformist suburbs dominated by television.

And so too had they missed the full import of the last fifteen years. The symbolism sustaining the aesthetic and intellectual pursuits of the Twentieth

Century was now meaningless. It was empty air. It was gone, vacant, missing, collapsed beneath the weight of two towers.

So much of the dialogue around literature and writing had become about the embrace of *human rights*, but a massive shift had happened and no one ever mentioned it.

For thousands of years, people had written with a wide variety of materials. Some used pens. Some used pencils. Some used typewriters. Some used papyrus. Some used foolscap.

Now writers used computers, which were the byproducts of global capitalism's uncanny ability to turn the surplus population into perpetual servants. All of the world's computers were built by slaves in China.

The business of American literature had become the business of exploiting slave labor. An example of this is the book that you are reading.

This bad novel, which is a morality lesson about the Internet, was written on a computer. You are suffering the moral outrage of a hypocritical writer who has profited from the spoils of slavery.

THESE LACUNAE meant that American writers were hopeless at writing about the Internet, which was nothing but the intellectual feudalism produced by technological innovation arriving in the disguise of culture.

By the time it became clear that the Internet was the dominant story of Twenty-First Century life, the survival strategy of many writers was to use the computer network as a marketing device.

In a curious approach for people whose intellectual and financial lives depended on the use of words and grammar, the primary Internet marketing technique of these writers involved the pretense that they, the writers, possessed worse literacy skills than a fifth grader.

"Luv u!" wrote the writers.

"Who r ppl?" wrote the writers.

"C u l8r bb!" wrote the writers.

The thought, anyway, was that these misspellings would help to sell books about tea time affairs in New York State.

OF COURSE, the *good novel* was a historical artifact and all the world's misspellings couldn't trick citizens of the future into caring about the sexual rutting of the useless.

The citizens of the future didn't care about the empty symbolism of the previous century. They had rejected the *good novel* and its false vision of American complexity. The citizens of the future had adopted the pop sizzle of the comic book and Science Fiction.

They wanted to read about the sexual rutting of supranatural creatures like werewolves, succubi, vampires, boy wizards, mermaids, minotaurs, centaurs, witches, fairies, jinn, ghosts, zombies, angels, incubi, hacktivists, genetically modified teenagers and ultrawealthy oligarchs.

There was only one solution if you were a writer who wanted to write about the Internet and you didn't want to write a *good novel,* and you weren't interested in pretending that your facility with language was worse than that of a fifth grader, and you didn't care about the sexual rutting of supernatural creatures like werewolves, succubi, vampires, boy wizards, mermaids, minotaurs, centaurs, witches, fairies, jinn, ghosts, zombies, angels, incubi, hacktivists, genetically modified teenagers and ultrawealthy oligarchs.

The only solution to the Internet was to write bad novels with central personages who do not appear.

The only solution was to write bad novels that mimicked the computer network in its obsessions with junk media.

The only solution was to write bad novels that mimicked the computer network in its irrelevant and jagged presentation of content.

chapter six

Adeline lived in San Francisco. San Francisco had two distinctions: (1) It was the most beautiful city in America. (2) It was filled with the most annoying people in America.

It had always been like this, from the beginning.

The merit of any moment in San Francisco could be measured by a simple question: was the beauty of the city outweighing its annoying citizens?

ADELINE HAD MOVED to San Francisco in 1996, which was a defining moment in the city's history. 1996 was not defined by Adeline's arrival.

1996 was defined by being the year during which the Internet economy exploded into the collective consciousness.

San Francisco had spent much of the Twentieth Century in decline, which meant that it was a bad place for people who liked doing business but a wonderful place for people who were terrible at making money.

San Francisco had been defined by the culture of people who were terrible at making money. It had become a haven for the misfits of America, most of who were living in the city's fabulous old houses.

When the Internet economy exploded into the collective consciousness, these people proved that resisting social change was the only thing at which they were less adept than earning money.

AFTER THE FILM VERSION of *Trill* was released in the late '00s and Adeline got kind of famous, she began attending an increased number of social events around San Francisco. Almost all of these events were associated with the arts and publishing.

One person whom she kept seeing around was a man named Kevin Killian. He lacked eumelanin in the basale stratum of his epidermis.

He was a very talented New Narrative writer. He stalked the city and looked like a mid-empire Caesar. He had been writing for decades. His finest books were *Shy* and *Impossible Princess*.

Adeline's best friend, a Science Fiction writer who called himself Baby, was well acquainted with some of the New Narrative people, but Adeline and Baby had never discussed the New Narrative movement.

She had no idea that Kevin Killian was on good terms with her best friend. She had no idea that Baby loved Kevin Killian and his work.

Sometimes the Earth seems very large and sometimes the Earth seems very small.

KEVIN KILLIAN was married to another wonderful writer named Dodie Bellamy. Kevin was a gay man. Dodie was a woman. Dodie didn't have much eumelanin in the basal stratum of her epidermis.

Kevin and Dodie had married each other and they had sex. Adeline knew this because she had read Dodie's truly excellent book *The Letters of Mina Harker*, which amongst many other things detailed the relationship between Kevin and Dodie.

Adeline found this beautiful.

WHEN THE WRITER J. Karacehennem moved to San Francisco from Los Angeles in late 2010, he started dragging Adeline to an even greater number of literary events. It was at just such an event, in the backroom of Alley Cat Books on 24th Street, that Adeline and Kevin Killian had a conversation.

Kevin told Adeline that he taught in the MFA program at the California College of the Arts. He asked if she would be interested in coming and talking to his students.

"Most certainly," said Adeline, "I'd be delighted to penetrate the kooky consciousness of all those bright young things. Why, I'm sure I'll simply destroy minds and reap souls with all the wonderments of my very own speech."

It was 2013.

It was twenty years since she'd agreed to draw *Trill*.

She still had the accent.

SO THERE ADELINE FOUND HERSELF at CCA, talking to Kevin's students. The students struck her as interesting and bright. She was talking about the realities of self-publishing.

Adeline loved situations in which she addressed a captive audience. She was surprised by how coherent she could be when speaking to a crowd.

This was unusual because she had grown up in California. She had lived in California for most of her life. Her coherence was unusual because people from California are the most inarticulate people in the world.

People from California punctuate every other word with *like* and *you know*. This is not an exaggeration. This is, like, you know, true.

IT WAS WHILE she was still in high school that Adeline adopted her Transatlantic accent. This accent sounds half-way American and half-way British. Other than upper class snobs and actors in early sound films, no human being has ever used this accent. It is entirely artificial. It died out around 1965.

Adeline had adopted a Transatlantic accent in 1984 after watching the film *Breakfast at Tiffany's*.

Breakfast at Tiffany's was about a male sex-worker who bullies a female sex-worker out of sex work so that the female sex-worker can submit to the male sex-worker's misogynistic love. Much of this bullying happens while a yellowfaced Japanese caricature screams in a stairwell.

The female sex-worker is played by Audrey Hepburn. She's reinvented herself from Southern White trash named Lula Mae into a resplendent glamour girl named Holly Golightly.

She is stunning. She is everything. She speaks with a Transatlantic accent.

29

FOR A WOMAN who loved a captive audience, Adeline had a bad habit when she spoke before crowds.

She displayed an inability to stay on topic. She had recognized this habit and fostered it. She liked the conversational drift. She thought it was charming.

Adeline had forgotten the ceaseless vigilance required of women who live in a society that hates women. She'd forgotten that only men were allowed conversational drift. She'd forgotten that conversational drift in women was not seen as charming.

Here were some of the adjectives that people, both men and women, had thought about Adeline's conversational drift: ditzy, flighty, silly, goofy, whimsical, crazy, scattered, self-important.

WHEN ADELINE WAS SPEAKING to Kevin Killian's students, she began with self-publishing. Then she moved to Kathy Acker, a writer whom Kevin Killian had known, and then she moved to Dorothy B. Hughes, a writer who died before Kevin Killian could know her, and then moved to Internet Piracy and then moved to *The One Thousand and One Nights* and then moved to the Middle East and then moved to Middle Eastern politics and then moved to the Arab Spring and then moved on to Beyoncé and Rihanna.

THE ARAB SPRING was a name given by people in America to events that occurred between the years 2010 and 2012.

The citizens of various Arabian nations had staged a series of protests and revolts against their governments. Americans called this the Arab Spring.

Some of these protests and revolts lead to the toppling of social orders. Other protests and revolts lead to the re-entrenchment of social orders and a brutal civil war in Syria.

AMERICAN JOURNALISTS loved the Arab Spring. The narrative of the Arab Spring in the American media was the same narrative that the American media perpetuated whenever any other country went into revolt.

This narrative was very simple. This is what it said: *People in a country without a tradition of European thought are staging a revolt with the inevitable end point being an embrace of human rights as devised by Enlightenment and post-Enlightenment thinkers.*

In other words, all revolutions happened because everyone everywhere wanted to be Americans.

THE HUMAN RIGHTS which the American media assumed all revolutionaries would embrace were rough analogues for America's own *Constitutional Rights.* The general belief was that these rights originated from the Constitution of the United States of America.

This very peculiar document had been written by slave holders and was cherished by a great number of Americans as a sacred text of human liberty, something inspired by The One True God.

THE ONE TRUE GOD was an idea that took many forms and shapes. More than anything, The One True God was a potent weapon used by sexually repressed members of society to inflict misery on everyone else.

American politicians were fond enough of The One True God that they had adopted IN GOD WE TRUST as the national motto. The national motto appeared on each piece of paper American money.

This was a spectacularly perverse marriage, but one exhibiting a peculiar and cruel logic.

After all, no other imaginary things had inflicted as much suffering on the American people as money and The One True God.

THE MANY FORMS AND SHAPES of The One True God did not come close to describing the actual God.

The actual God was wonderful and useless.

The actual God was nothing more and nothing less than the sound of Etta James singing "I'd Rather Go Blind."

The actual God was nothing more and nothing less than the sound of Shirley Collins singing "Lady Margaret and Sweet William."

The actual God was nothing more and nothing less than the sound of Elvis Presley singing "Long Black Limousine."

The actual God was nothing more and nothing less than the sound of Abner Jay singing "I'm So Depressed."

BECAUSE THE AMERICAN MEDIA was fueled by advertising, its narrative of revolution mimicked the method of advertising, presenting both a stated idea and an intended one.

The stated idea was the embrace of human rights, which is to say a replica of American *Constitutional Rights*.

The intended meaning was the idea that countries liberated by an embrace of human rights would be a great place to sell the goods of multinational corporations.

To the surprise of no one, these multinational corporations were generally the same corporations that fueled the American media with advertising revenue.

THE ARAB SPRING was the moment during which the American media collapsed both the stated and intended meanings into one thing. The reporting had focused on Facebook and Twitter.

Here are some headlines from the period:

Is Egypt About to Have a Facebook Revolution?

Egypt's Revolution 2.0: The Facebook Factor

The First Twitter Revolution?

Was What Happened in Tunisia a Twitter Revolution?

Social protests staged in countries thousands of miles away, on a different continent, were covered as advertisements for multinational corporations headquartered around and near San Francisco.

ADELINE'S FRIEND J. Karacehennem, whose last name was Turkish for *Black Hell,* went to Egypt one month after its Facebook revolution lead to the overthrow of Hosni Mubarak, a dumb asshole who had been in power for thirty years.

Lots of Egyptians talked to J. Karacehennem about the protests. Many had been in the protests.

No one mentioned Facebook. No one mentioned Twitter.

Mostly people talked about money and how they had none.

SPRING IS ONE OF THE FOUR SEASONS that occurs in temperate zones.

Almost all the territories hosting protests during the Arab Spring were located either in the Subtropics or the Tropics.

In the Subtropics and the Tropics there are, at best, two seasons. A wet season and a dry season.

So that was another miracle worked by American corporations headquartered near, in, and around San Francisco: the first ever arrival of Spring in the Middle East.

HERE IS WHAT ADELINE SAID about Internet Piracy, in response to a question posed by one of Kevin Killian's students about the impact of the Internet on sales of *Trill*:

"I couldn't give two shakes of a hangman's holler," said Adeline, "about my comics being online and freely available. The Internet hasn't, as far as I can tell, affected our sales one metric inch. My collaborator feels otherwise. He feels that the Internet has impacted our ability to make good money off our old work. That's probably wrong, darlings, but what do I know? I barely use email. Have you seen my website? It's *très pathétique*. I don't use Twitter or Facebook. What does send yours truly into a tizzy is when people won't admit that they're just stealing other people's shit. The Internet is a weird place. Everyone makes everything a moral crusade. Why can't you just steal my books? Why must you be justified? Why must you bore me to death with a loooooooooong speech about how copyright is actually copywrong?"

SO THERE ADELINE was in a classroom on the CCA campus over by Mission Bay, talking to a bunch of kids.

They were decades younger than her.

She was in her mid-forties. She was kind of famous. She was expressing a series of unpopular opinions. She was in public. It was 2013.

It was here that she made the one unforgivable mistake of the early Twenty-First Century.

She neglected to notice that someone was recording every word that she said.

chapter seven

Months before her appearance in Kevin Killian's class, Adeline had involved herself with a man named Erik Willems who didn't have much eumelanin in the basal cell layer of his epidermis.

Erik Willems worked in information technology and Internet startups. Erik Willems was rich. He was a kind of rich that Adeline had never encountered. And she was from Pasadena.

He had explained his money to her in abstract terms, saying, "During periods of economic and societal contraction, the value of labor falls and the value of capital rises. Physical work stops mattering. Money starts making its own money. Some people are good at helping money make money."

"Our dear old Mother," said Adeline, "made beaucoup bucks from Daddy's money, but even our decadence wasn't nothing like yours."

LIKE MANY OF THE MEN who worked with technology in the information economy, Erik Willems had a deep affection for juvenile literature.

Which is to say that he liked Science Fiction.

Which is to say that he also liked Robert Heinlein.

Which is to say that he also liked J.R.R. Tolkein.

Which is to say that he also liked Ayn Rand.

SCIENCE FICTION was a dying genre in which writers with no personal understanding of the human experience posited many theoretical futures of the species.

Robert Heinlein was a eumelaninless Libertarian maniac who had written tedious Science Fiction about futuristic group sex. The robots in Robert Heinlein's books were always horny. The aliens were even hornier. The aliens in Robert Heinlein's books were randier than dunghill roosters.

His most famous work was *Stranger in a Strange Land,* which was about a Martian named Michael Valentine who loves fucking and teaches Earthlings how to fuck like a Martian. *Stranger in a Strange Land* had influenced many straight people in the San Francisco Bay Area into adopting non-traditional sexual lifestyles.

The most common thing amongst straight people in the Bay Area who had adopted non-traditional sexual lifestyles was their need to discuss these non-traditional sexual lifestyles at every possible opportunity. This had the effect of making dinner parties both very annoying and very awkward.

J.R.R. Tolkein was the most abused author in the history of the English language. He had written *The Hobbit,* which was for children, and *The Lord of the Rings*, which was for adults. He had no eumelanin in the basale stratum of his epidermis.

Both of his books were informed by his terrible experiences in World War I during the Battle of the Somme, where he watched every thing around him die.

World War I was one of the biggest *wars* in human history. *Wars* were giant parties for the ruling elites, who sometimes thought it might be great fun to make the poor kill each other.

The poor were well-paid for their deaths and blown-off limbs and their scarred faces. The poor were called *heroes* and allowed to propagate the myths of noble battle and fraternity, which were ideas used to convince new generations of poor people that it was okay to kill other poor people.

Both of Tolkein's books were about elves, wizards and magic. Both books were read by morons. Both books had been turned into a series of idiotic films featuring a lot of flatulence.

Ayn Rand was a speed freak, a social welfare beneficiary and a sex cultist. She was quite possibly the most influential thinker of the last fifty years. There wasn't much eumelanin in the basale stratum of her epidermis.

She wrote books about how social welfare beneficiaries were garbage who deserved to die in the gutter. All of her books were terrible. All of her books were popular. Several had been turned into unpopular movies.

She was well regarded by very rich people unwilling to accept that their fortunes were a combination of random chance and an innate ability to humiliate others.

Ayn Rand's books told very rich people that they were good, that their pursuit of wealth was moral and just. Many of these people ended up as CEOs or in high levels of American government.

Ayn Rand was the billionaire's best friend.

SOME OF AYN RAND'S better known followers included:

Paul Ryan, the 2012 Republican candidate for Vice President of the United States of America.

Vince Vaughn, a dough-faced actor who had starred in such hilarious comedies as *The Watch, Couples Retreat, Four Christmases, The Internship,* and *Delivery Man. The Internship* was a film about two adults who receive internships at Google's headquarters in Silicon Valley.

Peter Thiel, a co-founder of PayPal, a billionaire weapons profiteer and incompetent hedge fund manager who wanted to build independent nation states on floating ocean platforms.

Jeff Bezos, the founder of Amazon.com, an unprofitable website dedicated to the destruction of the publishing industry.

Ron Paul, a septuagenarian medical doctor and perennial Presidential protest candidate.

Alan Greenspan, the Chairman of the Federal Reserve from 1986 to 2006. In his relative youth, Greenspan sat at the knee of Ayn Rand whilst she explained that poor people were garbage who deserved to die in the gutter.

None of these men had eumelanin in the basale strata of their epidermises.

ANOTHER OF ERIK WILLEMS'S favorite writers was Adeline's best friend, Baby.

ADELINE MET BABY during September of 1986 in an Alphabet City squat. She had lived in New York from 1986 to 1996. It was eleven years with only two instances of life beyond the city.

The first instance was in 1988, when she and Baby went to live with Suzanne in Pasadena. The second was in 1993, when Adeline went to live with Jeremy Winterbloss and his girlfriend Minerva, who shared an apartment in San Francisco's Lower Haight.

Back in 1986, Adeline was dating a punk rocker who lived in the Alphabet City squat. Baby had that very day arrived in New York on a bus from Wisconsin. He knew someone living in the squat.

The day ended with Baby's clothes being stolen by a junkie and Adeline's boyfriend screwing the brains out of another girl. Baby, a former high school athlete, beat the shit out of Adeline's boyfriend. Adeline invited Baby to crash at her dorm.

With the exception of a two year period in the mid-1990s, they had been simpatico ever since.

WHILE HE LIVED in New York, Baby had come into his own as a writer of Science Fiction. His first published story was entitled "Heroin of the Masses."

It was about a junkie alien who sang lead vocals in a post-post-post-post-post-post-post-post-post-post-post-post-post-post-post-post-post-post-post-post-post-post-post glam band at the Pyramid Club on Avenue A.

Baby's first novel was titled *Trapped Between Jupiter and a Bottle*. It was about a private eye in the future.

His second novel was titled *Saving Anne Frank*. It was about a time traveler who saves Anne Frank from Auschwitz and the Planet of Ashes.

Baby's first two novels had experienced some critical success.

There was something in his prose construction that was more literary than the average practitioner of Science Fiction, which lead to misinterpretations of his genre tropes as postmodern devices.

IN 2001, Jonathan Franzen published *The Corrections*, his *good novel* about people from the American Middle West without much eumelanin in their epidermises. They suffer from serious problems and a complicated family.

The Corrections arrived with great critical acclaim and massive commercial success. Baby took stock.

He too was from the American Middle West and, like Jonathan Franzen, he too lacked much eumelanin in his epidermis.

He was a young novelist of some critical reputation.

He was interested in leaving Science Fiction behind.

Baby decided that he too would write his own book about people who lived in the American Middle West. All of his characters would lack eumelanin in their epidermises.

He too would chronicle important problems and complicated families.

The resulting novel was the first instance of Baby writing fiction that wasn't about robots or aliens or time travel. The resulting novel was about a family in Milwaukee.

The patriarch worked in steel. The mother was on amphetamines. One son was attracted to danger. Another son was attracted to men. One daughter was attracted to men and to danger. Another daughter had an abortion.

Baby titled the book *Hot Mill Steam*.

It bombed.

AFTER THE FAILURE of *Hot Mill Steam*, Baby knew that he'd be stuck in Science Fiction forever. So he wrote a new novel of Science Fiction.

The average length of a novel is about 80,000 to 85,000 words. *Trapped Between Jupiter and a Bottle* and *Saving Anne Frank* were relatively short, both clocking in at roughly 70,000 words.

Hot Mill Steam was 150,000 words.

Baby had wanted to capture everything about having a lack of eumelanin in the American Middle West. All the suffering and joy that comes with being the color of a newborn piglet!

The bad novel that you are reading is about 72,900 words long.

WHEN BABY STARTED his new Science Fiction novel, he found that he could not shake the long-winded bullshit of *Hot Mill Steam*.

Long-winded bullshit was now in his blood. Long-winded bullshit had become part of his style.

The new novel was about 175,000 words.

Baby titled it *Annie Zero*.

The title was also the name of the book's protagonist, a French Neo-Maoist in the far flung future. The name was a pun on the French phrase *année zéro*, which meant Year Zero, suggesting that once Annie Zero instituted her neo-Maoist cypherpunk revolution in the Megaverse, the calendar would be reset.

AS PART OF HIS LONG-WINDED BULLSHIT, Baby fell into a genre trope that he had avoided in his first two novels.

He started inventing new words.

This was a common habit amongst Science Fiction writers. They couldn't help themselves. They were always inventing new words.

Perhaps the most famous example of a Science Fiction writer inventing a new word occurs in Robert Heinlein's *Stranger in a Strange Land*. Part of Heinlein's vision of horny decentralized alien sex involves the Martian word *grok*.

To *grok* something is to comprehend that something with effortless and infinite intuition. When you *grok* something, that something becomes a part of you and you become a part of that something without any troublesome Earthling attempts at knowing.

A good example of *groking* something is the way that members of the social construct of the White race had *groked* their own piglet pink.

They'd *groked* their skin color so much that it became invisible. It had become part of them and they had become part of it. That was *groking*.

People in the San Francisco Bay Area, especially those who worked in technology like Erik Willems, loved to talk about *groking*.

With time, their overusage stripped away the original meaning and *grok* became synonymous with simple knowledge of a thing.

In a weird way, people in the Bay Area who used the word *grok* did not *grok* the word *grok*.

BABY HAD ALWAYS BEEN POPULAR with people on the Internet, which was a wonderful place to deny climate change, willfully misinterpret the Bible, and denounce Darwin's theory of evolution.

Now that Baby had coined nonsense neologisms, he had become more than popular. He had become quotable.

Annie Zero was Baby's best selling book. *Annie Zero* was why Erik Willems approached Adeline at a dinner party.

He recognized her from a photo which accompanied an interview she'd done with the *SF Weekly*. The interviewer, a guy named Evan Karp who didn't have much eumelanin in the basale layer of his epidermis, had asked Adeline about her friendship with Baby.

Adeline spilled the beans.

ONE OF THE REASONS why Adeline liked San Francisco was that it retained a high degree of sexual freedom. She often said it was the last place in America where a person needed only 48 hours' notice to arrange a threesome with a baby crocodile and a pygmy dwarf.

Like many things in San Francisco, this high degree of sexual freedom curdled when adopted by straight people of the upper middle class.

Straight people of the upper middle class who'd adopted this high degree of sexual freedom had the bad habit of recommending books like *The Ethical Slut: A Guide to Infinite Sexual Possibilities* and *Stranger in a Strange Land*.

ADELINE WAS AT THE DINNER PARTY in question because she'd been invited by her friend Christine. Christine had disappeared, saying that she was going to powder her nose.

In *Breakfast at Tiffany's,* going to the powder room is a euphemism for the exchange of money between the female sex-worker and her clients. Christine was not a sex-worker. She really was powdering her nose.

She left Adeline sitting beside a middle-aged straight couple.

Adeline herself was middle-aged but was always surprised by the middle-agedness of others.

She still felt young, even if she'd been dyeing her hair for two years.

When she was in high school and college, Adeline had gone through a range of hairstyles and colors roughly coincident with her participation in a wide span of subcultural identities.

Her hair then had been every color other than grey, the color that she now hid beneath an unnatural black hue.

The middle-aged straight couple told Adeline about their non-traditional sexual lifestyle, about how it had liberated them from the institutional shackles of monogamy and shown them a new kind of happiness derived from basic human biology. The woman in the couple insinuated that she was adept at the usage of strap-on dildos.

Adeline listened, waiting for Christine, and wondered which of the following conversational turns was most likely: (1) A discussion of the differences, if any, between an open relationship and being polyamorous. (2) The recommendation that she read *The Ethical Slut*. (3) Someone using the word *grok*. (4) The suggestion of a threesome, with an offer to host if Adeline felt uncomfortable having the liaison at her place.

"Excuse me," said Erik Willems, leaning over the table, "but are you M. Abrahamovic Petrovitch?"

"Why yes," said Adeline, standing up, "I am."

THEY MOVED over by a window. Coit Tower was visible through the glass, rising above North Beach. Adeline found North Beach *très déclassé*, as it was chock-a-block with tourists and strip clubs and the kinds of tourists who went to strip clubs.

Her friend J. Karacehennem, whose last name was Turkish for *Black Hell*, loved North Beach. He was always in Caffe Trieste at the corner of Vallejo and Grant.

"I read *Trill*," said Erik. "In the omnibus."

"And whatever was your opinion, young man?" asked Adeline.

"I thought it was interesting."

"Only interesting?" asked Adeline.

"It was a *gootbluck*," said Erik.

"Darling, a what?" asked Adeline.

"A *gootbluck*."

There was a very awkward pause.

"I'm sorry," said Adeline, "but dost thou *sprechen ze German*? *Je ne parle pas allemand!*"

"How can you not know what a *gootbluck* is?"

"Should I?" asked Adeline.

"A *gootbluck* is a work of art that you recognize has high merit but doesn't appeal to you on the personal level. Some people don't like James Joyce but everyone knows that *Ulysses* is a good book. For some people, *Ulysses* is a *gootbluck*."

"Darling," said Adeline, "why ever would yours truly know the definition of *gootbluck*?"

"It's a word from *Annie Zero*," said Erik.

"Oh Jesus Christ," said Adeline. "Fucking Baby and his fucking book."

ADELINE HADN'T READ *ANNIE ZERO*. Baby told her to skip it. He said it wasn't very good. She took him at his word.

Later that night, Adeline ended up sleeping with Erik Willems.

Why not?

chapter eight

J. Karacehennem met Adeline during the run up to the feature film adaptation of *Trill*. They were both in Los Angeles.

He was asked by the editor of an ephemeral magazine to conduct an interview with the artist responsible for the original *graphic novel*.

They met in a house that was once owned by Walt Disney's Uncle.

WALT DISNEY was America's most beloved Anti-Semite and racist. He hated labor strikes, unions, organized labor and Communists. He named the names of troublesome employees before the House Un-American Activities Committee, saying that they were probably Communists.

In 1938, Disney granted a private audience to Adolf Hitler's favorite director, Leni Riefenstahl. After World War Two, Disney hired Werhner von Braun.

Werhner von Braun was a Nazi rocket scientist and a Major in the Schutz-staffel. He invented the V-2.

The V-2 was a rocket that bombed the living fucking shit out of London during World War Two. Werhner von Braun used slave labor to build the V-2s.

12,000 people died building the V-2. 9,000 people died being bombed to shit by the V-2.

After the war, the CIA's immediate precursor, the Office of Strategic Services, brought Werhner von Braun to the USA. They forgave the National Socialism because they wanted him to build rockets for the American military.

The rockets would be used to threaten the Russian government. The members of the Russian government were all Communists.

Like any member of any government, the Russians were a bunch of dumb assholes. The Russians were the reason that the CIA had funded literary fiction. It was thought that American writers and *good novels* could help destabilize Communism.

In the 1950s, Disney hired Werhner von Braun. The Nazi rocket scientist appeared in a Disney television program called *Man in Space*.

Forty-two million people watched the broadcast.

THE CREATION OF MICKEY MOUSE was the greatest achievement of Disney's studio, which was founded in the garage of the house where Adeline met J. Karacehennem.

Mickey Mouse was a scampish anthropomorphic rodent who hung around a barnyard. His friends were barnyard animals. Their existential concerns were underscored by barnyard humor.

Mickey's pals included Clarabelle Cow and Horace Horsecollar and Dippy Dawg. They appeared together in black-and-white synched sound cartoons and a newspaper strip.

A guy named Ub Iwerks invented the characters and drew the early animated shorts. A guy named Floyd Gottfredson drew the newspaper strip. Both men worked-for-hire.

Disney took all the credit.

THE COMPANY that Walt Disney founded in his uncle's backyard became one of the world's most metastatic entities, consuming every available piece of intellectual property.

Walt Disney's company ended up buying Marvel Entertainment.

This meant that Walt Disney's company owned the most valuable intellectual output of Ub Iwerks, Floyd Gottfredson and Jack Kirby.

DURING THE RUN-UP to Don Murphy's *Trill,* Adeline was living, temporarily, in Los Angeles. She'd picked up a storyboarding job. It was interesting work and gave her a chance to visit her hometown.

J. Karacehennem had moved to Los Angeles after the collapse of a seven year long relationship. He arrived with the unconscious idea that he'd join the swelling ranks of people who go to California to die.

Much to his surprise, dying required more than a move to Los Angeles.

THE INTERVIEW went well. J. Karacehennem hung around for hours.

They shot the shit. Off the record. He and Adeline exchanged cellphone numbers. He went home.

THEN J. KARACEHENNEM went through several interpersonal catastrophes and a month long trip to İzmir, Turkey. When he got back to America, he called Adeline. She was still in Los Angeles.

She'd been spending time with her mother Suzanne. The less said the better.

Adeline told J. Karacehennem to come on over.

They ended up sleeping together. Only a few times. This did not last long. The less said the better.

WHEN J. KARACEHENNEM moved to San Francisco in late 2010, he got in touch with Adeline. They hadn't spoken in about a year. Soon they were hanging out all the time. There was a distinct absence of romantic or sexual tension.

He'd moved to San Francisco because he was following a woman.

This woman wasn't Adeline. This woman was The Hangman's Beautiful Daughter.

J. Karacehennem and The Hangman's Beautiful Daughter had dated for a few years, long distance, with him going to San Francisco and her going to Los Angeles.

It was rocky until it wasn't. At some point it became solid.

J. Karacehennem went north.

HE MOVED into the apartment of The Hangman's Beautiful Daughter, which was located on Bryant between 23rd and 24th in the Mission District, a historically Latino and working-class neighborhood which was ground zero for gentrification driven by obscene Internet wealth.

The apartment sported several strange features.

It was 1,000 square feet but it had no interior walls.

It was one giant room.

The floors were all grey masonite.

The Hangman's Beautiful Daughter had installed a 15-foot tall tree into the middle of the room.

Moving into an apartment with no walls and a giant tree required not only a lot of love but also a great deal of trust. But that was his relationship with The Hangman's Beautiful Daughter. All love and all trust, with a dash of pointless arguments.

MOSTLY, J. KARACEHENNEM hung around writing, performing the daily chores of the common law househusband, and thinking about the lack of eumelanin in the basale stratum of his epidermis.

Before he moved to California and the Sun exacted its terrible vengeance, he was as pale as milk. This was unusual as he was Turkish.

His relatives in Turkey were loaded with eumelanin. They were dark. They were Brown.

The lack of eumelanin in J. Karacehennem's epidermis was a real world manifestation of the question asked on page 8 of the September 30, 1909 edition of the *New York Times*: "IS THE TURK A WHITE MAN?"

To answer this question and others, J. Karacehennem had checked Stormfront.org, which was the premiere website of the White Nationalist Community. It was a one-stop shop for racist discourse.

Perhaps unsurprisingly for the premiere website of the White Nationalist Community, the general consensus amongst its members was that Turk was not a White man.

The general consensus was that the Turkish people did not, alas, belong to the Aryan race. The general consensus was that the Turkish people were a mongrel breed.

THE STRANGEST THING about the apartment was its landlord. The landlord owned the building and lived above J. Karacehennem and The Hangman's Beautiful Daughter.

The landlord was five-foot-five. The landlord was a stocky middle-aged immigrant from England. The landlord was completely bald. There was not a scratch of hair on his egg-shaped head. There was no eumelanin in the basale stratum of his epidermis.

The lack of hair and the stocky build made the landlord look like a single column of flesh that tapered upwards from his thick waist to the pointy crown of his head.

SAN FRANCISCO was in the middle of massive economic upheaval. Its poorer citizens were displaced every single day. Its rents were rising. There was a housing shortage. This created a situation in which a person's life was defined by their apartment.

Rental agreements were documents of inequality codified under American law, which had always favored property rights over liberties of the individual. This made any landlord the most important person in his or her tenants' lives, capable of enacting terrible vengeance on the slightest whim.

Basically, the most important person in the life of J. Karacehennem was not The Hangman's Beautiful Daughter.

Basically, the most important person in the life of The Hangman's Beautiful Daughter was not J. Karacehennem.

Basically, the most important person in the life of J. Karacehennem and The Hangman's Beautiful Daughter was a man who looked like a giant penis.

THE LANDLORD SPOKE with a Received Pronunciation accent, which was the accent of the British Royal Family and actors who study with the Royal Shakespeare Company. To American ears, this accent sounds like the utter heights of refinement.

This is because each member of the human race is an idiot impressed from birth with a series of cultural assumptions that skew in favor of the upper classes.

In actuality, each language and dialect is as equally expressive any other language or dialect. There is no evolutionary difference between any language or dialect.

The only, like, exception, is, like, you know, the California dialect, which just, like, sucks.

FOR AN AMERICAN to accept the fact that there is no expressive advantage between languages and dialects would require this hypothetical American to admit that Received Pronunciation was as valid a tool of expression as Black English.

Black English was a dialect used by some members of the social construct called the Black race.

If there is one lesson that every American learned by the time of their fifteen year, it was this: to speak Black English is to speak improper English.

It's *common sense* that Black English is improper English, because *common sense* dictates a formal, unchanging relationship between the alphabet and spoken pronunciation.

This is one of the thousand places where *common sense* veers into intolerable bullshit.

THE LANDLORD not only looked like a giant penis but had begun to act like one as well. He had come to hate both J. Karacehennem and The Hangman's Beautiful Daughter.

The hatred started about a year after J. Karacehennem moved to San Francisco.

In December of 2011, J. Karacehennem had been standing beneath the giant tree. The Hangman's Beautiful Daughter came into the apartment and said that the vacant storefront a few doors down, at the corner of 23rd and Bryant, was getting a new tenant.

"What is it?" he asked.

"I have no idea," she said.

Several days later, one of the neighbors came and knocked on the door. She had a petition against the new business.

She said it was going to be an upscale luxury restaurant called Local's Corner. There would be a great deal of outdoor seating. Its clientele would be workers in the tech industry.

The neighbor started a petition because she found it strange there had been no discussion between the owner of the new restaurant and its neighbors.

The petition asked the city to consider blocking Local's Corner from moving into the location.

It may seem odd that anyone would expect a new business to alert the neighbors of its existence.

It is odd. But that's San Francisco.

NOT BEING on the lease, J. Karacehennem did not sign the petition.

The Hangman's Beautiful Daughter signed the petition.

Their landlord signed the petition.

IN RESPONSE to the petition, The Owner of Local's Corner held a community meeting in a location across the street from his proposed business. The Owner did not have eumelanin in the basale stratum of his epidermis.

This location for this community meeting was an arts space called Million Fishes.

Two years later, Million Fishes would be evicted. The building would be renovated. A tech startup called Bloodhound would move into the space.

Bloodhound had received $3,000,000 in a round of venture capital funding led by Peter Thiel, who was a co-founder of PayPal, a billionaire weapons profiteer and an incompetent hedge fund manager.

In addition to funding startups named after animals bred to hunt other animals, Peter Thiel wanted to build independent nation states on floating ocean platforms, where the citizens of these independent nation states would organize around the Objectivist principles of Ayn Rand.

Million Fishes paid $5,000 a month in rent.

The lease signed by Bloodhound would be for $31,667 a month. Plus $564 in fees.

By May 2014, Bloodhound would stop paying and skip out on the building.

THE HANGMAN'S BEAUTIFUL DAUGHTER and J. Karacehennem went to the community meeting. The landlord did not.

About seventy people attended.

The meeting played out in the manner of all community meetings. It was a forum for grandstanding and irrelevant grievances.

Only some of the grandstanding was about the restaurant.

As the night wore on, residents of the neighborhood expressed their concerns, or their compliments, and The Owner responded. Nothing was resolved, platitudes were offered. People talked through each other.

So J. Karacehennem asked The Owner if he felt like there was any reason to have a meeting.

To which The Owner replied.

So then J. Karacehennem asked The Owner if he felt like his restaurant was a *fait accompli* and if he believed that the concerns of the residents were things to be brushed off.

To which The Owner replied.

So then J. Karacehennem pressed the issue even further.

The Owner ended the meeting.

BECAUSE HE HAD BEEN OBNOXIOUS at the meeting, J. Karacehennem was approached by other people in the area, none of whom he had seen before. They asked if he wanted to go to a smaller meeting about Local's Corner.

So he went. The meeting was in someone's apartment.

The attendees were a ragtag group. Some were very old. Some were young. One of them had Alzheimer's disease, which was a disease that caused human consciousness to turn into mush. There was a whole spectrum of eumelanin and its lack.

As a result of this clandestine rendezvous, the next few weeks of J. Karacehennem's life got very weird.

He entered into a conspiracy with the other neighbors that necessitated his attending a secret rendezvous above a fried chicken store on 24th Street.

He went to a contentious meeting in City Hall. He went to an even more contentious meeting in a nearby cafe.

The Owner was in these latter two meetings. The one at City Hall happened in the office of David Campos, the neighborhood's elected City Supervisor, who had some eumelanin in his epidermis. It was unpleasant.

J. KARACEHENNEM never thought that they would win the fight against Local's Corner.

America was open for business. The civic statutes governing new businesses were written with the explicit purpose of encouraging as much commerce as possible.

You can't stop the gears of capitalism. But you always can be a pain in the ass.

ANYWAY, THE OWNER ended up opening Local's Corner.

It was an upscale, locally-sourced seafood restaurant crammed into 590 square feet. Its interior decor, which looked like someone's Victorian grandmother had puked up a diet of reclaimed wood and handprinted wallpaper, was designed by the architects at atelier KS.

The space was too small for an industrial oven. The restaurant seated about thirty.

By the end of 2014, it was closed.

J. KARACEHENNEM'S involvement with the anti-Local's Corner faction had caused a split with his landlord. Through an arcane process of mutual seduction, the giant penis went from being someone who had signed a petition against the restaurant to being one of its biggest supporters.

The landlord accused J. Karacehennem of not breaking down recycling boxes in the garage. The landlord accused J. Karacehennem of leaving the garage open at bizarre hours of the night.

The landlord refused speak to J. Karacehennem on the street.

Actually, that last one was kind of a relief.

chapter nine

It was the morning after Adeline spoke in Kevin Killian's class.

Adeline woke up late. She was in her apartment near Dolores Park.

Erik Willems had spent the night. Now he was gone. That was one reliable thing. He was always gone in the morning.

SHE HAD COME TO THE CONCLUSION that Erik Willems was an empty vessel. There was nothing behind the eyes. No soul, no intelligence.

This conclusion was long building. It arrived when Erik told Adeline about a sexual double entendre common amongst his social class.

"We call them," he said, "the cupcake and the pastry."

"You call what the cupcake and the pastry?" asked Adeline.

"The pussy and the ass. They are the cupcake and the pastry. Because one tastes sour and one tastes sweet."

"Darling," said Adeline, "which is which?"

"That's the mystery of the cupcake and the pastry. No one knows. It depends on your personal preference."

ADELINE HAD LONG BELIEVED that good sex was possible only with people in possession of a primal intelligence. There needed to be something behind the eyes.

Yet Erik Willems was empty and still he fucked like a beast. He understood both the cupcake and the pastry. The sex was a revelation.

SHE WAS APPROACHING the end of her socially acceptable sex life. She was a woman in a society that hated women.

Men could fuck well into their seventies without anyone blinking an eye. Women past a certain age were allowed to fuck but only as long as they adopted certain names of war.

Like: *MILF*. Like: *cougar*.

MILF was an Internet acronym for Mother I'd Like to Fuck.

A *cougar* was an older women with sexual interests in younger men.

Both terms categorize a woman's sexuality by its explicit relationship to men. Both terms suggest that an older woman's virility exists only as a tutoring device to school younger men in the art of lovemaking. Both terms contextualize an older woman's sexuality based on her willingness to offer men a taste of the cupcake and/or the pastry.

It was the same old intolerable bullshit dressed in a red pleather skirt.

But, really, are there any sexual colloquialisms for women that don't embed some intolerable bullshit about men?

ADELINE WAS OLD ENOUGH to know that some fights aren't worth having. She understood that time and energy are limited commodities.

And, to her mild embarrassment, most of her recent sexual partners had been younger men. Erik Willems was a full decade her junior.

So she let the world's intolerable bullshit wash over her.

"Oh, darling, here I stand, I cannot do otherwise," she'd said to J. Karacehennem. "I'm a *MILF.* I'm a *cougar.* I accept everything."

ADELINE GOT OUT OF BED. There was an impression where Erik Willems had slept. He'd crushed the pillow.

Adeline went into her kitchen and made some breakfast. Yogurt and uncooked oats.

It was about one in the afternoon.

She underwent an enforced social ritual necessary to her professional life. She checked her email.

ON THE AVERAGE MORNING, Adeline received about twenty emails. Fifteen of these would be junk, which is different than spam. Spam was the name for unsolicited emails which attempted to seduce the receiver into spending money.

She had received a lot of spam until she switched to GMail, a free e-mail service offered by Google.

In exchange for its free e-mail service, Google scanned its users' emails and served its users advertisements targeted to the content of the scanned emails.

If someone emailed about a table, then GMail would offer Adeline a deal on a table. If someone emailed about a musical performance, then GMail would offer Adeline a deal on concert tickets.

The junk came from organizations to which she had given her email address. Some prime examples of junk email were the daily inanities which she received from the Parsons School of Design.

Adeline had graduated from Parsons in 1990. She was an alumna. In a fit of nostalgia, she'd given Parsons her email address.

Parsons soon made her regret this unexpected visitation of school spirit.

The other emails would be work related. Stuff from Jeremy about *Trill*. Stuff from people with whom she'd worked in the past, offering new work. Requests for interviews. The usual crap.

ADELINE CHECKED her email. She discovered hundreds of messages.

This had happened before. Her old email address had leaked to members of a Yahoo Group dedicated to *Trill*.

She never discovered who'd leaked her email address. But she'd experienced its effects.

The countless stream of messages, the unfathomable tide, the tsunami of want and need and questions. The infinite desire for affirmation, for validation.

And from whom?

From someone who had drawn an anthropomorphic cat.

She started reading her email.

ONE OF KEVIN KILLIAN'S STUDENTS had recorded Adeline's every word. He had used his cellphone. The student then uploaded the video of Adeline to YouTube, which was a web service owned by Google.

YouTube's users uploaded video files in various formats. Other YouTube users then watched low quality versions of the uploaded video. Google made money from YouTube by serving advertisements both before and during the video.

The most popular videos on YouTube were: (1) Pretty girls giving hair-and-makeup advice. (2) Fast things captured in slow motion photography. (3) Ugly cats meowing in bathrooms. (4) Celebrities in the act of committing a social faux pas. (5) Ray Jay Williams crowing about the size of his genitals. (7) A Swedish videogame reviewer calling himself PewDiePie, who was indistinguishable from Božidar Boža of Petnjica, Montenegro, a man kicked by a mule as a child and doomed to live out life as the village idiot.

Adeline was kind of famous and had enacted the social faux pas of being a woman who expressed unpopular opinions in a society that hated women. She'd committed the only unforgivable sin of the Twenty-First Century.

So there Adeline was on YouTube.

Now she was making money for Google.

KEVIN KILLIAN'S STUDENT had not uploaded the video with bad intentions. The uploader was thrilled to meet someone responsible for a beloved childhood classic. He'd read *Trill* in the Scholastic omnibus.

Adeline spoke with such candor and wit. It was nice, wrote the uploader, to see someone with an opinion.

The uploader had emailed the video to websites that reported on the comics industry. These included Newsarama and Comic Book News and Bleeding Cool.

These sites tended to run breathless articles about Marvel's latest exploitation of Jack Kirby's intellectual properties. With the exception of

Bleeding Cool, these sites did not run many articles about Jack Kirby being royally screwed.

There were two reasons for this: (1) The necessity of maintaining a dialogue with Marvel. (2) The complete disinterest of comics fans in hearing about the way that Jack Kirby got screwed.

Bleeding Cool ran an article with the title: "*Trill* artist M. Abrahamovic Petrovitch in Epic Rant!" The video was embedded in the article. The accompanying text was positive.

Most readers of Bleeding Cool responded well to the display of wit and candor. Truth be told, most readers of Bleeding Cool liked Adeline's general weirdness.

Several negative responses appeared in the forums, employing the following words: ditzy, flighty, silly, goofy, whimsical, crazy, scattered, self-important.

Only a handful of people called her a stupid bitch.

READERS OF BLEEDING COOL shared the video. They sent emails. They posted links to Facebook and Twitter.

A few submitted the video to reddit. Most comments were favorable. Instant karma. One of the submissions was upvoted to the front page.

The video moved beyond the confines of comic book fans.

SOMEWHERE IN HER MONOLOGUE, Adeline had suggested that she couldn't understand why any woman would work in technology.

"These deluded young gals," she said, "who think that these companies will deliver them any single thing but grief need to see psychologists and explore the roots of their messy masochism. Probably something about Daddy, the poor darlings. These companies are the devil. Satan with a capital S. They're anti-women and they emerge from that dreadful masculine trait of engineering. I'm old enough to know what engineering means. It means weapons for the military. All technologies end up in the hands of warmongers. I suppose if these girls want to kill other people with their labor, they can, but we should be mature enough to admit when we've allied ourselves with evil. These girls ain't on the side of the angels. Many women have worked for the devil. It's a tradition, darlings. How else does one explain that ghastly thing known as Sarah Palin? All these crazy young ones are lining up to burn in their very own Shirtwaist Factories, screaming that they're empowered by the very technology that's set them aflame. Remember, the master's tools will never dismantle the master's house."

THE TRIANGLE SHIRTWAIST FACTORY FIRE was one of the great disasters in American life. It happened in 1911 on Washington Square in New York City. It happened in a building that is now part of New York University's campus.

Back in New York, whenever Baby and Adeline had walked past the building in question, Adeline asked odd questions like, "Baby, when you're attending classes in that building, do you ever feel as if a shade will reach out from the netherworld and clutch you in its grasp? If a shade does clutch you in its grasp, do you worry that its spirit will inhabit your body? If it does inhabit your body, what do you imaginate that you'll think and feel? Will you want to work as a slave laborer? Will you gag on ectoplasmic smoke?"

"Adeline," said Baby, "I have no idea what you're talking about."

"That's simply delightful," said Adeline. "Neither do I."

THERE WAS A GREAT WORRY amongst the owners of the Triangle company about their employees. They were worried that their employees would steal the same garments which they sewed for slave wages.

Each day, all of the exits were locked, allowing managers to check for pilfered goods before the employees left the building.

The system worked until it didn't. One day the building caught fire. The women and men couldn't escape. 146 people died.

Burning, smoke inhalation, jumping out of windows and splattering on the pavement. They were immigrants and they were poor and they were illiterate and they had no other opportunities for employment and they had no vested interest in the fruit of their labors and now they were dead.

Two of the deceased, a pair of teenaged brothers named Sam and Max Lehrer, had lived at 143 Essex Street. This was two doors away from 147 Essex Street.

147 Essex Street was where, six years later, Jack Kirby was born as Jacob Kurtzberg.

ADELINE HAD OFFENDED some of the women in tech.

Because these women worked in tech, they were avid users of Twitter.

Twitter was a system by which people broadcast short messages to computers and cellphones. Each of these messages was called a *tweet*.

The vast majority of *tweets* were written by narcissists interested in letting other people know the wide range of their opinions on every possible subject.

These subjects included: celebrities, the dinners that the narcissists were eating, politicians of the opposing party, celebrities, the names of people who were dumb assholes, the habits of Black people (pro and con), celebrities, the breakfasts that the narcissists were eating, celebrities, politicians, sports, the number of Asian-Americans on any given night in any given dance club in Los Angeles, corporations to which the narcissists held an allegiance as customers, fast food brands, celebrities, sports celebrities, celebrities, celebrities, celebrities, celebrities, celebrities, complex social and political trends, and the lunches that the narcissists were eating.

All of the other *tweets* were written in the service of corporations and non-profits which had adopted Twitter as a method of public relations.

On an average day, you might see: (1) Your sister *tweeting* about her salad. (2) Your boyfriend *tweeting* about Kobe Bryant. (3) The Los Angeles Public Library *tweeting* about different images of Hollywood through the decades.

KOBE BRYANT was a basketball player with eumelanin in the basale stratum of his epidermis. He was paid tens of millions of dollars to create the illusion of meaning while throwing round rubber balls around rectangular spaces.

Whenever he threw round rubber balls around a rectangular space, Kobe Bryant wore shirts that bore the name of the organization that paid him: the Los Angeles Lakers. These shirts also bore his last name, Bryant, and a number assigned to him by the organization.

The ostensible purpose of these shirts was to differentiate players from each other on the rectangular court.

The actual purpose of these shirts was to create objects imbued with an illusion of meaning that could be replicated on a mass scale.

People who believed in the illusion would buy replicas of Kobe Bryant's shirt. The prices of these shirts started at $34.95. Some shirts cost well over $100.

THE FORMALIZED SYSTEMS in which grown men threw around balls were called *sports*. *Sports* were big money for the men who threw around balls, and even bigger money for the men who paid other men to throw around balls.

Like any formalized system of control, *sports* were hugely contentious. *Sports*, like every formalized system of control, were about money.

Typically the men who paid other men to throw balls around would find their employees amongst the poor and ill-educated, as the poor and ill-educated were more likely to sign bad contracts. This was also the organizing principle of the early comic book industry, which preyed on Jewish men who lived in ghettos.

For the sake of both clarity and a lack of future headaches, a distinction should be made between being poor and ill-educated and being *stupid*.

Anyone could be *stupid*. Most people were. Stupidity wasn't the root cause of signing bad contracts.

The poor and ill-educated signed bad contracts because they lacked a social background which educated them in both contract law and its implication for one's future. The poor's lack of understanding made them attractive targets for exploitation, which was the organizing principle of American life.

IN THEORY, Twitter made its money by placing the *tweets* of its users alongside *tweets* which were paid for by advertisers. So the tweets about your sister's salad, about Kobe Bryant, about Hollywood would appear alongside tweets about the new Ford F-150.

The Ford F-150 was a truck. A truck was an over-sized *automobile*.

Automobiles were mechanized vehicles which transported human beings from one point to another while destroying the atmosphere and the planet.

ONE OF THE CURIOUS ASPECTS of the Twenty-First Century was the great delusion amongst many people, particularly in the San Francisco Bay Area, that *freedom of speech* and *freedom of expression* were best exercised on technological platforms owned by corporations dedicated to making as much money as possible.

People from all across the political spectrum loved Twitter. Instant activism with an instant response. There was the sensation that *things were happening,* that *people were listening.*

IN FACT, all of the people who exercised *freedom of speech* and *freedom of expression* on Twitter were doing nothing more and nothing less than creating content that they did not own for a corporation in which they had no stake.

In effect, they were working-for-hire like Jack Kirby. The only difference being that Marvel, like, you know, actually paid Jack Kirby before he was screwed. Twitter didn't pay its creators.

The only purpose of *tweeting* was the creation of new opportunities for advertisements. The only function of exercising *freedom of speech* and *freedom of expression* on Twitter was to make money for the people who had founded and invested in Twitter.

The founders of Twitter were named Jack Dorsey, Biz Stone, Noah Glass and Evan Williams. There was no eumelanin in the basale strata of their epidermises.

So that was radical activism in 2013. Hosted by a service owned by white dudes which displayed advertisements for Coca-Cola and Pepsi.

ADELINE HAD OFFENDED women in tech. She had offended advocates of *free speech.* She had offended people who believed that copyright was copywrong. She had offended people on the Left. She had offended people on the Right.

There was anger about her trivialization of the travails of women in the tech sector. There was anger on behalf of the victims of the Triangle Shirtwaist Fire of 1911. There was anger on behalf of the Arabs, still locked in political struggle and still not liberated by Twitter or Facebook. There was anger on behalf of the US Constitution, an inanimate document without feelings that had doomed millions to slavery. There was anger on behalf of the victims of incest and sexualized violence.

She'd only spoken for fifty minutes.

SHE HAD EMAIL from friends, asking if she'd seen Twitter. She had email from journalists, asking for an interview. She had emails linking to articles that had been written about her epic rant. She had emails linking to other articles rebutting the previous articles.

ADELINE'S REAL ERROR was criticizing both Beyoncé and Rihanna and their fans' relationship to their achievements.

Beyoncé and Rihanna were pop stars.

Pop stars were musical performers whose celebrity had exploded to the point where they could be identified by single words.

You could say BEYONCÉ or RIHANNA to almost anyone anywhere in the industrialized world and it would conjure a vague neurological image of either Beyoncé or Rihanna.

Their songs were about the same six subjects of all songs by all pop stars: love, celebrity, fucking, heartbreak, money and buying ugly shit.

IT WAS THE TWENTY-FIRST CENTURY.

It was the Internet.

Fame was everything.

Traditional money had been debased by mass production. Traditional money had ceased to be about an exchange of humiliation for food and shelter. Traditional money had become the equivalent of a fantasy world in which different hunks of vampiric plastic made emphatic arguments about why they should cross the threshold of your home.

There was nothing left to buy.

Fame was everything because traditional money had failed. Fame was everything because fame was the world's last valid currency.

BEYONCÉ AND RIHANNA were part of a popular entertainment industry which deluged people with images of grotesque success.

The unspoken ideology of popular entertainment was that its customers could end up as famous as the performers. They only needed to try hard enough and believe in their dreams.

Like all pop stars, Beyoncé and Rihanna existed off the illusion that their fame was a shared experience with their fans. Their fans weren't consumers. Their fans were fellow travelers on a journey through life.

In 2013, this connection between the famous and their fans was fostered on Twitter. Beyoncé and Rihanna were *tweeting*. Their millions of fans were *tweeting* back. They too could achieve their dreams.

Of course, neither Beyoncé nor Rihanna used Twitter. They had assistants and handlers who packaged their *tweets* for maximum profit and exposure.

They were famous in a time when fame was the world's last currency. Fame could purchase the illusion of being an Internet user without the purchaser ever touching a mobile phone or a computer.

That was a difference between the rich and the poor.

The poor were doomed to the Internet, which was a wonderful resource for watching shitty television, experiencing angst about other people's salaries, and casting doubt on key tenets of Mormonism and Scientology.

IF BEYONCÉ OR RIHANNA were asked about how to be like them and gave an honest answer, it would have sounded like this: "You can't. You won't. You are nothing like me. I am a powerful mixture of untamed ambition, early childhood trauma and genetic mystery. I am a portal in the vacuum of space. The formula for my creation is impossible to replicate. The One True God made me and will never make the like again. You are nothing like me."

IT IS WORTH NOTING that both Beyoncé and Rihanna had loads of eumelanin in the strata basale of their epidermises. The American media loved showing Black people who were successful at the performing arts and *sports.*

The American media almost never showed Black people achieving success through education and professionalism. These were not interesting narratives.

BACK WHEN she'd been in Kevin Killian's class, one of the students had interrupted Adeline.

"But, like, don't you like, think that, you know, Facebook and Twitter can serve, like, a role in the pursuit of, like, social progress?" asked the student.

"Pray tell, sweet flower, what is social progress?" asked Adeline. "Social progress might have had meaning twenty years ago when I was but a young thing, but these days it's become the product of corporations. But what do you people know, anyway? You're a lost generation. Even your drugs are corporate. You spend your lives pretending as if Beyoncé and Rihanna possess some inherent meaning and act as if their every professional success, which only occur because of your money and your attention, is a strike forward for women everywhere. Which is sheer nonsense and poppycock, oh my wretches."

A WIDE RANGE of humanity believed that Beyoncé and Rihanna were inspirations rather than vultures. Adeline had spit on their gods.

This wide range of humanity responded by teaching Adeline about one of America's favored pastimes, a tradition as time-honored as police brutality, baseball, race riots and genocide.

They were teaching Adeline about how powerless people demonstrated their supplication before their masters.

They were *tweeting* about Adeline.

chapter ten

Adeline called her friends. She asked for advice.

THE FIRST PERSON she called was Jeremy Winterbloss.

Jeremy Winterbloss and his wife Minerva lived in San Venetia, up in Marin County across the Golden Gate Bridge. It was half an hour from the city, traffic permitting.

Jeremy answered the phone. Minerva wasn't home.

When she and Adeline met, Minerva had been an anarchist punk who'd escaped the Soviet Union. They'd both been students at the Parsons School of Design. Now Minerva was a registered nurse.

Minerva wasn't at home. She was at a hospital, tending the broken bodies of the ill.

"I was waiting for your call," said Jeremy. "My email is going crazy."

"No one's put the frighteners on you, have they?"

"This is all you."

"What does one do?" asked Adeline. "They're saying so many cruel, cruel things about yours truly! You can't imagine the sheer frenzy of Beyoncé's fans!"

"Did you read the YouTube comments?" asked Jeremy.

"No," said Adeline.

"Promise me that you won't," he said.

EACH VIDEO hosted on YouTube was surrounded by an apparatus through which its users could comment upon the hosted video. This apparatus fostered debates between YouTube's users.

Typically these debates were about: (1) Whether or not the person in the video, who was often a 13 year old girl, was an ugly fucking slut who deserved to die. (2) Whether or not President Obama was destroying the country and/or sucking cocks in Hell. (3) Whether or not the other users commenting on the video were dumb assholes. (4) Whether or not Black people were %&$#?@s. (5) Whether or not Asian men had small penises. (6) How wetback Mexicans were stealing good jobs.

To participate in these debates, in which powerless people attacked other powerless people, YouTube's users would return to each video many times over.

Each time that the users returned to the video, renewed in their intentions of calling someone an ugly fucking slut deserving of death, Google served more advertisements and earned more money.

Google was making money off debates about whether or not President Obama sucked cocks in Hell while destroying America. Lightly sprinkled with comments about whether or not Black people were %&$#?@s.

That was okay. YouTube had the same reputation as Twitter. It was an activist tool that fostered *freedom of speech* and *freedom of expression*. It had brought Spring to the Middle East.

"WHAT EVER should I do?" asked Adeline.

"Well, what do you want?" asked Jeremy.

"I'm not certain," she said.

"You could always get an account on Twitter and apologize."

"But darling," said Adeline, "I'm can't. I'm not sorry about anything I've done."

THE NEXT PERSON she called was J. Karacehennem, whose last name was Turkish for *Black Hell*.

"It's simple," he said. "Viral content works like joke writing. So, okay, basically, a joke functions through the contrast of ideas. The first idea is the assumed one, the second idea is a tweak on the first. Here's the set-up to a joke: 'I just flew in from Pittsburgh.' Here's the punchline: 'And, boy, are my arms tired.' The humor rests on the tension between the assumed idea of flying in an airplane and the punchline's verbal tweak which reminds the listener that there are different forms of flight."

"Are you talking down again, darling?"

"Only a little," said J. Karacehennem. "Bear with me. So, okay, viral video works along the same principle. Things go viral when the action within the video exists as a tweak of the cultural assumptions embedded within the video's visual signifiers. Any time you have a grandmother who behaves in a strange way, like a grandmother who sings the latest hit song or talks about sex or does a backflip, that will have some inherent virality, because there is a standing set of cultural assumption about old people in general and grandmothers in specific. These are violated by hit songs and backflips and frank discussions of sex."

"This is getting terribly borrrrrrring," said Adeline. "What does any of this have to do with me?"

"The thing is," said J. Karacehennem, "And I hate to break it to you, but you're the god damned weirdest person alive. There you are in this video, an attractive woman of some years, a dressed-up version of those rock n' roll women in their mid-forties that you meet at the Rainbow Room—"

"Darling, are you calling me rockabilly?"

"—Then you open your mouth and you sound like a drugged out Dianna Vreeland and you've got an erudite range of insane opinions on every possible topic. It's fascinating. And you're kind of famous. People love watching celebrities self-immolate. People fucking love it. It's the spectator sport of the New Millennium."

"That's all very well and good," said Adeline, "What do I do?"

"I wouldn't worry," he said. "In two days, no one will remember. In six months, most of the links will depreciate. Just be glad you've published books. The only powerless people on the Internet are the ones with nothing to sell. Imagine being a spotty Paki chav in London. You'd be a suicide. There's a guy I know whose friend uploaded a picture of him when he was 15. He looks awful. This was almost twenty years ago. It's still the first image result for 'ugly nerd.' Did you talk to Jeremy?"

"Of course," said Adeline.

"Did he say anything about the impact on sales?"

"We've re-entered the Amazon Top 500. Not since the trailer for Don Murphy's *Trill* has our book sold so many copies."

"Ride the wave," said J. Karacehennem. "Everything is advertising. I wonder if you guys could push it any further."

"Sirrah," said Adeline, "Thou must knowest that this is one cow that don't need no milking. I only want the horror to end."

"Wait it out."

"Jeremy said I should acquire my own Twitter and argue my position."

"Trust me, the one thing you do not want to do in this situation is engage. I'd suggest following the rule of all celebrities who have successfully cultivated an air of mystery. Never explain or complain."

ADELINE'S NEXT CALL was to Baby. Baby didn't answer.

Baby was terrible with his phone.

ADELINE'S NEXT CALL was to Erik Willems.

"I don't *grok* virality," he said. "It's very mysterious to me and yet I've helped many startups based around viral content. One of the things that we try to pursue is a blue ocean strategy. What did you say, anyway?"

"Haven't you seen the video?" asked Adeline.

"I don't really care," said Erik Willems. "I'm not that interested in the content so much as the delivery."

"Yet we're sexually intertwined," said Adeline. "And still you can't be bothered to give two tosses of a tuppence?"

"It's all just gossip," said Erik Willems. "It's all just a *solsitre*."

Solsitres are one of the challenges that Annie Zero faces in *Annie Zero*, Baby's book about French Neo-Maoists in the Megaverse.

A *solsitre* is a difficult situation that has no solution but proves to be ultimately irrelevant. The danger of the *solsitre* is that, much like this bad novel, it wastes time.

Solsitres stand in the way of the Neo-Agrarian cypherpunk revolution. The mark of a good leader is her ability to tell *solsitres* from genuine problems. Problems that require attention are called *reprotens*.

"Great good God Almighty," said Adeline to Erik Willems. "You are making me run through my memories like some little Fräulein bolting in a Bavarian field, desperately searching for her runaway Schnauzer. I'm dying, darling, simply dying, to remember why it is that I fuck you."

ADELINE'S FINAL CALL was to Christine.

"I have no idea what I could tell you," said Christine. "This isn't my field of expertise. I'm more of a general Google person."

chapter eleven

While Adeline was learning what it was like to use the Internet, other people were suffering from technological platforms dedicated to *freedom of speech* and *freedom of expression*.

And unlike Adeline, they weren't kind of famous.

And unlike Adeline, they had nothing to sell.

A PRIME EXAMPLE would be Ellen Flitcraft, a twenty-two year old woman living in Truth or Consequences, New Mexico. She had no eumelanin in the basale stratum of her epidermis.

Truth or Consequences was called Hot Springs until the 1950s, when the city elders changed its name as part of a radio contest. People tended to call it *T or C*.

It was small. It was flat. It was in the desert. It was near Elephant Butte Lake, which was both beautiful and embarrassingly named.

Almost everything was painted a shade of brown or white. Less than seven thousand people lived in the city. No building was over two storeys. There were two main roads. Everyone knew everyone else.

The major feature distinguishing Truth or Consequences from other small cities was the plethora of spas near its southern border. Truth or Consequences was loaded with hot springs. Hence the spas. Hence the earlier name.

Spaceport America was about twenty miles out of the city. This was a facility constructed with tax payer dollars and private funding.

In the future, Spaceport America would be a staging ground for private space travel, which was a luxury targeted towards rich people who wanted to bring the wisdom of Ayn Rand to the Red Planet of Mars.

IF YOU WERE YOUNG and smart, you abandoned Truth and Consequences and went to college.

Ellen Flitcraft was class valedictorian at Hot Springs High School. She had a killer admission essay. She had high SAT scores.

She matriculated into the University of California, Los Angeles. She paid out the nose with student loan money. There was also a small merit scholarship.

She'd gone to UCLA thinking that she would major in biology, but upon arriving in Los Angeles, the city's culture seeped into her bones. She transferred into UCLA's film program.

The idea was to finish her degree and stay in Los Angeles and scrounge work in film production.

Ellen wasn't egotistical. She didn't expect to end up as a director, but she did hope that she'd eek out a middle class existence working on film and television productions.

Computers and an insane tax structure were shrinking the job market. But Ellen had hope.

Anyway, it beat being back in Truth or Consequences.

ELLEN FLITCRAFT was raised by her grandmother, who didn't have any eumelanin in the basale strata of her epidermis.

Ellen'd never met her father, who presumably didn't have any eumelanin in the basale strata of his epidermis.

Her mother, who didn't have any eumelanin in the basale strata of her epidermis, spent much of her life wrestling with Methamphetamine, the drug of choice for workers in the American Rust Belt and members of the Nationalsozialistische Deutsche Arbeiterpartei.

Ellen's mother died when Ellen was very young.

Ellen's grandmother did the best she could with the little that she had. Truth or Consequences was a poor city. The cost of living wasn't high.

ELLEN GRADUATED FROM UCLA. Her grandmother didn't attend the ceremony. She was too old for travel.

A few days after receiving her degree, Ellen's cellphone rang.

The call was from her grandmother's neighbor, who said that Ellen's grandmother was up in the Sierra Vista Hospital.

Ellen's grandmother had suffered a stroke.

Ellen drove her ancient grey Toyota Camry back to Truth or Consequences. Normally, the drive took about eleven hours but Ellen did it in eight.

She found her grandmother in the hospital. Her grandmother recognized Ellen but her grandmother couldn't speak. The left side of her body was crippled.

A doctor told Ellen that the effects of the stroke were less severe than they appeared. Her grandmother would never fully recover but with rehab and physical therapy, the old woman could return to a decent life.

It was clear that Ellen would have to return, temporarily, to Truth or Consequences.

IT WASN'T HARD FOR ELLEN to pack up her life and go back home. She'd been planning on moving.

"It's for a year, at most," she said to her Los Angeles friends. "I'll be back. Lots of people take a year off."

She offered her furniture to a wide circle of acquaintances. What wasn't adopted was put out on the street. To be honest, most of it was pretty shitty.

Ellen packed the rest of her belongings and drove back to Truth or Consequences.

HER LIFE NOW REVOLVED around her infirm grandmother. Much of this was simple chores like cleaning and helping the older woman perform bodily functions.

The harder stuff was taking her grandmother out of the house, ensuring that the older woman made her twice weekly appointments for physical therapy.

Her grandmother's Social Security cheque wasn't enough to pay for both Ellen and her grandmother. Not with the student loans.

A friend of her grandmother's neighbor's son had an opening at his place of business. He sold insurance. The pay wasn't great but the work was mindless. Anyway, it was only temporary. Ellen would be going back to Los Angeles.

When Ellen was at work, the neighbor would come in and check on Ellen's grandmother.

ELLEN HADN'T GOTTEN IN TOUCH with any of her high school friends. The few times when she'd come back from Los Angeles and hung out had been awkward. Whenever she talked about her life in Los Angeles, it sounded like bragging.

None of her old friends knew that she was in Truth or Consequences. This was a difficult feat to manage, as Ellen was connected with all of her friends on Facebook and Instagram.

Instagram was a social media platform acquired by Facebook in 2012 for $1,000,000,000. Instagram allowed its users to share photographs with the world. *Come, children,* Instagram said to its users, *upload your photographs of the world's beauty!*

Mostly, Instagram's users uploaded photographs of things on which they'd either spent money or wished to spend money.

It was an infinite sexless orgy of cars, guns, food, clothes, dogs, cats, yoga, bikinis, money clips, works of art, breast implants, buttocks implants, dream vacations, tattoos, vinyl records, cellular phones, footwear, laptop computers, country estates in England, airplanes, piercings, exotic pets, mid-century modern homes, bongs, crockery, bathroom mirrors, cameras, mojitos and other delicious alcoholic beverages, lip augmentation, handbags, watches, spiral staircases, suicidal ideation, caffeinated drinks purchased at Starbucks, motorcycles, protein supplements, suntan lotion, fake moustaches, novelty mugs, children's toys, sunglasses, guitars, Sno-cone machines, vape pens, scooters, crystal pendants and imported Japanese junk food.

Uncoincidentally, Instagram was also the first social media platform to which the only sane reaction was hate.

AFTER SHE RETURNED to Truth or Consequences, Ellen curtailed her activities on both Facebook and Instagram. She didn't want anyone to know she was back in town, which was a hopeless idea in a community with a population below seven thousand.

Still, it was worth a try.

WHEN A FEW WEEKS had passed, Ellen realized that she couldn't spend every night in the house with her grandmother. The older woman was particularly insistent that they watch re-runs of *Two and a Half Men,* an awful sitcom about the sexual innuendo which emerges from the unconsummated homosexual desire between two brothers. It was enormously popular with senior citizens.

Ellen made the decision to have a drink at Raymond's Lounge, a small dive bar next to the Circle K gas station. Its standing signage read: RAYMOND'S LOUNGE PACKAGED GOODS.

There were other bars in town but the lounge loomed in her imagination, from way back in high school when the other kids whispered about the place, bragging of exploits within its four walls.

She ordered a drink. She sat at the bar. She kept to herself. The clientele was the expected mixture of rummy desert rats and young men in cargo shorts. The ceilings were low. The ceiling fans rotated.

Ellen finished her drink and ordered another.

Somewhere through the second drink, she heard a voice calling her name. "Ellen? Ellen?"

She turned around. She saw her high school sweetheart, Maximiliano Rojas, who had some melanin in the basale stratum of his epidermis.

MAXIMILIANO AND ELLEN got to talking. He started buying her drinks.

"Don't get too excited," said Ellen. "I'm not going to fuck you."

"That's okay," said Max. "I couldn't anyway. I'm practically married."

"Who with?" asked Ellen.

"I don't know if you remember her. Ashley Nelson?"

Ashley Nelson didn't have any eumelanin in the basale stratum of her epidermis.

"Ashley," said Ellen. "You're lucky. Ashley's cute."

Ellen and Maximiliano dated from grade ten to grade twelve. They broke up about a month before graduation. Maximiliano had called it off.

Following the split, she saw him at school and occasionally ran into him around town. Each time was like being stabbed.

UCLA and Los Angeles were her salvation. Once Ellen was out of Truth or Consequences, she was amazed at how little she thought about Maximiliano. Time dulled the pain.

But the questions had never gone away, all the wherefores and whys. She'd always thought that if they met again, she'd make him tell her the reason he'd ended it.

Now, having their first conversation in four years, Ellen couldn't remember why she cared. So much had happened. There'd been a series of pointless sexual encounters in Los Angeles and one very bad relationship. She was so beyond Maximiliano. He was the past.

They talked. Mostly about their families. Maximiliano's sister had moved to Albuquerque. His dad still drank too much and still had his model trains, although he'd given up HO scale for O.

"I love your mom," said Ellen. "She was so sweet to me."

"You can always go see her. She'd love it."

"Maybe I will."

ELLEN FINISHED her fourth drink. It was time to go home.

"This was really nice, Max," said Ellen. "It was really great seeing you again."

"You're in town for a while, though?"

"Yeah, at least a year."

"We should hang out together again. Maybe we'll go bowling."

"Is that place still open? I haven't been bowling in forever."

"Hit me up on Facebook."

Ellen went home. Her grandmother was sleeping but otherwise fine. Ellen went into her bedroom and fell asleep.

She had a dream about someone falling from a high platform and cracking their skull. It was a clean break beneath the skin, running vertically from the forehead to the jaw.

ELLEN DID GO and visit Mamá Rojas, who had a fair amount of eumelanin in the basale stratum of her epidermis. The woman was sweeter than ever, taking Ellen into her house and insisting on feeding her. The food was unbelievable.

"I missed your cooking," said Ellen. "Los Angeles is okay but there's nothing like this."

"You need to eat, eat," said Mamá Rojas. "Too skinny."

Ellen noticed that Mamá Rojas's English was much improved.

When Ellen and Maximiliano were dating, the older woman had peppered her Spanish with a few English words and nothing more. This had been useful for Ellen, as she picked up a great deal of Mamá Rojas's native tongue.

"And how do you find my English?" asked Mamá Rojas.

"I wasn't going to say anything," said Ellen. "I didn't want to be rude. But you've learned so much!"

"I take the courses online," said Mamá Rojas.

They talked about Los Angeles. They talked about Ellen's grandmother. They talked about Maximiliano's hooligan cousins on his father's side, the boys who Mamá Rojas called *dos perros hermanos*.

When Ellen was leaving, Mamá Rojas asked Ellen if she'd met Ashley.

"In high school. I didn't know she was dating Max."

"I wish he stayed with you," said Mamá Rojas. "Ashley is no good. I tell him all the time. You lost the one good girl who will ever love you."

"Don't give him ideas," said Ellen.

ELLEN TOOK MAXIMILIANO up on his offer. They went bowling. The name of the bowling alley had changed and so had the sign and now the interior and exterior façade were done up to look like the dwelling of a cartoon caveman. But otherwise it was still T or C.

Somewhere around her fourteenth gutter ball, Ellen realized why she hadn't gone bowling in Los Angeles. She hated bowling. Bowling was awful.

Maximiliano was buying the drinks.

"I'm still not fucking you," said Ellen.

"I'm not trying," said Maximiliano. "You're out of my league."

"Shut up," said Ellen.

Maximiliano went to the bar to get the third round of drinks. He bumped into one of Ashley's friends, an unpleasant girl named Amanda Martinez, who was originally from New York City and had a very small amount of eumelanin in the basal stratum of her epidermis.

"*¿Hola cerote, cómo estás vato?*" she asked. "*¿Ashley estás aquí? La chica puta dijo se mantiene el culo en casa.*"

"*Está en casa,*" said Maximiliano. "*Estoy aquí con mi amiga Ellen.*"

"Ellen Fitcraft?" asked Amanda. "That *empollón* you fucked?"

"*Sí*", said Maximiliano. "Flitcraft. *Ella en la ciudad.*"

The bartender brought over the drinks. Maximiliano paid.

"*Hasta luego,*" said Maximiliano.

"Later," said Amanda.

AMANDA MARTINEZ watched as Ellen and Maximiliano bowled. She was using her cellphone. She was sending text messages to Ashley.

Amanda to Ashley: *BITCH WHERE U @*

Ashley to Amanda: *wot u on about now*

Amanda to Ashley: *BITCH Y IS UR MAN HERE WITH HIS*
RAGGITY ASS RATCHET X

Ashley to Amanda: *wot*

Amanda to Ashley: *BITCH HES HERE WITH EILEEN*
FITCRAFT

Ashley to Amanda: *u crazy*

Ashley to Amanda: *shes in la sucking hollywood dick*

Ashley to Amanda: *lol*

Amanda to Ashley: *BITCH I C THE BITCH WITH MY EYES*

Amanda to Ashley: *BITCH THE BITCH JUST FELL IN HIS ARMS*

Amanda to Ashley: *BITCH SHES HOLDING HIM*

Ashley to Amanda: *he said hes with his cousins tonite*

Amanda to Ashley: *BITCH HES HERE RITE NOW*

Ashley to Amanda: *where*

Ashley to Amanda: *?*

Amanda to Ashley: *BEDROXX*

Amanda to Ashley: *I NEVER LIKED THIS STUCK UP CUNT AND SHES BOWLING WITH UR MAN*

Ashley to Amanda: *im comin rite now*

BUT ASHLEY'S BROTHER, with whom she lived, had borrowed her car. She had to walk from the northern part of the city. By the time that she arrived, Ellen and Maximiliano had gone to their respective homes.

Amanda gave Ashley a ride over to Maximiliano's house. Ashley thought she'd catch Ellen and Maximiliano in the act of betrayal, but the only thing she found was her boyfriend sitting on his mother's couch, eating toxic junk food and playing *BioShock Infinite* on his X-Box 360.

"Where's your whore?" asked Ashley.

"What?" asked Maximiliano.

"Ellen," said Ashley. "Amanda saw you."

"Aw baby," said Maximiliano, "It wasn't nothing. We were just hanging out."

Maximiliano spent the next few hours explaining the situation. He was soothing Ashley. He was telling her the truth about why he hadn't told her the truth. He'd wanted to keep her from freaking out because he didn't think she'd believe him that nothing was going on. He stroked her head and let her cry. He kissed her face.

Mamá Rojas overheard everything. None of it improved her opinion of Ashley.

WHEN ELLEN WAS DATING MAXIMILIANO, they had a ton of sex. They had lost their virginities to each other and fucked in every possible way. They had seen each other clutched in orgasm. Countless times. They'd been in love.

On one evening late in the relationship, when they were both drunk and more than a little stoned, Maximiliano convinced Ellen to let him take photographs of them having sex.

"I just want to have something to remember," he'd said.

He used his cellphone.

Ellen knew this was a terrible idea but she lived in a culture enraptured with its consumer electronics. These consumer electronics were inevitably incorporated into people's sex lives.

Sometimes it was gross, like the unconscious symbolism of a television remote control employed as a dildo.

Most of the time it was simpler.

It was the Twenty-First Century.

Everyone fucked on camera.

THEY DIDN'T END UP HAVING VAGINAL SEX. While Ellen was performing oral sex on Maximiliano, he ejaculated into her mouth and onto her face. It was something about the combination of the camera and the act and the way that the camera made him see the act. He took pictures of it all.

While they were in bed, Ellen asked to see the evidence. She had sucked his dick with such love but none of that came across in the photos. She just looked awkward and weird.

"Can you delete these?"

"I wanna keep them," said Maximiliano. "For the future, you know. I love you, baby."

Ellen said okay, fine.

When they broke up, she insisted that he delete them.

"I'll come to your house and tell Mamá," she said.

He told her not to worry. He said he deleted them.

A WEEK after the bowling incident, Ashley Nelson visited the Rojas household. She screwed out Maximiliano's brains. He fell asleep.

While he was snoring, Ashley found his cellphone and looked for evidence of his infidelity. She'd never done this before. She couldn't find anything.

Ashley woke up Maximiliano.

"I don't feel so good," she said.

"What's wrong?" he said.

"Stomach ache," she said. "I need some medicine. Do you guys have Kaopectate?"

Maximiliano went into the bathroom and looked through the medicine cabinet. He remembered seeing a bottle of Kaopectate.

He couldn't find any. What he didn't know is that Ashley had removed the old Kaopectate. The bottle was in the bottom of her purse.

He returned to his bedroom.

"I couldn't find any," he said.

"Can you go get me some?" she asked. "It's killing me."

She gave her very best groan.

MAXIMILIANO TOOK HIS CAR and went to find some Kaopectate. Ashley sat down as his computer and started going through his files. She was seeking evidence of his infidelity. She had never done this before.

She found the pictures of Ellen performing oral sex on her boyfriend.

Now Ashley's stomach really did hurt. She wanted to throw up. She felt like she could die. The sky had crashed in on her head.

She logged into her email account. She emailed herself the pictures.

When Maximiliano came back home, Ashley thanked him for the medicine. She drank some Kaopectate and said she had to go home. He offered to drive her. She said it was okay. She'd be okay. She just wanted to sleep in her own bed.

IT STARTED SOMEWHERE around eight in the morning. Ellen's phone beeped out the arrival of phonecalls and text messages and voicemail. The first text message was from her second cousin. That was weird. They hadn't texted in years.

CHECK YR EMAIL.

Ellen checked her email.

There were about thirty messages.

The nicest read, "I'm sorry to tell you this but I think you were hacked. There are some pictures of you online with your name that you should probably see. You probably recognize them but maybe you don't."

The email concluded with a link to a webpage.

And it was on that webpage that Ellen saw herself performing oral sex on her high school boyfriend. Her full name was attached. She was on the Internet.

ASHLEY EMAILED THE LINK not only to Ellen but also to everyone who knew Ellen. Old friends, people from high school, teachers from high school, Ellen's boss at the insurance company. Ellen's family.

Because Ellen was a normal human being, she didn't know that she could hide her friends list on Facebook. Her friends were visible to the world.

Ashley sent links to all of Ellen's friends. The ones who didn't read the message from Ashley received the link in messages from other people to whom Ashley had sent it.

Almost everyone who knew Ellen saw photographs of Ellen performing oral sex on her high school boyfriend.

All the while, Facebook was making money. Every message that people sent each other about Ellen's public shame arrived alongside advertisements for electric razors, pet food and the Child Brain Health Research Institute.

All the while, Google was making money. Whenever anyone searched for Ellen's name, Google serving targeted advertisements and collecting user data for future exploitation.

There was not going to be a move to Los Angeles. There was not going to be any career in film. There was only a long stretch of crippling student debt and elder care in Truth or Consequences, New Mexico.

There was only life in a city where at least half the population had seen photographs of Ellen performing oral sex on her high school boyfriend.

She could change her name and hope that no future employers would make the connection, but this meant giving up her identity and did nothing whatsoever to alleviate the mental trauma.

She wasn't kind of famous like Adeline and, unlike Adeline, she had nothing to sell.

Ellen was twenty-two years old and her life was over.

chapter twelve

Christine worked as an assistant librarian at UCSF's Parnassus campus. Adeline had never inquired as to how she got the job.

Adeline never asked about anyone else's work or living situations. It seemed rude.

ADELINE MET CHRISTINE at an event for Baby's *Annie Zero*.

The event was held at City Lights, a bookstore in North Beach famous for its association with the Beat Writers of the 1950s and 1960s.

It was the best bookstore in San Francisco. It was also the best bookstore in America.

EVENTS AT CITY LIGHTS were planned by a man named Peter Maravelis, who didn't have eumelanin in the basale stratum of his epidermis. If Peter Maravelis believed that an event would draw a large crowd, the event was held downstairs. Smaller events were held upstairs in the intimacy of the poetry room.

The event for *Annie Zero* was held downstairs.

BECAUSE OF THE FICTIONAL CONCEITS within *Annie Zero*, Baby was being mentioned alongside a certain class of contemporary writers.

These writers were influential amongst the men who ran Silicon Valley. These writers were also influential amongst the men who worked in subservient positions to the men who ran Silicon Valley.

Baby had joined the ranks of writers like William Gibson, who wrote *Neuromancer.*

Baby had joined the ranks of Neil Stephenson, who wrote *Snow Crash* and *Cryptonomicon.*

Baby had joined the ranks of Cory Doctorow, who wrote fantasies about rebellion aimed at a teenaged audience.

Despite being aimed at a teenaged audience, Cory Doctorow's books were read by adults. Typically, these adults were UNIX systems administrators, network engineers, and Ruby developers who'd been rendered functionally illiterate by their collegiate computer science programs.

WHEN BABY WAS WRITING *ANNIE ZERO,* he needed a conceptual space for the French Neo-Maoists to stage battles against the entrenched social order.

Because Baby was realistic about the future, he couldn't conceive of a world in which these battles happened in any traditional context.

So he invented the Megaverse.

In *Annie Zero,* after global warming and an accidental nuclear winter, all the world's citizens live out their lives in the Megaverse. The Megaverse was a significantly upgraded version of an old online multiplayer roleplaying game called *Ultima Online.*

When the tattered shreds of the world government modded *Ultima Online* into the Megaverse, there were many notable enhancements, including wetware interfaces for biological needs like fucking, eating and shitting.

The central conceit of *Annie Zero* is that life in the Megaverse has evolved to a point where its social structure is an almost exact mirror of life in 1990s. The Neo-Maoist revolution happens in a world that is a virtual duplicate of our own.

Despite the inference of this narrative, Baby didn't believe in teleological social progress.

He did believe in recognizable fictional settings. He knew that a recognizable setting would help draw in an audience. From his experience with *Trapped Between Jupiter and a Bottle*, he also knew that a recognizable fiction setting was the best way to convince readers that his work was an *allegory.*

Allegory was a word used by self-important writers and readers to suggest that the flaws of an above average novel were, in fact, virtues.

When someone suggested that a narrative was *allegorical,* they meant that the narrative's symbolism was intentionally gauzy. They meant that a narrative's ill-thought out structure possessed a *secret meaning.*

Many, many people called *Annie Zero* an *allegory.* They saw parallels between Baby's Megaverse and the work that they were doing on the Internet and in Silicon Valley.

They also found the struggles of the Neo-Maoists very inspiring. What was the Internet if not an outlet of constant revolution and social change?

These men were confused about the basic nature of Neo-Maoism. Their formal educations in computer science had rendered them historically as well as functionally illiterate.

They didn't realize that Maoism had been, you know, like, an actual thing.

THUS DID BABY find a wider audience, elevating himself out of the common gutter of Science Fiction and into the echelons of digital prophecy.

Baby didn't care about the Internet's potential for free speech or world revolution. He only wanted to tend his own garden.

But Baby was realistic. For a long time, he'd known that the Internet was a propaganda engine through which he could trick people into buying his books.

He began *tweeting* cryptic phrases about new technologies, futurism and dystopias.

CHRISTINE CAME TO THE EVENT as a favor to a friend, who didn't want to attend Baby's event by himself.

Adeline went to the event because Baby was Baby and Adeline was Adeline. She hadn't read *Annie Zero.*

BEFORE BABY ARRIVED IN SAN FRANCISCO, he did fifteen other events. Most were on the East Coast. A few in the American Middle West. Some in Southern California.

He had pressed the flesh of his audience and in turn his audience had pressed their flesh against him.

One member of Baby's audience had given him a terrible cold.

He'd since swallowed a near overdose of remedies, including: Vitamin C, Vitamin E, NyQuil and Sudafed. Nothing helped.

As he walked through the door of City Lights, Baby was one of America's sickest men. He leaked mucus from all the orifices of his countenance. His eyes blurred with tears.

The only saving grace was that, forty-eight hours earlier, the vomiting and violent diarrhea had disappeared.

BABY STOOD AT THE PODIUM and talked and talked. About the abuses of Maoism, about its vogue with young Parisians of the upper middle class during the May '68 revolt, about the suicide of Guy Debord, about the Khmer Rouge, about the novelist Michèle Bernstein, about the conceptual structure of the Megaverse.

While he talked, he coughed. While he talked, he blew his nose. While he talked, he expelled phlegm into a handkerchief.

The event was standing-room only.

Baby spoke for an hour, scattering germs in every direction.

BABY FINISHED SPEAKING. People queued in line. They wanted Baby to sign copies of *Annie Zero*. Adeline hung around near the front of the store.

Christine was in the same area. Her friend was queued in line. Christine had no interest in Baby's autograph.

"What's the matter with you, sweetheart?" asked Adeline. "Aren't you simply dying to touch the author of *Annie Zero*? Or is it his germs that you fear?"

"I haven't read it," said Christine. "I'm just waiting for a friend."

"Me too," said Adeline. "Do you know, I gather that *Annie Zero* is rather stuffed full of interesting new words. There might very well be a word in *Annie*

Zero for the chance meeting of two people at an event for a book neither person has read."

"Is there a glossary?" asked Christine. "Some of these books come with their own glossaries."

They checked. There was no glossary.

BABY FINISHED SIGNING BOOKS. Peter Maravelis asked Baby to leave an artifact on an altar in the basement. Maravelis said that every writer left a relic.

Baby couldn't think of anything, so he ripped a random page from his reading copy of *Annie Zero* and blew his nose.

"The very first thing on here was a cum rag," said Peter Maravelis.

BABY WAS STAYING with Adeline. The plan was to go for drinks after the event. Adeline asked Christine if she wanted to come along.

"What about my friend?"

"Is he a square?" asked Adeline. "Does he have four equal sides and angles?"

"It'd be kind of embarrassing," said Christine. "He might gush the whole night."

"Baby's simply been gushing for days. It might be nice to have someone else do the dirty deed."

Christie ditched her friend. Christine told her friend that she was taking a cab home.

Christine walked out of City Lights, headed down Columbus towards Market. She waited five minutes and doubled back on Pacific, Grant and Kerouac Alley. Her friend was gone.

BABY INVITED his own set of people. Adeline didn't know any of them. One was a gorgeous *twink*.

Twink was slang for a young gay man without any personality or body hair.

jarett kobek

EVERYONE WENT across the street to a bar called Specs, an old wooden place decorated with a wide-range of curios.

Adeline let Baby hold court. She didn't interrupt. She talked to Christine.

"Tell me, you charming girl," said Adeline, "Do you think Baby is going to screw the brains out of this *twink*? If so, do you posit that this screwing out of brains will occur at my apartment?"

BESIDES THE *TWINK*, Baby brought along five other sycophants. Adeline and Christine listened as they asked Baby pointless questions about *Annie Zero*.

Like: *In chapter fifteen, when Annie Zero demands that the agrarian class enter a state of permanent revolution, does this preclude allies from the proletariat?*

Like: *Who does Annie Zero marry in the end?*

Like: *How did you think of the thing with the anteater?*

NEITHER ADELINE NOR CHRISTINE were part of the conversation. Adeline suggested that they pass the time by doing what Baby had done, which was to invent a lot of bullshit words.

Adeline came up with *pregnot:* the time between the last unprotected sex and the onset of ovulation.

Christine came up with *jeejoonjaz:* the sensation of existing, simultaneously, within three different calendar months.

Adeline came up with *celebusikenz:* being made sick by the accidental radiation of a D-list celebrity.

Christine came up with *shizpaz:* the problem of needing to urinate and defecate at the same time and the confusion that arises when a person can't figure out which to do first.

Adeline came up with *haksiksad:* the feeling a person gets when they hear their cat wretch but before the feline has vomited.

Christine came up with *disaguit:* when a handsome young man invites you back to his place only to take off his shirt and play the guitar.

Adeline came up with *terrofucked:* the moment when an empire is destroyed by 19 guys carrying box cutters and a few cans of mace.

Christine came up with *sloslopped*: the slowing of time as you spill liquid across a linoleum floor.

Adeline came up with *twinkiwink*: when you're not sure whether your best friend, who is leaking mucus from every orifice of his countenance, will bring a *twink* to your apartment for sex.

Christine came up with *oldthunked*: when you conceive, in totality, the full life of a person who you have met in their final decade.

ADELINE AND CHRISTINE exchanged numbers.

They started hanging out.

They saw each other about once a week.

BABY SCREWED OUT the *twink's* brains. He took the *twink* to Adeline's apartment. They made orgasms and earthquakes of pleasure. They shook the guest bedroom.

Baby was coughing and leaking the whole time. The *twink* didn't care. Adeline put on headphones.

EVERYONE WHO'D BEEN AT CITY LIGHTS came down with a cold. This included Adeline. This included Peter Maravelis. This included the *twink*. This included Christine.

Baby had coughed all over the audience and infected them with his germs. This was only slightly metaphorical.

chapter thirteen

J. Karacehennem had moved to San Francisco at an insane moment in its history. The beauty of the city was not outweighing its annoying residents.

THE WORD USED TO DESCRIBE the insanity of the moment was *gentrification,* but no one knew what *gentrification* meant, not really, and most people did not understand what was happening.

Christine was one of these people. She had lived in the city for almost two decades. She was caught up in a whirlwind of change. She had no idea what the fuck was going on.

It was as if she'd been hit by one of the Ford F-150s advertised on Twitter.

GENTRIFICATION WAS WHAT HAPPENED to a city when people with an excess of capital wanted their capital to produce more capital while not attributing any value to labor.

THE POINT WAS THIS: in 2007, the American economy had crashed.

In the decades leading up to the crash, a series of US Presidents had done everything they could to make sure that capital, rather than labor, was the driving force of the American economy. This process was called *deregulation.*

These Presidents were: Ronald Reagan, George Bush I, Bill Clinton, George Bush II. None of them had any eumelanin in the basale strata of their epidermises.

RONALD REAGAN was a former actor who had starred in a movie in which he taught morals to an ape. He was the Governor of California before he was President of the United States.

George Bush I came from such an old money family that his father sat on the board of a bank under Nazi control. George Bush I had been the director of the Central Intelligence Agency.

Bill Clinton grew up poorer than dirt. He positioned himself in the imaginary political center, which was a polite way of saying that he governed from the Right while mouthing platitudes of the Left. He loved three things: (1) Women. (2) The sound of his own voice. (3) *Deregulation.*

George Bush II was the son of George Bush I. He was a draft dodger. He was President when America was *terrofucked.* His brother, Neil, was a sex tourist who caught herpes from a sex-worker in Southeast Asia.

George Bush II was an alcoholic and one of the worst Presidents in history. His inexperience led to him being manipulated by his Vice President, another draft dodger who loved three things: (1) Torture. (2) War. (3) Self-righteousness.

THE PRESIDENCY, which was limited to eight years, had an incentive for *deregulation.*

The incentive was simple. The short term gains caused by *deregulation* appeared very fast. The damage took decades to arrive.

IT'S WORTH NOTING that the one constant in all four Presidencies was the presence of Alan Greenspan, the Chairman of the Federal Reserve.

Alan Greenspan loved *deregulation.*

He was also one of Ayn Rand's disciples. He'd sat at her knee whilst she talked about poor people being garbage who deserved to die in the gutter.

Ayn Rand was the most formative intellectual influence on the man who oversaw the Federal Reserve during a period of intense *deregulation.*

The predictable result of this *deregulation* was a series of speculation bubbles that destroyed the economy.

It's arguable that Ayn Rand's finest achievement was not the authoring of two shitty novels. It's arguable that Ayn Rand's finest achievement was crashing the economy twenty-five years after her death.

A SPECULATION BUBBLE was a scheme in which people with money convinced people with less money that things have value greater than their actual worth.

People who get in at the beginning of a bubble and then get out before the bubble pops make a ton of money. Everyone else gets screwed.

WHEN THE ECONOMY IMPLODED, the response of the Federal government was to institute a series of half-assed reforms which kept the status at quo.

Part of keeping the status at quo was lowering short term interest rates to near zero and instituting a series of quantitative easing programs which pumped billions of dollars, monthly, into the economy. The latter had the effect of lowering long term interest rates to almost zero.

If interest rates were near zero, traditional outlets—savings accounts, treasury bonds—would no longer offer returns on investment. This would force people with capital to move that capital into other parts of the economy.

By putting money into investment opportunities, cash circulated and the economy was stimulated.

In theory.

ONE OF THE MODELS by which people invested their money was venture capital. Venture capital was the dominant investment model of the San Francisco Bay Area.

Erik Willems was one of the men who worked in venture capital. He moved money in the desired directions of his masters.

Before Erik Willems worked in venture capital, he had a job with Fear and Respect Holdings Ltd., the firm run by His Royal Highness Mamduh bin Fatih bin Muhammad bin Abdulaziz al Saud.

HRH MAMDUH BIN FATIH BIN MUHAMMAD BIN AB-
DULAZIZ AL SAUD disliked using his given name with people who
weren't native Arabic speakers. To grease the gears of global capitalism, he'd
adopted many names in different languages.

In Chinese, he was called 野生花卉, which meant Wild Flower.

In Spanish, he was called *El Diablo árabe,* which meant The Arabic Devil.

In Turkish, he was called *Küçükkutsaldağ,* which meant The Little Holy
Mountain.

In German, he was called *Der Meister der Weltschmerz,* which meant
Master of the World's Sorrow.

In English, he was called *Dennis,* which meant Dennis.

ERIK WILLIAMS MET DENNIS at Harvard University. They were
both graduate students.

Erik was earning an MBA at the Business School. He spent his days
arguing case studies and pretending as if future success could be predicted
from past failure.

Dennis was earning a Masters of Public Policy at the John F. Kennedy
School of Government, an institution where war criminals taught the global
elite how to rule with an iron fist.

Erik met Dennis at a party on Commonwealth Ave in Brighton. The
apartment was rented by another student at the Kennedy School. The rentee's
father was prominent in Mid-East politics.

The apartment was small. Dennis asked the rentee why he hadn't chosen
accommodations more befitting someone whose father was prominent in the
governance of his native country.

"We afford only so much," said the rentee. "My father isn't too corrupt."

"All things in time, my friend," said Dennis. "In the domains of the
Prophet, Peace Be Unto Him, even the agèd learn on which side their bread
is buttered."

Dennis was living in a Victorian mansion on Chauncy Street. His father
owned the building.

ANYWAY, ERIK AND DENNIS were at a party in this apartment on Comm Ave in Brighton. They both arrived alone. The guests were boring.

Dennis noticed that Erik was examining the rentee's bookshelves. He walked over and introduced himself.

He told Erik to call him Dennis.

"Do you recognize any volumes befitting of your tastes?" asked Dennis.

"They're all textbooks."

"I myself am a man of some refined literary avarice," said Dennis.

This was before Erik had moved to the Bay Area. He'd yet to develop a taste for juvenile literature.

No one had heard of *Annie Zero* because *Annie Zero* didn't exist. Baby was licking his wounds from the failure of *Hot Mill Steam*. He hadn't begun to think about the Megaverse or Neo-Maoists.

"I don't know much about books, really," said Erik to Dennis.

"As of late," said Dennis to Erik, "I have cultivated a hunger and passion for the words and philosophy of the Russian émigré Ayn Rand. I find that engagement with her work relieves the vital center."

The friendship was formed.

ERIK AND DENNIS graduated at the same time.

Dennis would have graduated earlier but America got *terrofucked*.

In the aftermath, when dark accusations were flying about the Saudi royal family, Dennis took a leave of absence from the Kennedy School.

On September 13, 2001, he and several relatives charted a private jet out of Rhode Island's T.F. Greene airport.

Dennis spent the next year in Paris. His father co-owned a hotel in *le 8ᵉ arrondissement*. Dennis crashed in a palatial suite on the penultimate floor. He ingested a great amount of Bolivian cocaine and fucked a copious number of high priced sex-workers while listening to the albums of Iron Maiden. His favorites were *Seventh Son of a Seventh Son* and *The Number of the Beast*.

One time, when he was high on Bolivian cocaine and listening to Iron Maiden and in the company of a sex-worker with a great deal of eumelanin in the basale stratum of her epidermis, Dennis imagined that he himself was the seventh son of a seventh son.

"I am not a simple prince of The Kingdom of Saud," he told the sex-worker, "But also am I born the seventh one, born of woman, the seventh son! I have the power to heal! I have the gift of the second sight! So it is written! So it shall be done!"

"*Mais oui, bien sûr, mon mari,*" said the sex-worker in Tamil-inflected French. "*Mais ma chatte ne ronronne. Passe-moi la Blanche neige.*"

When America was back to business and using cluster bombs to transform illiterate Pashtuns into scattered chunks of bruised meat, Dennis returned to Harvard.

A FEW MONTHS after graduation, Dennis offered Erik a job with Fear and Respect Holdings Ltd.

Dennis formed Fear and Respect with a capital seed of $100,000,000. The money was a graduation present from his father.

For over three decades, the old man, His Royal Highness Fatih bin Muhammad bin Abdulaziz al Saud, had run his own company. He'd built it into a powerhouse and made himself the third richest man in the Middle East.

One of Fatih bin Muhammad's few failures came during the dotcom era of the 1990s, when he'd lost a lot of money on bad investments. The most notorious was Kozmo.com.

Kozmo.com was a one-hour delivery service that sold goods below cost and hoped to make up the money on delivery fees. The hysteria of the moment was such that even with a business model dedicated to losing money, the company raised about $250,000,000 in capital.

Dennis's father had invested $20,000,000. The money disappeared in about a year. Fatih bin Muhammad was convinced that while the Internet offered growth opportunities, he himself didn't understand the burgeoning online world.

As he was learning this lesson about the new digital economy, Fatih bin Muhammad was also wracked with concern about his son.

Heretofore, Dennis had proved to be little more than a useless layabout. His only appreciable skills were: (1) An internal radar which allowed him to land at any major airport in the world and immediately locate the city's upscale drug dealers. (2) Fucking high priced sex-workers.

Fatih bin Muhammad would be damned to Karacehennem before he allowed Dennis to become another useless Saudi playboy. He combined his two problems and decided that Dennis would run a company which invested in Internet and media.

"My son, my son," he said, "I'm too old for the Internet. My body grows weak and betrays me. Such illness. No longer shall I be called Abū Mamduh. All now shall know me as Abū al-Amrāḍ.

"But you, my child, you are yet young. The swift blood of your mother runs through those veins. The Internet is for the young. Mass entertainment is for the young. Do not shame your father. Go and prove yourself. Conquer the Internet! Conquer new and old media!"

Fear and Respect Holdings Ltd. was formed.

ERIK WAS DENNIS'S FIRST HIRE. On the whole, the situation worked. They had some successes. They had some failures. They made more money than they lost. Fatih bin Muhammad was happy.

Erik only lasted about two years with Fear and Respect. He hated the constant travel and he couldn't handle Dennis's frequent insistence that they smoke DMT in brothels.

"I'm good with whores," Erik said while giving notice. "And I can deal with elves revealing universal secrets in 360° vision, but I can't handle elfin revelation in Castilian whorehouses. It's too much for me."

Erik left Fear and Holding with a decent severance package and a few words of Dennis's advice: "Get to San Francisco! I am certain there is money awaiting your conquest. Fear not, dear friend, for I will come and visit. My father owns two buildings in the Haight and another in the Financial District."

Erik went to San Francisco and found a job at Sequoia Capital. Sequoia Capital was a venture capital firm.

VENTURE CAPITAL firms offered opportunities in venture capital funds.

Venture capital funds provided money to up-and-coming companies.

In exchange for this funding, the firms purchased a certain amount of equity in these up-and-coming companies.

The funds were managed by general partners like Erik. The investors, either very rich individuals or very rich institutions, were limited partners.

The general partners found opportunities and, using the money of the limited partners, invested in these opportunities.

THE BASIC UNDERLYING APPROACH of venture capital firms was to invest in a wide range of companies. Most of the companies in which venture capital firms invested would fail.

The hope was that one or two of these companies would make a great deal of money. This great deal of money would offset the losses from the bad investments.

It was like shooting at a flock of birds with a sawed-off shotgun.

AFTER A FEW YEARS at Sequoia, Erik Willems and some of his co-workers decided to found their own venture capital firm. They named it MoriaMordor.

The co-founders arrived at this name by combining two imaginary locations in J.R.R. Tolkein's *The Lord of the Rings*. Having lived in the Bay Area for some years, Erik and the other co-founders were well versed in juvenile literature. They *groked* Sci-Fi/Fantasy.

Before anyone could join MoriaMordor as an official co-founder, they had to pass a trial by fire. Each needed to land at least one limited partner.

Some of the co-founders tapped clients for whom they'd worked at Sequoia Capital. Erik chose another route. He called Dennis.

IT TOOK A FEW DAYS of wrangling with Fear and Respect's apparatchiks, but Erik got Dennis on the telephone.

When Erik spoke to Dennis, the latter was staying in the Hürrem Sultan suite at Hôtel Les Ottomans in Istanbul, Turkey. His father was entertaining the idea of purchasing the hotel, which was a renovated old mansion overlooking the Bosphorus.

"How's Istanbul?" asked Erik.

"My mother, as I am sure you remember, she herself was a Turk. As was my grandmother. I always love this country. The only unpleasantness in Turkey is the Turks. Still, a person admits their hospitality. Their name for me here is Küçükkutsaldağ. 'Hoşgeldiniz Küçükkutsaldağ,' they say. 'Nasılsınız, Küçükkutsaldağ?' they ask. A beautiful thing. But Istanbul, eh, what words might a man offer about Istanbul? It is the most wonderful city in the world if a person's sole desire is to encounter ten thousand red-faced Germans wearing t-shirts which read either 'NYC' or 'Brooklyn.'"

Erik told Dennis about MoriaMordor. He asked Dennis to contribute to MoriaMordor's limited fund.

Dennis said yes.

MORIAMORDOR'S FIRST FUND had an initial capitalization of $50,000,000. The general partners were working for Fear and Respect Holdings Ltd. They were working for the endowment of the University of California. They were working for Indiana's Public Retirement System. They were working for other, smaller entities.

This fund had a limited term.

After ten years, the fund would disappear.

The partnership would dissolve.

The incentive, as with *deregulation*, was on short term gain.

MORIAMORDOR WAS FORMED at a fortuitous moment. It arrived only one year after the release of the iPhone.

The iPhone was a smartphone introduced into the market by Apple. Smartphones were small computers which performed almost all the tasks of bigger computers but also functioned as a cellular telephone.

The iPhone was a leap forward for smartphones because of two features: (1) Its display and interface employed multitouch glass, which meant that its users dragged their fingers around its physical surface to make the iPhone do their bidding, smearing the grease of their flesh as they commanded the technology. (2) Apple built an interface for the iPhone which allowed its users to both create and buy additional iPhone software while using the iPhone.

This type of software was called an *application*, but was better known by the colloquial name *app*. You could buy *apps* in the Apple App Store.

IN 2010, Apple had introduced a new product called the iPad.

The iPad was an iPhone with a bigger screen and no ability to function as a cellular phone. The iPad was a *tablet*.

It could run all of the *apps* that people used on their iPhones.

MOST *APPS* WERE DEVELOPED on the principle of the lowest common denominator, working off the general assumption that stupidity was the baseline of the human experience.

If an *app* was developed with stupidity in mind, and if stupidity was the baseline of the human experience, then perhaps hundreds of thousands, if not millions, would download this *app*.

Some *apps* cost money. Others were free and served advertisements.

Apps were incredible growth opportunities. The burgeoning mobile market was creating hundreds, if not thousands, of new businesses around the Bay Area. Each of them needed funding.

AROUND THE TIME that Adeline committed her unforgivable sin, Erik had begun a formal monetary relationship between MoriaMordor and a company called Lifechoosey.

Lifechoosey was a platform with a social media overlay which focused on men's fitness. It offered good deals on gyms and personal trainers. It allowed its users to recommend the best places to workout. It had both a website and multi-OS smartphone *apps*.

Between rounds of power masturbation and screwing out Adeline's brains, Erik Willems had analyzed the market research and feasibility studies on Lifechoosey. He spoke with its founders, a pair of undergraduate students at Stanford University.

MoriaMordor gave Lifechoosey $5,000,000 in funding.

In exchange, MoriaMordor gained an equity stake in the company, represented by a significant amount of stock options, and some controlling interest in the company's destiny, represented by two seats on its board.

Contingent upon his investment of the limited partners' money, Erik Willems demanded that Lifechoosey change the company's name.

Lifechoosey became Bromato, which was a portmanteau of *bro*, a slang term for young straight men interested in physical pleasure, and the three syllables of tomato without the determining 't.'

A *bro* was the target audience. *Omato* induced visions of the ripe healthy swollen fruit.

Thus was Bromato born.

THE THING TO REMEMBER is that the venture capital fund managed by Erik Willems could not make long term investments. It had a limited term of ten years.

He was bound to find quick returns on the invested money.

Limited terms ensured that venture capital outfits like MoriaMordor had a unique metric by which they measured a company's success.

To be a success for MoriaMordor, Bromato did not need to make a profit.

IF ERIK WILLEMS invested $5,000,000 in Bromato for a 20% equity stake, this would set the valuation of Bromato at $25,000,000.

This valuation was determined by ideas and processes developed through years of investing. In theory, the valuation was meant to reflect the growth potential of the company and its potential earnings.

In actuality, the valuation of Bromato was meaningless. It existed in a complex and random system. Bromato offered an entirely new and untested service in an ultra-niche market.

Erik Willems could have arrived at an equally valid number by standing in Golden Gate Park's Sharon Meadow, the place where all the old hippies held drum circles, counting the number of farts that drifted beneath his nose and multiplying the number by one million.

Everything existed for the sole purpose of making Dennis and his father and their friends and rivals richer. They wanted their capital to produce more capital without paying the costs associated with labor.

They had crashed the global economy before. They would crash it again. But they themselves would never suffer.

THERE WERE HUNDREDS AND HUNDREDS of Bromatos all over San Francisco. Each attracted new workers and each rented office space.

Because Bromato had been given its money by Erik Williams in an investment scheme, and because there was no expectation that Bromato earn a profit, Bromato could sign bad leases at egregious price.

Businesses that actually made money, that actually had a profit, were losing their leases to businesses like Bromato. Businesses that made actual money were generally run by responsible people who couldn't sign bad leases at egregious prices.

These business were referred to as *lifestyle businesses*. They allowed their owners to maintain their *lifestyle*. This was a bad thing.

THE NEW WORKERS had a detrimental effect on the real estate market. San Francisco was seven miles wide by seven miles long. Housing was limited.

People with salaries in the six figures could afford to pay $3500 for a 1BR apartment in a traditionally working class Latino neighborhood.

The other employees, the dopes who came West with promises of deferred compensation, would bunch together.

They lived eight people to a 2BR apartment. They paid $5,000 a month in rent. They had two sets of bunkbeds in each room.

THE CITIZENS OF SAN FRANCISCO were being victimized by low interest rates.

That was capitalism and it was simply grand, darling.

A FEW MONTHS after the initial investment, Erik Willems helped Bromato stage another round of funding. The equity being sold during this round had a higher cost than the equity purchased by MoriaMordor.

When another fund bought in at $10,000,000 for a 10% equity stake, the company's valuation increased to $100,000,000.

The mutual fund's original stake went from a value of $5,000,000 to $20,000,000.

On paper, he had produced a significant return on the initial investment. He was making money for Dennis and Dennis's father.

THE LIKELY FATE of Bromato was total failure. It would survive for some time, but as with most venture backed companies, it too would disappear.

The dominant model of investing in the San Francisco Bay Area was the business of investing in companies that failed.

TO GET TO THE POINT where it could be acquired by a bigger company or offer its stock on a public exchange, both of which could transform MoriaMordor's initial investment into a ridiculous amount of money for Dennis, Bromato had to mimic the outward edifices of a functional business.

It would have to attract workers.

These would be either: (1) Young ignorants who'd heard of a gold rush out West. (2) Tech industry veterans with actual experience at other companies.

The big catches, the ones with skills and experience, would earn salaries somewhere in the six figures. A few would get signing bonuses.

The small fries, the interns, and the young ignorants would be sucked into miniscule salaries and deferred compensation. This deferred compensation would come with promises of vested equity.

ALL OF THESE HIRES were expendable.

Everyone was expendable.

The people of San Francisco. The entry level workers. The experienced stars. The co-founders. The managing partners.

chapter fourteen

The video of Adeline in Kevin Killian's class became public domain. Adeline was making money for the Internet.

The Internet was a wonderful resource for sermons about inequality amongst the 1,000 Americans who cared about contemporary poetry, moral outrage about governmental policy, and arguing that religious figures from previous millennia understood the social conditions of the present.

Adeline used the cupcake and the pastry to explain her situation.

"I'm being victimized," she said to Baby, "People are separating me from them and taking offense. They think I'm the cupcake and they're the pastry. Or they think I'm the pastry and they're the cupcake. The peculiar part is that the vast majority of these people harbor very similar political positions as yours truly. One could argue that I am both the cupcake and the pastry and my accusers are also both the cupcake and the pastry."

"What are you talking about?" asked Baby over the telephone. "All I know is that I have requests for interviews about your epic rant and you're rambling about delicious kitchen treats."

BABY WAS SPEAKING to Adeline from his Cape Cod home. Cape Cod was a land mass jutting off the coast of Massachusetts that looked like a flexed human arm.

Baby had left New York City after people from Wall Street ran up the rents.

Rent wasn't his problem. His apartment on 7th Street had been rent controlled. Plus, he could've afforded the market rate. His agents were good at selling film options on his books and Baby's money manager used Baby's capital to produce more capital.

Trapped Between Jupiter and a Bottle, which Baby titled after an ex-boyfriend's mishearing of a Bob Dylan lyric, had sold to a eumelaninless film producer and director named Alan Pakula.

Alan Pakula never made *Trapped Between Jupiter and a Bottle* into a movie, but he had directed *All the President's Men,* one of the films featuring an Academy Award winning performance by Jason Robards.

Jason Robards was Adeline's father's last patient.

Sometimes it feels like there are only eleven people in the world and that the rest are paste.

BABY DIDN'T LEAVE New York because of the rent on his own apartment.

He left because all the wonderful queers were chased off Manhattan island. All the beautiful freaks. They were chased away because they had no money. Manhattan had experienced extreme *gentrification.*

Some moved to Brooklyn. Others left the city.

Baby refused to move to Brooklyn. He was too much of a snob.

HE CHOSE MASSACHUSETTS because he decided to marry his long term boyfriend, a failed architect named Massimo Colletta.

At the time, Massachusetts was the only place in America where gay people could get married to other gay people of the same gender.

Weirdly, anywhere in America, gay people could marry other gay people of the opposite gender. This tended to defeat the purpose of marriage, a social tradition by which sex is legitimized through shared bank accounts.

PROVINCETOWN, WHERE BABY LIVED, was full of gay people and the pleasantries of gay culture. It was beautiful in the summer and filled up with beautiful homos who expressed their faggitude in the Summer sun.

You could go to parties thrown by the film director John Waters, who didn't have any eumelanin in his epidermis.

The winters were hard but Baby was from Wisconsin. New Englanders complained about the snow, but it wasn't much compared with Baby's childhood.

Sometimes, Baby liked looking at Norman Mailer's house. Norman Mailer was a writer who didn't have eumelanin in the basale stratum of his epidermis.

Back in the early 1990s, Baby and his friend Regina, who had some eumelanin in her epidermis, were at a party. So was Norman Mailer. Norman Mailer made a leering advance at Regina and called Baby sweetheart. Baby threatened to beat Norman Mailer like a dusty broom.

This incident raised Baby's profile with New York's literati.

A few years later, Baby and Adeline crashed a party at Norman Mailer's apartment in Brooklyn. There was another confrontation. Baby was asked to leave the premises.

When Norman Mailer died in 2007, Baby stopped looking at the house.

"I CAN'T GET OVER that you know Kevin Killian," said Baby.

"What's peculiar about that?" asked Adeline. "Every one in this demimonde of ours has made the acquaintance of Kevin Killian. Not only is he a great writer, he's also a social butterfly."

"I've known Kevin for years. He's very supportive. He's such a nice person and such a good writer."

"Why do you think I talked to his bothersome students?" asked Adeline. "It isn't for everyone that yours truly wanders around spouting objectionable opinions. I only go viral for Kevin Killian."

"I'VE GOT A NEW BOOK COMING OUT," said Baby. "It doesn't have a title. What if I called it *The Cupcake and the Pastry?*"

"What's the book?" asked Adeline.

"It's an official sequel to *Annie Zero*. It takes place fifty years after the Neo-Maoist revolution has failed. Annie Zero's daughter Annie Terminay is a fugitive from justice. Her best friend is a sentient computer virus with a drinking problem."

"A sequel," said Adeline. "Can you recollect those olden days when you cared about your scribblings? Remember how sick it made you to try and read *Infinite Jest?*"

"I remember, but I live in Barack Obama's America. We got a huge advance and sold it into foreign territories. I need the money."

BARACK OBAMA was the President of the United States. He'd been elected in 2008 and then re-elected in 2012. The basale stratum of his epidermis was full of eumelanin.

George Bush II, the predecessor of Barack Obama in the office of the Presidency, was a truly horrible President.

George Bush II had driven America insane. Things were bad enough that a majority of the country temporarily put aside their racism and elected an African-American into the highest office of the land.

Eight years earlier, this was thought impossible. Most people believed that they would be dead before America elected a Black man to the Presidency.

So that was something like a functioning model of American progress: change is only achieved once half the country is crazy enough to forget that they participate in a system of institutionalized racism.

AMERICA HAD BEEN DRIVEN CRAZY BY: (1) A possibly stolen election. (2) A twice crashed economy. (3) An episode of being *terrofucked.* (4) An Army scientist mailing Anthrax. (5) Two foreign wars in the Middle East. (6) A guy trying to blow up an airplane with his shoes. (7) Revelations of torture. (8) A hurricane that destroyed much of New Orleans and in particular its African-American communities. (9) The failure of two foreign wars in the Middle East. (10) Tens of thousands of American causalities during two failed foreign wars in the Middle East.

It was a terrible time to be alive. It was like being kicked to the ground and then being kicked while you were on the ground. Again and again and again and again and again and again and again and again.

The kicking never stopped and because the kicks were a simile, you could never lose consciousness. You could never be kicked to death. You had to live and watch and be kicked.

If you didn't live through the kicks, you can never know how awful it was.

HERE ARE THE TWO MOST INSANE THINGS that happened:

(1) The United State of America, a warrior culture filled with good people, became a nation that embraced torture and unprovoked war. 4,487 American soldiers were killed in Iraq. 32,223 were wounded.

(2) After France's President, Jacques Chirac, refused to help the US invade Iraq, there was a movement to rename French Fries, which were apolitical strips of deep-friend potatoes.

The new name for French Fries was Freedom Fries. This actually happened in the commissaries of the United States Congress.

JACQUES CHIRAC refused to go to war in Iraq for a very good reason. He believed that George Bush II's main motivating factor was a crackpot interpretation of the Bible.

George Bush II had telephoned Chirac and said, "Gog and Magog are at work in the Middle East... The biblical prophecies are being fulfilled... This confrontation is willed by God, who wants to use this conflict to erase his people's enemies before a New Age begins."

Chirac got off the phone with Bush II. He asked his staff if they knew anything about Gog and Magog.

As French people are hedonists who write actual *graphic novels* about people fucking on beds of their own shit, no one in Chirac's office remembered that Gog and Magog were proper nouns which appear in the Bible.

Chirac's staff contacted a Professor at the University of Lausanne named Thomas Römer.

Thomas Römer was an expert in Old Testament studies. They asked him for a report on Gog and Magog.

"ARE YOU going to explore the metaphor?" asked Adeline, "Or will you bury it beneath a bunch of new words that no human tongue has ever spoke?"

"I'm trying to get away from that," said Baby. "I hate my audience."

"Are you sure calling it *The Cupcake and the Pastry* is a good idea? You'll send Erik over the moon. He is your audience, darling. Did you know that he's pressured Bromato into renaming one of their services after a word he found in *Annie Zero?*"

"Which one?" asked Baby.

"Oh, darling," said Adeline, "my attention is too dreadful. Anyhow, all you need do is wait for when someone uses the service to kill a queer or bully a teenager into suicide. The news reports will draw the connection. And then, my sweetness, you'll be ever so proud. You're the guru of San Francisco, Baby, you're the yogi with the mostest. Erik's education was so poor. The child seeks profundity in your very big words. So are you sure about that cupcake and that pastry? Dost thou really want the influence to go both ways?"

"I've got to call it something, don't I? You can't have a nameless book."

"But I didn't call to talk about your book!" said Adeline. "I wanted your opinion."

"My opinion on what?"

"On what I should do! Beyoncé's fans hate me!"

chapter fifteen

The furor died on a Friday. Like Jesus Christ, it was reborn on a Sunday.

JESUS CHRIST WAS A SOCIAL RADICAL from the Roman province of Galilee. Jesus Christ was executed in the Roman province of Judæa. He preached the radical ideas of total love and total forgiveness.

J. Karacehennem was fixated on the idea that Jesus Christ was a White Magus initiated into a system of sexual magick by Apollonius of Tyana.

Apollonius of Tyana was another mystic. Like J. Karacehennem's family, Apollonius of Tyana was from the land mass now known as Turkey. No one really knows much about Apollonius of Tyana.

The major theme in this imaginary system of sexual magick was the use of seminal fluid as a remedy for death. The idea was nonsense but Karacehennem had snuck it into almost all of his writing.

ON SUNDAY, someone found an interview with Adeline that appeared in the July 1997 issue of *Wizard* magazine.

Wizard was a news publication which covered the comic book industry. It told its readers about Marvel's latest plans to exploit the intellectual properties created by Jack Kirby.

Wizard folded in 2011.

THE INTERVIEW OCCURRED when the true nature of Adeline's pseudonym was not yet known. It was conducted over email not long after Adeline bought her first computer.

Believing that Adeline was a Russian man living in Moscow, the interviewer asked some very stupid questions, like: *Are the girls in Russia really as sexy as them seem?*

Adeline answered with even stupider answers, like: *Russia girls are sexier than Americans! Here in Russia we have word* блядь! *It is nice word use on street with girl! American girls are very willing for sex! I come America for their sexy and see how they serve men!*

блядь was the Russian word for *bitch* or *cunt* or *whore*.

Unlike the speakers of English, who had hundreds of words for degrading women, the Russians believed in economy.

AYN RAND was a Russian who didn't believe in economy.

Her endless novel *Atlas Shrugged* was about 800 pages long. The book was about how money is awesome and rich people are awesome and everything is awesome except for the poor people who are garbage that should die in the gutter. The big thing that happens in *Atlas Shrugged* is an asshole named John Galt convinces all the world's rich people to move to a valley where they can be rich together. Then he gives a speech that runs for 60 pages.

THE PERSON who found the old copy of *Wizard* uploaded digital replicas of its pages.

IN LIGHT OF THIS NEW MATERIAL, the original video of Adeline in Kevin Killian's class was reanalyzed and reblogged and retweeted and retumbled and reshared. It was joined with links to the newly rediscovered interview.

Amongst the outraged, there was the sense of a specific connection between Adeline's appearance in Kevin Killian's class and the objectionable opinions which she had expressed sixteen years earlier.

Journalists were writing articles.

They had noticed the trend.

JEREMY WINTERBLOSS emailed Adeline a series of images which were circulating on the Internet. When she saw them, she knew that the situation had become impossible.

The central visual was the same across the images. It was a screenshot from the video of Adeline in Kevin Killian's classroom. The only variation between images came in the form of captions superimposed over the screenshot.

The superimposition of captions over images was one of the Internet's great pastimes. There was an explosion of free services ensuring that the world's great wits could caption photos with ease.

Most of the captions were stupid. Some called Adeline old. Some called her a whore. Some just quoted things that she'd said in Kevin Killian's classroom or in her interview with *Wizard*.

One image made Adeline furious. There she was in Kevin Killian's classroom. Captioned over her own face were the words: PRETENDS TO BE A RUSSIAN MAN. HATES OTHER WOMEN.

"How can anyone think that I hate other women?" Adeline asked her computer. "This is bullshit!"

And then Adeline realized that she was talking to an inanimate object, as if by vocalizing her disgust she could somehow put the genie back in its bottle.

The situation had become impossible.

Adeline did the only practical thing that had been suggested.

She opened her own account on Twitter.

chapter sixteen

For years, Adeline's choice of pseudonym had worked out. She found something hilarious about having the name of a Russian man. It seemed distinct enough that no one would ever mistake the name for anything else.

JOEL SILVER let slip the truth about both J.W. Bloss and M. Abra-hamovic Petrovitch right around the time that the performance artist Marina Abramović, who didn't have much eumelanin in the basal cell layer of her epidermis, went from being a star of the art world to being a flat out star.

In 2010, Marina Abramović did a performance piece at the Museum of Modern Art in New York. She sat in a gallery and invited the museum's visitors to stare into her face. She in turn stared back.

The performance was called *The Artist is Present.* It ran for several months and was broadcast live on the Internet, which was a wonderful resource for artist engagement, expanding a fan base, and reading about the feud between Alan Moore and Grant Morrison.

Something about the piece resonated far beyond the normal impact of performance installations. *The Artist is Present* generated massive coverage. Print and digital.

Then Lady Gaga showed up.

LADY GAGA was a pop star without any eumelanin in the basal cell layer of her epidermis.

The word GAGA had become the metonymy by which any person in the industrialized world could summon up a vague neurological image of Lady Gaga's face. It was a magickal invocation. It was a brand.

Lady Gaga's songs were about the same six subjects of all songs by all pop stars: love, celebrity, fucking, heartbreak, money and buying ugly shit.

A COMMON ARC in the narrative of pop stars was their desire to be recognized as cross-platform successes.

Clothing and accoutrement were the easiest. Every pop star sold shoddy clothing to their guileless fans. Many sold their own perfumes and jewelry. Many attempted acting in feature films.

Lady Gaga went to the Museum of Modern Art and visited Marina Abramović's *The Artist is Present*. Lady Gaga did not stare into Marina Abramović's face and Marina Abramović did not stare into Lady Gaga's face.

Lady Gaga just walked around. She was shitting gold and pissing honey and she wanted to be part of the Art World.

A KEY ASPECT of pop stardom involved the creation of a lexicon for various aspects of the experience. Every pop star needed fans who were willing to adopt a slightly ridiculous group name.

Lady Gaga's fans called themselves *Little Monsters.*

Lady Gaga called herself *Mother Monster.*

By the time that Lady Gaga visited Marina Abramović at the Museum of Modern Art, over 5,000,000 *Little Monsters* were following *Mother Monster* on Twitter.

A few months later, *Mother Monster* would become the most followed person on Twitter.

By March 2012, she had over 20,000,000 followers.

AMERICAN JOURNALISM was morally bankrupt and bereft of ideas. As a result, the number of a person's *followers* on Twitter was treated as a metric of influence.

To a certain degree, this was true. The *tweets* of *Mother Monster* did indeed reach a large number of *Little Monsters*.

But other than endorsement deals, it was very difficult to turn *tweets* into money, which is the only measure of merit in a capitalist society.

Mother Monster's first album, *The Fame* (2008), sold 4,572,000 albums in the United States of America. *Mother Monster's* second album, *Born This Way* (2011), sold 2,326,000 albums in the United States. *Mother Monster's* third album, *ARTPOP* (2013), sold under 1,000,000 albums in the United States.

All the while, her number of Twitter *followers* was on the increase. A *follower* was someone who received notification of the *tweets* generated by any given individual account.

By the end of 2013, *Mother Monster* had about 40,900,000 Twitter followers.

Letting *I* stand for influence, *AS* stand for total album sales, and *TF* stand for Twitter followers, now comes a general formula for calculating the waning influence of *Mother Monster's* influence via Twitter:

$$ I = \frac{AS_2 - AS_1}{TF_2 - TF_1} $$

FOR ANOTHER METRIC, one might use the methodology invented by Zhang Xi, a visiting scholar at the University of California, Berkeley. In 2012, Zhang Xi published a paper entitled *Positiv/Negative Einfluß: Digitale Hebelwirkung entfalten mit Twitter*. Zhang Xi had some eumelanin in the basale stratum of her epidermis.

Zhang Xi's paper suggested that a user's Twitter influence was best measured by establishing a connection between three principle data points: (1) The number of users following a Twitter account. (2) The number of users followed by a Twitter account. (3) The number of *tweets* sent from a Twitter account.

As she was well read in the Frankfurt School, Zhang Xi had encountered the early works of Augustus Erhard Ernest Pfeiffer-Phol. Like all members of the Frankfurt School, Augustus Erhard Ernest Pfeiffer-Phol didn't have any eumelanin in the basale stratum of his epidermis.

Zhang Xi admired Pfeiffer-Phol's much ignored paper on Kant's *Critique of Pure Reason*, in which the writer repeated a phrase to dismiss much of what he found lamentable in the Prussian thinker. This phrase was *Wenn alle Nerven kaputt sind!*

When Zhang Xi was writing her paper on Twitter, she had given a great deal of thought to the relationship between her writing and Pfeiffer-Phol's work. The fundamental thesis of her paper was based on Pfeiffer-Phol's idea that the most powerful person in any social situation is the one who speaks the least.

As a tribute to the Pfeiffer-Phol, Zhang Xi had turned his phrase into an acronym which had unfortunate connotations in English. It appeared as such:

$$WaNks = \frac{T}{fw - fd}$$

The lower a Twitter user scored on the WaNks Index, the greater the influence. Users with very high scores had very little influence.

On the day of March 8, 2013, Lady Gaga's WaNks Index Score was 0.0000765202785228534. She was very influential.

WHEN *MOTHER MONSTER* went to see Marina Abramović at the Museum of Modern Art, her media presence may have been at its very peak.

It was between *The Fame* and *Born This Way.*

Marina Abramović became very famous. She never looked back.

MARINA ABRAMOVIĆ'S fame became a problem when people started to imagine a linguistic closeness between Marina Abramović and the pseudonym of M. Abrahamovic Petrovitch.

Adeline even looked a little like Marina Abramović. They were both women over forty with long dyed black hair and a lack of eumelanin in their epidermises.

Marina Abramović was older than Adeline by about twenty years, but this didn't matter. People remember at most three characteristics about other people's appearances. Usually, it's two: the color of skin and the style of hair.

Whenever someone like Kevin Killian introduced Adeline as M. Abrahamovic Petrovitch, it was almost inevitable that she would be mistaken for Marina Abramović.

These conversations went something like this:

"This is Adeline. You might know her better as M. Abrahamovic Petrovitch. The artist."

"OH MY GOD, YOU'RE MARINA ABROMOVIĆ? I TOTALLY WATCHED YOUR THING ON THE INTERNET."

"No, darling, I'm not Abramović. I'm M. Abrahamovic Petrovitch. I'm not a performance artist. I draw comic books."

"Oh. Like Spider-Man?"

"No."

FOR THREE YEARS, this was the most annoying aspect of Adeline's modest dose of fame. She didn't find it that bad, really, as she was being mistaken for someone else and could easily shut down conversations.

THE DAY BEFORE someone found Adeline's old interview in *Wizard* magazine, she went to brunch with Erik Willems at a bakery near Dolores Park called Tartine.

Tartine was a twee little place. Adeline tolerated it. Erik Willems loved it. Tartine was a tourist destination. There were usually long lines on weekends.

Adeline and Erik Willems had experienced a very rare occurrence. They were able to find a table.

Tartine's renown was due to the high quality of its baked goods and the fact that it kept getting write-ups in a wide range of publications like *Vogue* and the *New York Times*.

THE *NEW YORK TIMES* was transitioning from America's newspaper of record into a website that catered to the perceived whims of affluent, youthful demographics.

This meant a lot of articles about ephemeral music. This meant a lot of articles about ephemeral technology. This meant a lot of articles about Tartine.

The *New York Times* was not very good at reporting on ephemeral music. It was even worse at reporting on ephemeral technology.

It was excellent at reporting about Tartine.

THE *NEW YORK TIMES* was extraordinarily bad at reporting on the run-up to George Bush II's War in Iraq.

After America was *terrofucked*, the *New York Times* had run all manner of ridiculous articles about how Saddam Hussein, the dictator of Iraq, was building and stockpiling Weapons of Mass Destruction.

The leaders of countries like America, who ran countries which possessed weapons capable of killing billions of people, disapproved of Weapons of Mass Destruction.

Whereas a conventional bomb, like the ones that America dropped on Iraq, would turn a family of illiterate peasants into red mist and chunks of meat and then incinerate the chunks of meat, Weapons of Mass Destruction would poison entire families of illiterate peasants and cause them to choke to death. Weapons of Mass Destruction would cause entire families of illiterate peasants to blister and suffer chemical burns until they died.

The moral being: when obliterating illiterate peasants, there's a right way of doing things.

Both George Bush II and the *New York Times* said that Saddam Hussein had a metric fuckload of Weapons of Mass Destruction.

This was the principle justification for the War in Iraq.

GEORGE BUSH II's War in Iraq should not be mistaken for George Bush I's War Against Iraq, which was justified by Saddam Hussein's invasion of the oil rich country Kuwait.

Like his son, George Bush I had worked in oil. He knew the value of gas.

America was a country where a father and son, both with the same name, had waged war against the same dictator.

This is why more than half of the country forgot about their culturally imbued racism and decided it was time to elect an African-American to the Presidency.

WHEN AMERICAN TROOPS under the command of George Bush II reached Iraqi soil, they discovered that there were no Weapons of Mass Destruction.

The administration of George Bush II was wrong.

The *New York Times* was wrong.

They had cocked-upped the story about Weapons of Mass Destruction. They had really fucked up.

MOST OF THE WORST REPORTING on Weapons of Mass Destruction was done by a woman named Judith Miller. Judith Miller relied on bogus sources like the Iraqi exile Ahmed Chalabi, who had some eumelanin in the basale stratum of his epidermis.

Another reporter named Michael Gordon helped Judith Miller in her bad reporting.

While Judith Miller was writing her intolerable bullshit, there was another reporter working for the *New York Times* named Jayson Blair. He was African-American. His basale stratum was loaded with eumelanin.

Both Judith Miller and Michael Gordon had a conspicuous lack of eumelanin in their epidermises.

Jayson Blair filed stories about domestic issues.

Like Judith Miller's articles, the articles written by Jayson Blair were also intolerable bullshit.

Unlike Judith Miller, who asked Ahmed Chalabi to supply her with nonsense, Jayson Blair just made up his own crap.

He faked sources. He faked quotes. He faked being on location.

Eventually all of the bad reporting was exposed.

In the case of Blair, who wrote stupid little articles that were forgotten the day after publication, the *New York Times* printed an enormously long front-page article.

The article called the situation "a profound betrayal of trust" and a "low point in the 152-year history of the newspaper." The article contained a long digression as to whether or not Jayson Blair had been promoted due to his plethora of eumelanin.

In the case of Judith Miller and Michael Gordon, whose articles were cited by George Bush II as evidence in the run-up to America's invasion of Iraq and were thus responsible for 36,710 American casualties and hundreds of thousands of dead Iraqis, the *New York Times* published a short editorial that said its coverage of Weapons of Mass Destruction was not "as rigorous as it should have been."

Jayson Blair was fired and disappeared in disgrace. Judith Miller got a hefty severance package and continued to work in the news media. Michael Gordon stayed with the *New York Times.*

So this was the lesson, then, from America's paper of record: if you're going to publish intolerable bullshit, don't make up lies.

Do what a good journalist does.

Go out and push your nose to the grindstone and wear down the soles of your shoes and find someone else's lies and repeat those.

And don't be Black. And don't be a woman.

ANYWAY, THE REPORTING on Tartine was excellent. The croissants were called "flaky, buttery, crisp, greasy."

This was true. This was right. The croissants of Tartine were indeed flaky, buttery, crisp and greasy.

So there's always hope.

ADELINE AND ERIK WILLEMS were sitting in Tartine. They were having brunch. The night before, Adeline had screwed out Erik's brains.

This proved to be a welcome distraction from the fact that she'd spent several days being excoriated on the Internet, which was a wonderful resource for feigning interest in professional wrestling, hacking corporate websites, and inspiring inchoate longing for the bassist of the Los Angeles band Warpaint.

Adeline was picking at a croissant and drinking coffee. Erik Willems was eating a ridiculous banana creme tart.

Adeline was staring into the blankness of Erik Willems's eumelaninless face and wondering how it was that he fucked like a beast.

"There used to be a girl who worked here," said Erik Willems, "Every startup guy in the city was obsessed with her. They were always talking about the Tartine Girl."

"Did you ever lay eyes upon her, *mon frère?* Were you too smitten by her manifold charms?"

"I did," said Erik. "I didn't see the appeal. She was cute I guess, but I tend to prefer older women."

Adeline looked out of the windows at 18th Street, which served as a direct line between Valencia Street and Dolores Park, extending all the way into the Castro. Tartine was between Valencia and the park, which meant that it was on the main corridor of annoyance.

"WOW," SAID A GUY standing over their table, "You're, like, totally her, aren't you?"

"Darling," said Adeline, "You must have me mistaken."

"No," said the guy, "You're totally like her. You're that woman from the Internet. Me and my friends have been watching that video, like, all week."

"You have me sorely mistaken," said Adeline. "I'm not her."

"C'mon," said the guy, "I, like, recognize you."

"Like, no," said Adeline. "You know, I've totally been getting this for a few days, right? The problem is that there's a little, like, confusion. You've got me mistaken with M. Abrahamovic Petrovitch, but I'm not her. Like, I'm also, like, famous, which is why you recognize me, okay? My name is Marina Abramović. Do you, like, remember when Lady Gaga, like, went to the MoMA and stared into someone's face? That was totally my face. I'm not M. Abrahamovic Petrovitch. I'm somebody else who's somebody. I'm Marina Abramović. You know, *The Artist is Present?*"

"Oh, whoa," said the guy. "My mistake. Can we take a selfie?"

ADELINE AND ERIK WILLEMS left Tartine. They walked towards Adeline's apartment.

"I had no idea you could do other accents," said Erik.

"Some of us," said Adeline, "can be both the cupcake and the pastry."

Erik Willems didn't say anything. Adeline had long made him regret mentioning the cupcake or the pastry.

The whole time they were in Tartine, Erik Willems had sat clutched with anxiety. He was waiting for Adeline to mention the cupcake and the pastry. Tartine was, after all, a bakery.

"Do you know, I wonder if this is going to keep happening? It happened yesterday."

"Someone recognized you?"

"For *certainement*, my dear," said Adeline. "I was at the corner store. I let them take a picture. After that, I decided I'm simply going to lie to everyone and say that I'm Marina Abramović. They've been tormenting me with her name for three years, so why not embrace the pain? Do you think it's possible that people out there in New York Land might be inquiring with Marina Abramović as to whether or not she's M. Abrahamovic Petrovitch?"

Just then, a *Google bus* drove past.

chapter seventeen

The most visible sign of San Francisco's *gentrification* was the appearance of white luxury buses which roamed the streets like vampires in search of a hissing blood feast.

These buses provided transportation to people who lived in the city and worked at tech companies in Silicon Valley.

They were private buses, which meant that they were available only to employees of companies in Silicon Valley.

The name around town for these buses was *Google buses*, after Google, the company with which they were most associated.

The *Google buses* worked on the theory that employees of tech companies had different ideas about life than their parents. They didn't want to be in the suburbs and they didn't want to own houses in Silicon Valley and they didn't want to own cars.

So the buses allowed these employees to work for giant corporations while living in the city and experiencing the rich tapestry of the urban environment and its pleasures.

THE NECESSITY OF BEING A UNIQUE INDIVIDUAL who cared about living in the city while working for a faceless multibillion dollar corporation was one of the legacies of the Bay Area's intolerable bullshit. This bullshit had been generated during the late 1960s and early 1970s by young people who mistook participatory capitalism for enlightenment.

In Dallas, the guys who worked for Exxon Mobil knew that they were destroying the environment and loved every minute, funneling oil lucre into

God and Guns while having a good ol' hoot and holler and venting their lust into sex-workers with poor literacy skills and breast implants.

On Wall Street, the guys who made capital from capital hung around in three piece suits, screaming in New Jersey accents about fucking people's mothers in the ass while pouring gold flake champagne on their own genitalia.

In San Francisco, the generation of capital came with an oppressive narrative about both the investors, and the companies they invested in. They were offering services that *changed the world* and helped individuals *achieve their greatest potential.*

Twitter could not be described as it was: a mechanism by which teenagers tormented each other into suicide while obsessing about ephemeral celebrities and on which Adeline argued about whether or not she hated the victims of the Triangle Shirtwaist Fire of 1911.

Twitter was described as an outlet for *freedom of speech* and *freedom of expression.* Twitter was *changing the world.*

TWITTER WAS HEADQUARTERED in the Tenderloin on Market Street. Mayor Ed Lee had some eumelanin in the basale stratum of his epidermis. He had given Twitter a $22,000,000 tax break to move into the Tenderloin.

The Tenderloin was full of homeless people, drug addicts, and sex-workers. Many of these people were in very poor health.

There were people in the Tenderloin who were so poor that they were infected with tuberculosis, a disease which had been eradicated almost everywhere else in America.

A vast majority of the people with very poor health in the Tenderloin had a plethora of eumelanin in the basale strata of their epidermises.

This concentration of eumelanin was unusual. Between 1990 and 2010, the number of Black people in San Francisco had declined by 35.7%.

Twitter had been given $22,000,000 from the City of San Francisco to try and revitalize the Tenderloin.

Revitalization was institutionally racist code for adopting a policy of racial cleansing which made the neighborhood less welcoming to Black people.

While Twitter was changing the world on the seventh, eighth and ninth floors of 1355 Market Street, its employees could look down at Market Street and see crack addicted sex-workers having the stuffing beat out of them by people infected with tuberculosis.

It was a nice time to work for Twitter.

It was a shitty time to have tuberculosis.

GIVEN THE FACT that it was displacing an African-American population, the curious thing about Twitter was its popularity with Black people. Twitter was fashionable enough with Black people that this popularity had its own name: *Black Twitter.*

Like so much in American life, *Black Twitter* was a sinister burn engineered by people without eumelanin in their epidermises to exploit the labors of people with eumelanin in their epidermises.

The users of *Black Twitter* were supplying White people with effortless access to a body of language and thought which could be harvested and transformed into content on websites owned by White people.

The managers of these websites were very interested in demonstrating a fluency with Black culture but had little-to-no interest in hiring the people who lived it.

A fluency with Black culture would attract more advertisers. Actual Black people would scare advertisers.

Back in the good ol' days, when White people wanted to steal culture, they actually had to, you know, like, spend time around Black people.

But in 2013, the story was very different.

The iPhone had *changed everything.*

TWITTER ITSELF USED *Black Twitter* to serve advertisements.

Twitter's leadership and ownership structures were both remarkable and unremarkable for their total absence of Black people.

The only people making money off *Black Twitter* were White people.

According to eumelanin-rich Byron Crawford, who was the best writer of the new Millennium, there was a word for this.

Slavery.

GOOGLE WAS NOT the only corporation with buses. Apple, eBay, Electronic Arts, Facebook and Yahoo had their own buses. So did a multitude of smaller companies. Tens of thousands of workers were making a daily commute via the buses.

J. Karacehennem was mildly obsessed with the *Google buses* and told Adeline that they were the best evidence of J.G. Ballard having been a High Priest of the Future.

J. G. Ballard was a eumelaninless British author who came to prominence in the middle of the Twentieth Century. He had lived in a prison camp during World War Two. He wrote about weird sex and weird technology and weird sexual technology.

"At first," said J. Karacehennem, "I thought the buses signaled that we were living in an early Ballard book, like maybe *Crash* or *The Atrocity Exhibition*, where he writes about how people of the future would move beyond the perversions of the Nineteenth and Twentieth Centuries and create new eroticisms. You know *Crash* is all about people who fuck whilst they crash cars. So I was thinking that maybe all the Google people were riding dirty in their buses with enormous erections and wet vaginas and spontaneously orgasming through the simple pleasure of the bus's vibrations.

"Then I read *Super-Cannes*," continued J. Karacehennem, "and realized we're living in late period Ballard. *Super-Cannes* is about a complex on the Riviera where various corporations have their campuses and house their workers. The narrator discovers a crimewave that no one wants to discuss. He further discovers that it happens because there's an organized program of barbarism for the complex's corporate residents. They're all taken out on buses and get into fights with Arab gangs in the surrounding cities and the cops are paid off to look the other way. Who's gonna fuck with the big companies, and who really cares if their engineers are beating the shit out of a bunch of fucking ragheads, right?

"That's my theory," said J. Karacehennem. "I think the Google buses are taking employees around and getting them in gang fights. Why else are they so interested in maps? Do you think all that bullshit is really about making information free? Fuck no! Google is mapping the world so that they have a huge database of primo locations filled with the dispossessed. Google Street View is a map of the blood to be spilled.

"But they can't fight Muslims, not in San Francisco. This city doesn't have enough Muslims to ensure that every Google employee has the same opportunities for cross-faith violence. You can't achieve peak Muslim-bashing with such a small sample of Mahometans. Which leaves Latinos and Asians. So that's what happens. Every night at 4am, a prearranged number of Google employees gather together and get into huge fights with members of the Jackson Street Boyz and the 22 Boys and MS-13."

"Whatever does your lady think of this bright idea?" asked Adeline.

"If I bring it up in polite society, she pretends that she doesn't know me."

"DARLING," SAID ADELINE. "I hadn't the slightest you were so fascinated by the buses. You must break bread and exchange heap big wampum of words with my friend Christine. She's harboring some very dubious ideas about the whole thing."

"Why haven't I met her, anyway?" asked J. Karacehennem.

"Oh, Pip," said Adeline, "Don't you recollect our unfortunate encounter with that woman Sonja at Margaret Tedesco's gallery? If so, do you perhaps recall your own behavior with regards to the poor girl?"

"What did I say?" asked J. Karacehennem. "I never remember."

"As we three waited at the corner of 25th and Guerrero, she placed her winsome hand upon your shoulder. Which caused you to have rather an unfortunate response. You walked into out into the traffic and said that you'd rather be dead than spend a moment suffering her touch."

"Oh right," said J. Karacehennem. "Now I can remember."

"I considered that perhaps you had revealed your inner bigot. I worried, darling, that a meeting with Christine might end the same."

"You thought I was unpleasant to Sonja because she's trans?"

"That's the obvious conclusion," said Adeline. "You're very progressive, dear, but you're so unpredictable. And you're from Southeastern Massachusetts, darling. There's an inner Masshole in you."

"What the fuck, Adeline?" asked J. Karacehennem. "I wasn't horrible because she's trans. I was horrible because she's a fucking dullard. I'm not transphobic! I'm just a snob! I'm a flaming liberal who believes in Jeffersonian Democracy!"

WHEN J. KARACEHENNEM said that he believed in Jeffersonian Democracy, he was using *irony*.

Irony was a spoken or written device that presents an intended meaning opposite of the stated one.

If you were speaking with irony, you might say of a very stupid person, "Yes, she is a very smart woman." If you were speaking with irony, you might say of a very ugly man, "Yes, he is a handsome gentleman."

Irony was not that different than the mechanism of advertising, with its two meanings, except that in advertising the second meaning was not inherently oppositional to the first.

Most Americans used the adjective *ironic* to denote something other than a situation involving *irony*. When they were being *ironic*, or when something was *ironic*, they generally meant that there was a *coincidence*. Sometimes the *coincidence* was unfortunate.

If you were from California and the year was 2013, you might say something like, "It was, like, so *ironic*, because, you know, we both totally bought, like, red cars."

There was nothing *ironic* about two people buying red cars. There was no underlying secondary meaning. Two people buying red cars is a *coincidence*.

MANY MORAL SCOLDS had adopted grammar as a place where they could make other people feel bad about themselves. These people tended to be disturbed by the apparent misuse of the words *ironic* and *irony*.

On one hand, they had a point. There really wasn't anything ironic about two people buying cars of the same color.

On the other hand, the words *irony* and *ironic* were just symbols with shifting meaning given their value by a general agreement amongst members in a society.

They were like *money*. They were imaginary.

Or maybe they were more like the bullshit words in Baby's *Annie Zero* or Robert Heinlein's *Stranger in a Strange Land*.

Just some crap that someone made up once.

WHEN J. KARACEHENNEM said that he was a flaming liberal who believed in Jeffersonian Democracy, the *irony* did not derive from J. Karacehennem being a flaming liberal. He was indeed a flaming liberal.

As a flaming liberal, J. Karacehennem believed in an equality of people regardless of social constructs like sexual preference, race, gender and creed. As a flaming liberal, J. Karacehennem believed that the best way to achieve this equality, and address other ills, was through a reordering of society via governmental policies and the redistribution of wealth.

The *irony* in his statement derived from the fact that, as everyone knows, Jeffersonian Democracy was a wonderful fantasy about a nation comprised of farmers who hated a centralized government and embraced agrarian freedoms.

Being a flaming liberal was old-fashioned and almost totally discredited, because the national dialogue had been hijacked by an oligarchy of the ultra-wealthy. This oligarchy recognized that, in a reordering of society via governmental policies, it was their wealth which would be redistributed.

So they had thrown their resources behind corrupting the terms of the argument. The ideas of flaming liberals were verboten.

Instead, people were told to embrace intolerable bullshit like *pulling themselves up by their bootstraps*, which was a figure of speech that meant nothing.

People were told to embrace intolerable bullshit like Jeffersonian Democracy, which decentralized the importance of the Federal Government.

People loved talking about Jeffersonian Democracy. It was mentioned with an astounding frequency in the national dialogue, considering that it was a stupid fantasy about farmers.

WHAT PEOPLE DIDN'T LOVE talking about was the personal life of Thomas Jefferson, the man for whom Jeffersonian Democracy was named.

Jefferson was American's third President. He had been one of its richest men. He was its greatest theoretical architect of *freedom*. He believed in *self expression* and *freedom of speech*.

He was also one of the twelve Presidents of the United States to own slaves, which is a larger figure than the number of Presidents who had beards.

jarett kobek

EVEN AMONG THE ONE-FOURTH OF PRESIDENTS who owned slaves, Jefferson stood out.

After Thomas Jefferson's wife died, Thomas Jefferson started venting his lust in his wife's half-sister, Sally Hemmings.

Sally Hemmings had eumelanin in the stratum basale of her epidermis. Sally Hemming was Thomas Jefferson's wife's sister and she was Thomas Jefferson's slave.

Sally Hemmings was Thomas Jefferson's dead wife's sister because Thomas Jefferson's dead wife's father enjoyed venting his lust in Sally Hemmings's mother. Sally Hemmings's mother was Thomas Jefferson's dead wife's father's slave.

The venting of lust into slaves was also known as rape. So Thomas Jefferson was a rapist and Thomas Jefferson's dead wife's father was also a rapist.

If you were from California and the year was 2013, and you were discussing Thomas Jefferson's sex life, you might say, "It's, like, so *ironic,* because Thomas Jefferson was, like, totally a rapist who, you know, was raping a woman who, like, you know, herself was totally produced by a rape."

You'd be wrong.

It wasn't *ironic* that Thomas Jefferson raped a woman who was created by rape. It was *coincidence* that Thomas Jefferson raped a woman created by rape. Well.

It was either *coincidence* or it was symptomatic of institutionalized racism that devalued the agency and individual rights of people based on their race and economic status.

You know, like, either one.

FOUR OTHER PRESIDENTS have been accused of raping children into their slaves. These Presidents were: George Washington, William Henry Harrison, James K. Polk and John Tyler.

A great number of rich White men had vented lust into their slaves, and a great number had produced children in their slaves, but very few had produced a body of written work about the necessity of human freedom.

Thomas Jefferson was the rare slave holder who enjoyed raping his property while writing declarations and essays and letters about the dignity of man.

He was enslaving people at home while crafting a philosophical system that advocated the spread of liberty throughout the world.

It was a hell of a time to be alive.

chapter eighteen

Christine was under pressure.

She had rented the same apartment since 1997.

The apartment was rent-controlled, which meant that her landlord could raise the rent by only a small yearly percentage. This percentage was set by the San Francisco Rent Board.

The highest increase had been 2.9%.

The lowest had been 0.1%.

Christine rented her apartment in 1997 at $1,000 a month.

With all the percentage increases, Christine at present was paying $1350 per month. By the halfway point of 2013, the median price of 1BRs in San Francisco was $2,800.

Rent control is a miracle.

CHRISTINE LIVED in an apartment complex with six units spread across two buildings. This rendered her a less likely candidate for eviction, thanks to technicalities in the laws that governed evictions. But it was still possible.

The most important of these laws was the Ellis Act.

The Ellis Act had been passed by the California State Legislature in 1986. It was a way for landlords to get out of the business of renting.

But laws are weird. They create loopholes and manufacture unexpected consequences.

An unexpected consequence of the Ellis Act was that it created market incentives for landlords to convert their properties into condo buildings or rip down pre-existing structures and erect new gargantuan buildings in their stead.

Created for one purpose, it had assumed another. It had become the *de facto* method of evicting the elderly and ethnic minorities.

The elderly and ethnic minorities were living in rent controlled apartments. They were taking up space that could be occupied by employees of Google.

THE BIGGEST PROBLEM with Christine's living situation is that all six units had been occupied for years. All of the apartments were rent controlled.

The landlord had inherited the buildings from his mother in the late 1970s. He didn't have eumelanin in the basale stratum of his epidermis.

He tried to be a patient man, but every day the news media bombarded him with stories about the city's rising rents. He couldn't help but calculate how much money he would be making if his tenants paid the market rate.

He was losing tens of thousands of dollars a month.

CHRISTINE HAD STARTED DATING a new guy. He was named Bertrand. He was from Belgium and had no eumelanin in the basale stratum of his epidermis. Things were going well. Christine was in love.

But her rental situation was terrible.

Her landlord was considering using the Ellis Act. She knew this because Christine was the only tenant in the buildings with whom the landlord had a decent relationship.

He liked calling her up and complaining about how the property was ruining him.

When these telephone conversations began, Christine had not yet transitioned her outward conforming gender appearance. She'd been a woman living with the exterior appearance of a homosexual man.

At first she thought the landlord might be a closet case chasing a piece of strange, but years went by and he made no move or improper suggestion. Christine realized that the landlord just needed someone with whom he could talk about the buildings.

They became friends.

"Honey," he said to her, "These buildings are murder! A girl like you knows from murder and isn't this just the worst? You're wonderful, you're clean, but the others, they're dogs! They pay so little. Do you know that Daria moved in when my mother was still alive? We're talking 1973. My mother never raised the rent! I hate to do it but I'm going to have to get out of this rotten business."

Daria was a woman without much eumelanin in the basale stratum of her epidermis. She had moved to San Francisco during the druggie heyday of the late 1960s and early 1970s.

She had been in her twenties and believed that enlightenment came in the form of vinyl records and sugar cubes laced with LSD. Now Daria was a senior citizen. She was paying less than $500 a month for a two bedroom apartment.

"Don't even start me on Rafael," said the landlord. "He lives like a pig."

This was true. Rafael really did live like a pig.

"Honey," said the landlord. "I must sell these buildings or do something. I can't keep letting myself be robbed by animals!"

"You don't think I'm an animal, do you?" asked Christine.

"You're a doll," said the landlord. "You're the only star in my life."

IF CHRISTINE'S LANDLORD did evict her, there was no feasible way that she could stay in the city. Low interest rates, venture capitalists and the tech industry had removed her ability to remain in San Francisco.

Christine's biggest concern was that she was trans, which meant that she was a woman born with male physiology.

San Francisco was just about the friendliest place in America for a transperson. And even San Francisco was pretty bad. You still got heckled and threatened. Sometimes you would be beaten. Sometimes you would be killed.

Anywhere else that Christine moved would increase the likelihood of her being heckled, threatened, beaten and killed.

The threat of an Ellis Act eviction was the literal threat of violence.

More than ever, she felt the need for prayer.

IN HIGH SCHOOL, Christine had gone through a *Wicca* phase.

Wicca was the name for a hodge-podge of beliefs centered on the idea that witchcraft retained validity in the modern world. Its practitioners thought that they could affect change through the use of spells and sorcery and invocations of pagan deities like Ba'al and Bast.

As with every religion, it was a comforting bit of nonsense that some people took too seriously.

Christine hadn't really clicked with Wicca. Mostly, she'd used it as a way to have sex with awkward boys. She abandoned it after a few months.

Now that she'd developed the urge for prayer, she discovered a little splinter of Wicca was lodged in her heart.

She couldn't see herself praying to Jesus or Allah or HaShem. Not even to Aten.

If she were going to pray, then her prayers must be pagan.

SHE HIT UPON THE IDEA when she was thinking about Google.

Google was a company that was transforming the city. Google was the company that had flooded the city with its buses. Christine was sure that if she did get evicted, one of Google's employees would end up in her apartment. Google was the company sending Christine to an increased likelihood of violent death at the hands of bigots.

Christine realized the names of the new gods. She knew where to direct her prayers.

chapter nineteen

Adeline was *tweeting*. She was defending herself on Twitter. Her WaNks Index Score was 5.

She'd asked J. Karacehennem if he would read her *tweets* and see how they played. He refused.

"Twitter makes everyone sound like a whinging fifteen year old," he said.

AT THE END of her first week on Twitter, Adeline had about three thousand followers and had involved herself in countless disjointed conversations and arguments.

"I'm rather settling into this Twitter thing, darling," she said over the phone to Baby. "After all, I've seen so much of life and I'm what the pornographers call a mature woman. I'm a *MILF* and all these young things are asking for life advice."

"People on the Internet are completely insane," said Baby. "Don't open yourself up too much."

"Darling, haven't you been tweeting since 2008?" asked Adeline. "Weren't you an early bird?"

Baby's WaNks Index Score was 1.31411317.

"That's professional obligation. You can't really write Science Fiction without being on Twitter. It's a necessity. But if you look at my tweets, I almost never say anything. It's usually just jokes or random thoughts."

"How can you stand it? How can you tolerate all the pretense?"

"It's just a job," said Baby. "It's how I go to work."

AFTER ADELINE GRADUATED from Parsons, back in the early '90s, she had worked as a freelance illustrator. Then she transitioned into *Trill* and comic art.

She had never gone into an office. She had no idea that most people woke up every weekday morning and went to a place where they were disrespected and worked for people they hated. Adeline didn't realize that when people went to their place of business, they put on a spiritual mask which hid their true selves and their actual opinions.

She'd never really had a job. There'd been two days when she clerked at Tower Records on Sunset Boulevard. That was back in 1984 and she'd taken the gig to prove a point.

She no longer remembered to whom.

ERIK WILLEMS had a Twitter account but he never *tweeted*. He used his account to read *tweets* written by people to whom he'd given money. His WaNks Index Score was 0.002.

When Adeline had asked him to critique her *tweets,* he said, "If you're so concerned, you should hire a social media consultant."

To which Adeline replied: "It is a truth universally acknowledged, that a single man in possession of a good tongue must be in want of the cupcake or the pastry."

THE PEOPLE ON TWITTER were furious. Adeline couldn't accustom herself to the anger.

They were outraged about sports figures.

They were outraged about politicians.

They were outraged about injustice.

They were outraged about world events in countries thousands of miles away with complex and impenetrable political systems.

They were outraged about comic books.

They were outraged about the privilege of others.

They were outraged about criminal cases.

They were outraged about poor people.

They were outraged about rich people.
They were outraged about the death of the middle class.
They were outraged about everything.
And no one would stop *tweeting* about television.

ADELINE HADN'T OWNED a television since 1992.

She'd suffered fifteen years hearing about how the Internet would transform American culture and open new avenues of expression.

But in the end, it was only more people talking about television.

BEFORE SHE STARTED using Twitter, Baby had been the major source of Adeline's information about television. Baby watched everything.

He liked *The Sopranos,* which was a television show about rich criminals. He liked *Arrested Development,* which was about a rich family whose patriarch is arrested for corruption. He liked *The Wire,* which was about the criminal justice system violating people's civil liberties. He liked *The L Word,* which was about rich lesbians in Los Angeles. He liked *Six Feet Under,* which was about the sex lives of rich morticians. He liked *Mad Men,* which was about rich advertising executives. He liked *The Shield,* which was about the criminal justice system violating people's civil liberties. He liked *Breaking Bad,* which was about a poor teacher who becomes a rich drug dealer. He liked *The Borgias,* which was about a rich family of Spanish nobility during the Renaissance. He liked *Oz,* which was about the criminal justice system violating people's civil liberties. He liked *The Trip,* which was about two rich guys eating in restaurants. He liked *Curb Your Enthusiasm,* which was about a rich television producer. He liked *Dexter,* which was about the criminal justice system violating people's civil liberties. He liked *Sex and the City,* which was about rich socialites in New York City. He liked *24,* which was about the criminal justice system violating people's civil liberties. He liked *Game of Thrones,* which was about rich aristocracies in a quasi-medieval world. He liked *Weeds,* which was about a rich drug dealer who goes broke and ends up rich. He liked *Californication,* which was about a rich writer in Los Angeles. He liked *How I Met Your Mother,* which was about rich socialites in New York City. He liked *Reno 911!,* which was about the criminal justice system violating people's civil liberties. He liked *House of Cards,* which was about rich politicians. He liked *30 Rock,* which was about rich actors on television playing rich actors on television. He liked *Sherlock,* which was about a rich private detective violating people's civil liberties.

Baby liked *Girls,* which was about four rich socialites in New York City. Each role was played by the daughter of real world socialites, the actresses' parents having experienced success in the media and performing arts, thereby making the program the most perfect demonstration of the fact that, in the Twenty-First Century, America had abandoned its aversion to *dynasties.*

Dynasties were the very thing that America's Rapist-in-Chief, Thomas Jefferson, had decried in a letter to George Washington: "I did not apprehend this while I had American ideas only, but I confess what I have seen in Europe has brought me over to that opinion; & that tho' the day may be at some distance, beyond the reach of our lives perhaps, yet it will certainly come, when a single fibre left of this institution, will produce an hereditary aristocracy which will change the form of our Governments from the best to the worst in the world."

Baby hated *Doctor Who.*

DOCTOR WHO premiered on the BBC in 1963. The BBC was the British Broadcasting Company. The citizens of the United Kingdom paid for the BBC. It was nationalized television rendered as a service to the home nations.

Doctor Who was about an alien who traveled through time and space. The titular role of the Doctor had been played by many actors.

Because the Doctor was an alien, whenever an actor relinquished the role, the Doctor would suffer a fatal injury and then *regenerate.*

Regeneration was supercontained reincarnation. In the fictional context of *Doctor Who,* a *regeneration* meant that bright light would engulf the Doctor and then his body would change from one incarnation to another. His personality and face would be different. All of his memories were the same.

In the real world, *regeneration* meant the transition between actors was orchestrated with the dodgy special effects endemic to public television.

The one real constant in the various *regenerations* of the Doctor was that he always talked and acted like a British eccentric, thereby making *Doctor Who*, like *Girls*, a program about *dynasties*.

The most recent Doctor, played by the actor Matt Smith, was going to regenerate at the end of 2013. People on Twitter speculated about which actor would take up the role of the Doctor, and whether or not this actor would be a woman or a *Person of Color*.

A wide range of people on Twitter found this casting decision to be a very important issue. They believed that having a woman or a *Person of Color* as the Doctor would be a step forward for the representation of the disenfranchised in media.

Almost everyone alive, members of disenfranchised groups or not, wanted to be legitimated by intellectual properties in which they had no vested interest. The human species was a bunch of assholes.

THIS VOCAL SEGMENT of *Doctor Who* fans had a sophisticated understanding of the process by which television shows were made.

They understood that actors were cast. They understood the function of a head writer and executive producer.

Yet whenever an episode of *Doctor Who* aired, these very same people would *tweet* as if the fictional events depicted were really happening.

The *tweets* would contain outrage about the Doctor's choices and the implications of those choices, and all the privilege and microaggressions revealed in those choices.

It was impossible to tell whether or not the users of Twitter understood that *Doctor Who* was fictional. It was impossible to tell whether or not the users of Twitter understood that the Doctor wasn't real.

THIS INABILITY TO DISTINGUISH FICTION from reality was also present in the world of comics.

Many comic book fans *tweeted* their complaints about the creators working for Marvel and DC. Some comic book fans *tweeted* their complaints about the editorial decisions made by Marvel and DC.

Almost none of these outraged *tweets* were about the ill-treatment of Jack Kirby or Steve Ditko or Joe Simon or Martin Nodell or Bill Finger or Jerry Robinson or Bill Mantlo or Alan Moore or Lew Schwartz.

Mostly, comic book fans were *tweeting* about Batwoman's lesbian relationship with Maggie Sawyer or the death of Batman's son Damian or the retcon of Superman's marriage.

It was impossible to tell whether or not the users of Twitter understood that Batwoman and Maggie Sawyer and Batman and Damian and Superman were fictional characters.

HAVING WORKED in the comics industry, Adeline had experience with the interstitial space in which fictional characters were both real and not real. This was because Adeline had attended comic book conventions.

These events were, in theory, mass gatherings dedicated to the celebration of what the French termed *le neuvième art*.

In actuality, comic book conventions were an excuse for people to dress up like the intellectual properties of major corporations. Typically, the costumed would have encountered these intellectual properties in television, film, video games and comic books.

This pageantry was called *cosplay*. An example of *cosplay* would be when, for instance, a 45 year old man attends the annual San Diego Comic Con and dresses like Thor, a piece of intellectual property owned by Marvel/Disney and created by Jack Kirby.

This theoretical 45 year old man dressed as Thor will wander through the post-Brutalist architecture of the San Diego Convention Center. As he walks its white hallways, passing beneath its curved glass, people will approach the 45 year old man and speak with him as though he is Thor.

They will say, "Hi, Thor!" They will say, "Hey, Thor! How's it going?" They will ask, "Yo, Thor, how's the hammer hanging?"

They will pose for photographs with the 45 year old man. They will later post these photographs to Facebook and Twitter. They will ask for Thor's opinions on matters large and small. The 45 year old man will answer these questions in character.

In the liminal zone of the comic book convention, trapped within the magick circle of *cosplay*, it will be impossible to determine whether this 45 year old man has any conception that he is not, in actuality, the intellectual property of a major corporation.

Whenever Adeline attended a comic book convention and encountered *cosplay*, she was sure that she was witnessing the ultimate state of late period capitalism.

People who spent their leisure time *tweeting* and creating intellectual property for Twitter were going out into the world and dressing themselves as the intellectual properties of major international conglomerates.

They had transformed their bodies into walking advertisements for entities in which they had no economic stake. These advertisements would later appear in photographs on Facebook and Twitter and Instagram and Tumblr and Pinterest and Flickr and be collated on advertising supported websites like Newsarama and io9 and The Mary Sue.

Brand identity was complete.

ANYWAY, THAT WAS TWITTER in 2013. A system designed to tell Adeline that she should feel like shit via short messages from people who believed Batman was real.

These lessons in ethics and morality were conveyed through computers and cellular phones built by slave labor in China.

BUT TWITTER was only the symptom. The Internet was the disease.

The Internet was an excellent way to distribute child pornography, stolen autopsy reports and pirated copies of 1970s Euro Horror. It was also the dominant method of recorded communication in the early Twenty-First Century.

Despite the Internet's tyrannical reign over billions of people, very few of those billions understood how the technology worked. These billions were subject to a complex mechanism about which they knew nothing and over which they had no control.

Very few cared that they didn't understand the complex mechanism. They had been inoculated against any such concerns through repeated exposure to another complex mechanism about which they knew nothing and over which they had no control.

This other complex mechanism was called *governance*, an organizing principle used by societies to determine which individuals were granted homes on higher ground and which individuals were forcibly executed.

Many of the pointless men who built the Internet had done so under the delusion that their complex system could exist as a check on *governance*.

These pointless men believed that *freedom of speech* and *freedom of expression* were necessary to the functioning of a society and thus designed the Internet to prevent *governance* from impeding the free flow of discourse.

This wonderful fantasy disappeared around the time that another, more powerful fantasy took hold in the minds of the useless men who worked in technology. The second fantasy was *money*.

The men who championed *money* recognized that a platform where any old asshole could say any old bullshit was a zone without any rules of discourse. A lie was as powerful as the truth.

This made the Internet a wonderful place to *advertise*.

The champions of *money* understood that the best advertisements were those that involved a degree of interactivity with an audience. Here, too, the Internet, with its emphasis on *freedom of expression* and *freedom of speech*, proved its worth.

A POPULAR DELUSION in the Twenty-First Century was the belief that new technologies, which appeared every day, were neutral arrivals.

The thinginess of each thing was wrested from the field of Forms and brought into the world through nerdy Parthenogenesis.

But all technology was the product of its creators' spoken and unspoken ideologies. The Internet was not a neutral environment dedicated to *freedom of speech*.

It was something else, the result of paranoid Cold War thinking mixed with hazy San Francisco Bay Area notions like the idea that enlightenment could be achieved through sustainable polar fleece and organically grown fruits.

The Internet was bad ideology created by thoughtless men.

Consider, in contrast, the camera, another supposedly neutral technology which also become an arbiter of truth. If something was captured by the camera's lens, then it was true, then it had happened. Everything else was lies.

The camera was invented by middle class French men during a period of extensive Colonial expansion. Thus the camera operated, in perpetuity, on the spoken and unspoken ideologies of Nineteenth Century France.

The camera was very good at capturing sexualized images of women and even better at capturing dehumanizing images of poor people and people with eumelanin in the basale strata of their epidermises.

THE INTERNET was a heaping mass of ideologies, spoken and un-spoken, that reflected the social values of its many creators. Some of these men believed in *freedom of expression*. Some of these men were afraid of the Russians. Some of these men believed in nothing but money.

The system was designed with the sole purpose of maximizing the amount of bullshit that people typed into their computers and telephones. The greater the interconnectivity, the greater the profits. It was feudalism in the service of brands, and it rested on inducing human beings to indulge their worst behavior.

This was the world into which Adeline had wandered.

A place where complex systems gave the mentally ill the same platforms of expression as sane members of society, with no regard to the damage they caused to themselves or others. A place where complex systems induced the destruction of human beings like Ellen Flitcraft with no purpose other than making money for Google and Facebook.

Alas for the men who had designed the Internet whilst enthralled by Ayn Rand and shitty Science Fiction, it turned out that an open forum of ideas was impossible when the vast majority of vocal users were no more than babbling shit-asses.

WHAT COULD ADELINE DO? How do you reason with people who believe that Thor is real? How do you reason with people who make arguments about human dignity on machines built by slaves in China? How do you reason with people whose primary expression comes pre-branded by Twitter?

SO SHE PLAYED THE GAME. She was tweeting. Her first week went well. Kids were asking her for advice.

Then the most important kid reached out.

Emil called her.

chapter twenty

Emil was Adeline's son. He was nineteen years old. Emil was estranged from Adeline. Emil lived in Los Angeles with Suzanne, Adeline's alcoholic mother who had been an extra on the television show *Gidget*.

Emil was attending CalArts, an arts university founded by Walt Disney. Emil was working towards a Bachelor of Fine Arts.

EMIL WAS NOT an expected pregnancy.

Adeline got knocked up back in 1993, while she lived with Jeremy and Minerva on Steiner in the Lower Haight. Her bed was a couch in the living room.

The man who impregnated Adeline was born Nasir Mahmoud but called himself Nash Mac. He had a moderate amount of eumelanin in the basale stratum of his epidermis.

Adeline did not get pregnant on the couch in Jeremy and Minerva's living room. Adeline knew that good houseguests don't have sex on the premises.

No one who has opened their home has any desire to wake up at 11 in the morning and discover the nude entangled forms of their guest and another person or persons. No one who has opened their home wants to wake up at 11 in the morning only to find the blurry, drooping visages of the freshly fucked.

Adeline screwed out Nash Mac's brains in Nash Mac's apartment out in the Sunset District near the Pacific Ocean.

NASH MAC'S PARENTS were a pair of Iranian doctors who flew a little too close to the Sun and had to flee their native country during its Revolution.

Iran had vexed America for decades. It had been ruled by the Shah, a despotic King propped up by the CIA. The CIA was the same American organization that had funded the development of literary fiction and the *good novel.*

Anyway, in 1979, a bunch of Shi'a Muslims led the country into Revolution. The Shah was deposed and died in exile. The Revolution ended up installing a repressive Shi'ite Theocracy, which was a rather different outcome than the general American narrative of revolutions.

In 2009, a full thirty years later, the American and European users of Twitter and YouTube convinced themselves that they understood the political protests occurring in Iran and that the apparent use of Twitter by the protesters heralded the dawn of a new democratic era.

But this was wrong. Barely any Iranians were *tweeting.*

Almost all of the *tweets* were coming from Americans and Europeans taking a break from freaking out about the Doctor's next *regeneration* to *tweet* about democracy in the Middle East.

These *tweets* by Americans and Europeans against the Theocratic regime in Iran contained all the power, force and velocity of a banana-cream pie three feet in diameter when dropped from a stepladder five-feet high.

Nothing changed.

NASH MAC'S PARENTS moved to Virginia and became Americans. They brought their ten year old son.

Nash Mac did his undergraduate degree in computer science and then moved to the Bay Area, where he ended up working at LucasArts, a division of LucasFilm, the company owned by George Lucas.

George Lucas was the director and writer of the film *Star Wars*. He didn't have any eumelanin in the basale stratum of his epidermis.

STAR WARS WAS A TOTAL PIECE OF SHIT that had spawned billions of dollars in merchandise and sequels and books and games and pajama bottoms. It was an infinite reservoir, it was an endless void. It was responsible for a cornucopia of made up words like *Jedi,* the *Force* and *lightsaber.*

A *lightsaber* was a sword made of light. A sword was a weapon used to murder people.

A *Jedi* was a knight who believed in an idea of relative good and performed supernatural feats using the *Force.* A *Jedi* used supernatural feats and his *lightsaber* to murder people with opposing ideas of relative good.

The *Force* was an ill-explained mystical energy which ran throughout the fictional universe of *Star Wars.* It was a device which allowed characters to perform supernatural feats whenever a lull was created by poor writing in the screenplay.

As might be imagined, the *Force* was used with great frequency.

IN 2012, *Star Wars* and LucasFilm were sold to Disney.

George Lucas was different than Ub Iwerks, who created Mickey Mouse, or Jack Kirby, who created the comic book industry. George Lucas had worked in a Hollywood where there was a Director's Guild and agents and managers and lawyers who negotiated every deal. He had worked in an industry where labor had made some efforts towards organization.

When Disney bought *Star Wars,* they bought it from George Lucas because George Lucas owned *Star Wars.*

He made $4,000,000,000 on the deal.

TWO DECADES BEFORE the sale of *Star Wars* to Disney, George Lucas was paying the salary of Nash Mac.

George Lucas was paying Jeremy Winterbloss's salary. Jeremy Winterbloss was also working for LucasArts. Which is how Winterbloss met Nash Mac.

It was Jeremy who introduced Nash Mac to Adeline.

During the months when Adeline was screwing out Nash Mac's brains, Jeremy proposed the idea of *Trill.* It's entirely possible that Adeline became pregnant with Emil on the very same day that she started drawing her comic book.

BOTH JEREMY WINTERBLOSS and Nash Mac joined LucasArts about a year after a guy named Ron Gilbert had left the company. Ron Gilbert was the only genius who'd worked in video games.

He was responsible for *Maniac Mansion*. He was also responsible for *The Secret of Monkey Island* and *Monkey Island 2: LeChuck's Revenge*. These were the three greatest games ever made.

Ron Gilbert didn't have much eumelanin in the basale stratum of his epidermis. All of the intellectual property that he created at LucasArts was owned by George Lucas until it was owned by Disney.

ADELINE'S RELATIONSHIP with Nash Mac was never good. It was a thing that Adeline did because she was in San Francisco and bored.

1993 was a confusing time. She wasn't talking to Baby. She was estranged from Suzanne.

Adeline never understood much about Nash Mac. She never cared to understand much about Nash Mac.

Her lack of understanding became a problem after she flew home to New York City and discovered that she was pregnant.

THE + SIGN on the pregnancy test, bought in a Korean deli on Avenue A, reminded Adeline of being a teenager. She remembered being 14 years old.

The first year of high school. Her father was dead. She lived with Suzanne in Pasadena.

Adeline was deep in her deathrock phase, listening to beautiful and terrible bands like 45 Grave, Monitor, Flap, T.S.O.L and Christian Death. She hung around the Atomic Cafe. She saw The Castration Squad, the greatest band of all time, play Halloween gigs at Lazaro's Latin Lounge. Her hair was dyed black with blue highlights. She wore an unbelievable amount of kohl around her eyes.

She was dating this preppie guy named George Whitney. George Whitney attended the Buckley School. A deathrocker dating a preppie was one of those teenaged relationships that no one understands and no one can explain. Being young is terrible.

Suzanne was a realist who'd lived through her own adolescence and the chaos of the 1960s and 1970s. She knew that whenever George Whitney visited, he and Adeline were getting up to funny business in Adeline's bedroom.

Suzanne couldn't remember the mixture of terror, bluffing and desire that characterizes early sexual interactions. She couldn't remember a time when every sexual encounter didn't end with a male ejaculating into, or on, a woman.

She presumed that Adeline and George Whitney were having full-on penetrative sex. This wasn't true.

Adeline was only giving George Whitney handjobs and wondering about the quality of sex-ed classes at Buckley, as George Whitney had some difficulty identifying the clitoris.

Suzanne was worried about Adeline becoming pregnant. She resolved to deal with the issue.

"Adelllliiiiiiiiiiinnnnnnne!" she screeched from the living room.

Adeline was in her bedroom on the second floor. She opened the door and yelled, "What?"

"Adeliiiiiiiiiiiiine!" yelled Suzanne. "Please come down here and talk with me."

This all happened before Adeline developed her Transatlantic accent. This happened before Adeline saw *Breakfast at Tiffany's*. Adeline still sounded like a regular Californian teenager.

"Okay, fine," said Adeline. "Like, whatever."

Adeline went down into the living room and sat on the love seat.

"Adeliiiiiiiine," said Suzanne, "I think we need to talk about you and George."

"What's to talk about? George is just, like, you know, this guy I met on the beach," said Adeline.

"I've never wanted to be your enemy," said Suzanne. "I've always thought we could be best friends and talk about things like girlfriends."

Oh, no, thought Adeline. *She wants to talk about sex.*

"Look, Mom," said Adeline. "I'm not, like, totally stupid, okay? Me and George aren't fucking and I know all about birth control. We've have, like, sex-ed, remember? It's not like when you were young. It's the 1980s."

"You're an old soul," said Suzanne, "I thought you'd probably be too embarrassed to talk about it, so I taped something for you off the television."

"Who, like, are you?" asked Adeline.

"Please," said Suzanne. "I think it'll help."

Suzanne walked over and put her gentle hand on Adeline's shoulder. Adeline smelled whiskey on Suzanne's breath.

"Fine, okay?" asked Adeline. "I'll totally watch it. Right now. Let's get this over."

Suzanne turned on the television. She inserted the VHS tape. She turned on the VCR. She used the remote control to play the tape. She left the room.

Adeline watched. Her eyes were ringed with kohl. She was thinking about Tiffany Thayer, the astounding keyboardist in The Castration Squad.

It was an episode of ABC's *Afterschool Specials*, a series of moralizing dramas that aired in the early evening and dealt with issues which teenagers faced in the uncertain social climate of America's Cold War.

Suzanne had taped an episode called *Schoolboy Father*, starring Rob Lowe and Dana Plato.

Rob Lowe was an actor who would later be videotaped, twice, having group sex. Dana Plato was an actress who would later star in softcore pornography and die of a drug overdose. Neither of them had any eumelanin in the basale cell layers of their epidermises.

In *Schoolboy Father*, Rob Lowe plays a young teenager. He discovers that a girl he met at summer camp has given birth to a child. He suspects that he is the child's father. The girl is played by Dana Plato. She hasn't told Rob Lowe that she's pregnant. He finds her in the maternity ward. She tells Rob Lowe that she's planning to put the baby up for adoption. They fight. A social worker tells Rob Lowe that before the baby can be adopted, he has to sign a consent form. He decides to bring the baby home to live with him and his mother. He thinks he can handle it. His fantasy of parental competence conflicts with the reality of caring for an infant while trying to maintain an age appropriate social life. Rob Lowe realizes that he can't take care of a baby. The baby is put up for adoption.

Adeline wasn't sure what point Suzanne was trying to make with *Schoolboy Father*, but she knew enough not to ask for clarification. Suzanne was a drunk.

Adeline showed the tape to a gaggle of her deathrocker friends. They found the dialogue hilarious. They took great pleasure in quoting the film.

"Those sneakers are a national disgrace!" they yelled.

"You used precaution, didn't you?" they asked.

"We didn't think she'd get pregnant!" they yelled.

BUT NOW IT WAS 1993 and Adeline was pregnant. And all she could think was that she'd failed to learn anything from *Schoolboy Father*.

She'd been caught with her hand in the cookie jar. Her sexual encounters with Nash Mac had been so pointless. The sex itself hadn't been particularly good.

Now there was a child. A child was like a life sentence of Nash Mac.

She'd considered an abortion but didn't do it. This was not due to ideology.

Adeline had been the person in high school who helped other girls get abortions. She'd driven them to clinics and held their hands in reception areas painted the color of Norman Mailer's living room in Brooklyn.

Adeline believed that abortions were a social good.

Which, of course, they were.

She still brought Emil to term.

ADELINE'S OLDER SISTER DAHLIA flew out from Los Angeles to help with the pregnancy.

Dahlia had a husband named Charles. She'd had two children with Charles. No one in Dahlia's nuclear family had any eumelanin in the basale strata of their epidermises.

Charles and the children loved Dahlia but they were happy to have a break. Dahlia was a total pain in the ass.

AS SOON AS DAHLIA got off of the plane, she told Adeline that Adeline had better prepare for giving birth because giving birth felt like shitting out a baby seal.

"Dahlia, you blithering idiot, I'm not even close to my due date!"

"A baby seal, Adeline! A big wet baby seal!" said Dahlia. "You'll be shitting out a big wet baby seal!"

This all happened in a terminal at JFK Airport, long before America was *terrofucked*, so Adeline met Dahlia at her gate.

DAHLIA HELPED OUT. She talked with Suzanne and asked for money. Dahlia dealt with doctor's appointments and prenatal care and the hospital.

And she stayed with Adeline for a few months after the birth, which meant that Adeline never missed a deadline on *Trill*.

THERE ADELINE WAS IN A PRIVATE ROOM at Roosevelt Hospital, experiencing the miracle of childbirth, bringing a beautiful human life into this world and the only thing that she could think was about how she was shitting out a baby seal.

When she held the child in her arms, she knew that she'd call him Emil. Emil was the name of her older brother.

The first Emil was a suicide.

He'd been caught soliciting tricks on Selma Boulevard in Hollywood. Because of their father's forays into local politics, Emil's name and face ended up in the *Pasadena Star-News*. In the photograph, Emil was wearing a white tuxedo.

He threw himself off the Colorado Street Bridge into the Arroyo Seco.

THE CIRCUMSTANCES AROUND HER CHILD were what convinced Adeline to leave New York and move to San Francisco. Nash Mac was making noise about not having custody and never seeing his son.

Adeline wasn't going to get herself in a situation where Emil flew out to California to spend court mandated time with his father.

Suzanne'd suggested that they sue Nash Mac into oblivion.

"Adeliiiiiiine," she said, "You know that we've used Bert Fields in the past! I'm sure he could recommend an attorney who would pound your sperm donor into the dust!"

Adeline had grown up in Los Angeles. She'd been around Suzanne's friends and gone to private school out on the Westside.

She'd attended the Crossroads School for the Arts & Sciences, which was an alternative education relic of the 1970s. It was at Crossroads that Adeline had helped several pregnant girls procure their abortions.

She'd seen what lawsuits did to people. Divorce proceedings and custody battles seemed, more than anything, to harm children.

So she packed up and moved to San Francisco. Her boyfriend at the time, a former East Village punk rocker turned legal assistant, came with her. He didn't last.

AS A SINGLE MOTHER drawing over 30 pages of comic art every month, Adeline didn't have much time for a social life.

This was okay. She was in her thirties. She'd whittled away her teens and her twenties with questionable sex, drug use, and novels in translation. There wasn't much left undone.

Suzanne visited regularly. And Jeremy and Minerva came into the city from San Venetia. And Baby showed up from time to time. Even Dahlia was around.

The early years were wonderful. Emil had a sweet personality. He was a bright child.

LOOKING BACK, one of the things she remembered most was the sense of dread that arrived whenever Emil handled inflated balloons.

Balloons were a state of existential terror. You waited for the rubber to pop. You waited for the explosion of sound. You waited for your child to start screaming. You waited for your child's incomprehension about its imploded and disappeared toy.

WHEN EMIL TURNED 12, he began finding Adeline embarrassing.

She could see why.

Don Murphy had optioned *Trill*. Scholastic was sniffing around. Adeline spoke in a Transatlantic accent. Most people in her chosen field thought that she was a Russian man. Her best friend wrote Science Fiction. Sometimes an actual Russian woman would come over and swear about how capitalism had ruined her vagina.

When Emil turned 13, and it was clear that things weren't getting any less weird, he asked if he could go live with Nash Mac.

NASH MAC had transitioned out of computer games and was working for IronPort, which had been acquired by Cisco. Adeline didn't know what he did for a living. She didn't care. She didn't ask.

It was hard to maintain a pretense of civility, even for Emil's sake. Every time she saw Nash Mac's dumb face, it reminded Adeline of how stupid and pointless it is to be young.

Nash Mac had married another woman and fathered two other children. His new wife had blonde hair and no eumelanin in the basale stratum of her epidermis. Her name was Stephanie. She tried very hard to forge a working relationship with Adeline.

DESPITE HER EFFORTS, Stephanie couldn't bridge the gap. She and Adeline were very different.

While Stephanie was writing her Master's thesis on Barbara Kruger at Stanford, Adeline was stepping over dope sick East Village junkies and drawing Felix Trill's misadventures with amorous cephalopods.

AND THE SHARED SEXUAL PAST weighed on Stephanie's mind.

Aware of the distance between them, Stephanie spoke to Adeline in an unusually slow and loud manner, which wasn't that far from how some people talk to the foreign, the blind and the mentally backwards.

This manner of speaking made Adeline assume that Stephanie herself was mentally backwards.

Her responses to Stephanie's perceived mental backwardness did not foster conversation, as Adeline tended to talk to Stephanie as a person might speak to a favored pony.

"HELLO... ADELINE... YOU... LOOK... NICE... TODAY!"

"Many thanks, darling. You yourself are rather fetching."

"ADELINE... WOULD... YOU... LIKE... SOMETHING... TO... EAT?"

"Aren't you just a breath of fresh air? You're like a mint julep. I could simply drink you down in one gulp, princess."

"EMIL... SEEMS... LIKE... HE... IS... ENOYING... SEVENTH... GRADE!"

"Yes he does, doesn't he? We all must enjoy things in this world of ours. I do hope you have some things that you enjoy. You do? Well, aren't you a good girl!"

STEPHANIE AND NASH MAC lived out in Milpitas, one of the endless California suburbs comprised of strip malls and decaying erotic fervor.

Emil had his own room for the nights that he slept over. Both Stephanie and Nash Mac said that Emil was more than welcome to live with them.

So Adeline agreed.

She had regretted the decision ever since.

EVEN WITH THE NEW LATITUDE OF MOVEMENT, the loss of Emil was a sucking wound which would not heal.

"Baby," she said while visiting Provincetown, "It's like a creature has ripped asunder my soul. I knew he was going to grow up and leave me but why did it have to happen so soon?"

"For fuck's sake, Adeline," said Baby, "Go and take him back. You have custody. You're his mother. Can't Suzanne sue somebody?"

"He doesn't want me," she said. "He doesn't want anything to do with the weird life I've made for myself. He wants to be with his father and that dreadful woman. She talks so loud, Baby, and so slow. I suspect that she might be mentally backwards. I suppose she's his new mother."

"She's not his mother," said Baby. "You're his mother. He's supposed to hate you. You aren't supposed to take it seriously. You aren't supposed to let him move out of your apartment."

"No, Baby," said Adeline, "It's different. I remember hating Suzanne. This isn't hate. If he hated me, it wouldn't present a challenge. This is different. He doesn't hate me. He's just disinterested in my silly little life."

Baby rolled his eyes. Of all Adeline's strange decisions, he considered this the strangest.

ADELINE'S MOTHER HAD LEFT PASADENA and bought a condo in Downtown Los Angeles. Adeline couldn't imagine Suzanne anywhere other than Pasadena. It was too strange.

Suzanne kept her house but wanted something in the city. Downtown was revitalizing. "It's gentrifying, Adeliiiiiiiine!" said Suzanne. "All the swinging people are swinging again and they've cleaned out all that nasty burned out trash!"

When Adeline was young, she'd loved all the nasty burned out trash.

NOW EMIL WAS LIVING with his grandmother. This turned out to be worse than when he had lived with Nash Mac.

At least when Emil lived with Nash Mac, Adeline could see him when she wanted. At least he was still forced to stay with her on the weekends.

Now he'd fallen off the radar. Now he was out in Los Angeles. He didn't return her phone calls. He very rarely sent her email.

WHENEVER ADELINE needed to hear about the actual details of Emil's life, she had to call her mother and ask about her son. Whenever Adeline wanted to see an idealized self-portrait of Emil's life, she would check his presence on various websites owned by multinational corporations.

But she attempted to avoid the latter. She found it creepy to stalk her son's Internet presence. Emil's WaNks Index Score was 83.21223121.

ADELINE TRIED to take things in stride. Whenever she worried about irreparable harm to her relationship with Emil, she remembered the years when she wasn't speaking with Suzanne. And now she and her mother were on better terms than ever.

Besides, what was there to be afraid of?

Adeline herself had been a young waif on the streets of multiple urban environments. And that had been when the cities were dangerous, before they cleared away the burned out trash. That had been when cities were scary and before Internet pornography had anesthetized an entire population.

WHEN SHE SAW EMIL'S PHONE NUMBER come across her cellphone, she was thrilled. She answered on the first ring.

"Emil?" she asked.

"Mom," he said.

"How's Los Angeles, darling? Are you simply baking in the sunny sunshine with Mommy Dearest?"

"Mom," said Emil, "You've, like, got to stop using Twitter. You're so fucking embarrassing. It's totally awful."

"They've been saying some very terrible things about your mother on the Internet."

"I totally saw what you said about Beyoncé," said Emil. "All of my friends saw it. Do you know how many people, like, sent me it?"

"I'm sorry," said Adeline. "It wasn't my fault."

"When has it ever been your fault? When has a single thing ever been, like, something that you admitted was your fault? Our whole lives are so fucking crazy and it's never because of you."

THIS WAS UNFAIR.

As the daughter of an alcoholic, Adeline knew all about people who refused to see the relationship between the course of their lives and their own poor decisions. Adeline wrestled with as much responsibility as she could bear. She knew that her life was her own creation. It was nobody's fault but hers.

But Emil was young and his mother was dispensing relationship advice on Twitter.

"YOUR OPINIONS," said Emil, "are like, really, offensive. I totally don't know why you'd say any of those things in, like, public."

On the Internet, Emil offered a very different self-portrait than one might deduce from his California dialect. His intellectual output was full of words that he'd learned during his foundation year at CalArts.

He had been taught theory. His fellow students had recommended essential books, most of which were post-theory novels.

Whenever Emil posted something on the Internet, he included a great deal of jargon like *epistemology, ontology, intertextuality, binaries, intersectionality, extrarationality* and *improvisational impulse.*

Yet whenever Emil was involved in a vocal conversation, his California roots betrayed him. He sounded like a media stereotype.

The split between his written and spoken selves was startling, but not unusual for kids involved in the Los Angeles art scene. There were thousands of them. They all used the Internet to articulate what they could not articulate in person.

For all of her flaws, Adeline was flush with a mother's forgiving love. She had never noticed that her son sounded like an idiot.

A THING THAT ADELINE had never told anyone, not even Baby, was the real reason why she let Emil go live with Nash Mac.

It wasn't that Adeline didn't take responsibility. It was that Adeline took too much responsibility. She let Emil go live with Nash Mac because she'd felt guilty.

Guilty about bring a child into her weird life, guilty about subjecting Emil to her family and her friends, guilty about putting Emil into a situation beyond his control, guilty about robbing him of his own choices, guilty of sticking him on a planet that had less than a century left.

The only thing a parent need do, thought Adeline, was to inflict as little damage as possible and give their children the tools to handle future damage done by others.

She honored the feeling. She let Emil live where he wanted and hoped that things would repair themselves.

She was waiting for the verdict. The jury was still out.

$$))><(($$

"ENOUGH ABOUT THIS TWITTER NONSENSE, darling. Tell me, how are you? How ever is your band?"

"It's not a band, Mom," said Emil. "I've told you, like, a million times. We're not a fucking band. No one plays instruments. It's really not a fucking band."

"Sorry, darling," said Adeline.

chapter twenty-one

J. Karacehennem left his apartment near the corner of 23rd and Bryant. He was alone. He was going to a literary event where he would read aloud some of his own writing.

The Hangman's Beautiful Daughter was not coming along. The Hangman's Beautiful Daughter did not like his writing.

When he published his novel *ZIAD*, The Hangman's Beautiful Daughter read it. She said there were some nice parts but she didn't think the book was that interesting.

"What do you mean it's not interesting?" asked J. Karacehennem. "It's about Ziad Jarrah! One of the 9/11 pilots! It's a book about a psychopath who wants to crash a hijacked plane into the Capitol building! He fucked up your whole world forever! What could be more interesting?"

"It's just more masculine bullshit," said The Hangman's Beautiful Daughter. "Men are always writing books about killing each other. When they aren't writing books about killing each other, then they're just killing each other."

Anyway, The Hangman's Beautiful Daughter had been to a great number of J. Karacehennem's literary readings. She had seen enough. She didn't need to keep going.

She was skipping this one.

THAT VERY MORNING, J. Karacehennem had woken up and walked past Local's Corner. Local's Corner was the public relations disaster of a restaurant opened at 23rd and Bryant.

The previous evening, someone had vandalized the restaurant. They had used purple spray paint to tag its windows with graffiti. The graffiti read:

KEEP MISSION BROWN

Mission was the neighborhood in which Local's Corner was located. *Brown* was a colloquialism indicating the writer of the graffiti's desire to maintain the historically Latino character of the Mission.

A FEW WEEKS EARLIER, on Cesar Chavez Day, a woman named Sandra Cuadra and her family went to Local's Corner. They were a party of five. They all had eumelanin in the basale strata of their epidermises.

They were turned away.

The server would not seat Sandra Cuadra.

An explanation floated later was that Local's Corner didn't accommodate parties bigger than four people.

Sandra Cuadra was a long time resident of the Mission. She was Latino. She was Brown. She was an activist and a former city employee.

She sent email to a wide group of people. She detailed her experiences with Local's Corner.

Latino people were feeling squeezed by the forces of gentrification. Their neighborhood was being pulled apart by the whims of mega-capitalists, low interest rates, investors from out of town, and corporations located in Silicon Valley.

And there was Local's Corner, the most obvious and tone deaf symbol of the changes wrought on the neighborhood.

It had denied a Latino family service. On Cesar Chavez Day. Its owner had a bad reputation around the neighborhood. The matriarch of that Latino family was a beloved neighborhood fixture.

So the vandalization and graffiti began.

LATINO PEOPLE were the genetic descendents of both the Western hemisphere's indigenous peoples and the Spanish colonialists who had invaded the Americas. The Spanish colonialists started showing up at the end of the Fifteenth Century.

The Spanish colonialists had murdered and poisoned and infected the indigenous peoples of the Americas. Because the human race is driven by reproductive urges, the Spanish colonialists also vented their lust into the indigenous peoples of the Americas.

There were Portuguese colonists, too. From the perspective of the indigenous peoples who were being murdered and poisoned and raped and infected, the Portuguese were just Spaniards with a shittier accent.

LATINO PEOPLE were a diverse group of nationalities. Some Latino people had some eumelanin in the basale strata of the epidermises. Others did not.

The presence of some eumelanin in some Latino people is why someone had suggested keeping the neighborhood *Brown.*

WHEN SPANISH CONQUERORS invaded the San Francisco Bay Area, the indigenous people were the tribes of the Ohlone people.

The narrative history of the Ohlone people was the same terrible narrative visited upon all the indigenous people of the Americas. Death and depopulation through infection, murder and rape.

Before the Spanish arrived, there were tens of thousands of Ohlones in California. There were about 2,000 in 2013.

THE THING WITH THE OHLONES wasn't simply a Spanish problem or a California problem. All of the United States of America was stolen land.

The treatment of the indigenous people of the United States of America was the world's biggest genocide.

Americans loved doing things in a really big way. They couldn't help it. They were maniacs for obscene consumption. Americans were nuts for the enlarged and its attendant dramas.

HERE IS AN APPARENTLY TRUE STORY.

Prescott Bush was the father of George Bush I and the grandfather of George Bush II. He was the guy who worked for a Nazi bank.

The story goes that Prescott Bush and five other guys dug up the grave of Geronimo.

Geronimo was an Apache warrior. The Apaches were a grouping of indigenous people of some eumelanin in the basale strata of their epidermises whose way of life was destroyed during the genocide.

Prescott Bush and the five other guys were all students at Yale. They were all part of a secret society called Skull and Bones.

YALE WAS A UNIVERSITY. Universities were confidence games which pretended to ennoble their students through pedagogy. What universities really did was simple: they were research institutions that created better weapons for future wars.

Many universities, like Yale, used the *humanities* as a cloak for their development of better weapons for future wars.

The *humanities* were inquiries into the nature of human beings and their ability to create culture and have emotions and thoughts.

The *humanities* were also unprofitable.

Some institutions of higher learning, like Worcester Polytechnic Institute and the Massachusetts Institute of Technology and the California Institute of Technology, didn't bother with the cloak of the *humanities*.

The teachers at these institutions pretty much ignored things like reading and critical thinking and focused their efforts on devising new ways to kill more humans.

Humans killing other humans was part of the human experience, but what Worcester Polytechnic Institute and the Massachusetts Institute of Technology and the California Institute of Technology wanted was *peak efficiency*. This term meant the most dead humans in the least amount of seconds.

Peak efficiency was very profitable.

SKULL AND BONES was a secret society of elite students who attended Yale. Skull and Bones had a disproportionate influence on America society.

Prescott Bush's son, George Bush I, was a Bonesman. His grandson, George Bush II, was a Bonesman. Both George Bushes ended up as Presidents of the United States.

In 2004, Bush II ran for reelection. His opponent was John Kerry. John Kerry was a Senator from Massachusetts. He was another eumelaninless Bonesman.

PRESCOTT BUSH dug up Geronimo's skull and sent it back to Yale.

The skull remains in the clubhouse of Skull and Bones. Both his son and his grandson had regular interactions with a skull taken from a grave robbed by their paterfamilias.

IF YOU WERE FROM CALIFORNIA, and it was the year 2013, and you were talking about Prescott Bush robbing a grave, you'd say, "It's, like, so *ironic,* because America is, like, totally a country ruled by both, like, laws and, you know, human decency and, like, the people who rob graves totally bring a stain upon, you know, themselves and, like, their families forever."

You'd be right. It would be *ironic.*

You'd mean the opposite of what you were saying.

Because Prescott Bush ended up as a Senator in the United States Congress and a banker who worked with Nazis.

His son ended up as President of the United States.

His son's son ended up as President of the United States.

His son's other son ended up as Governor of Florida and a Presidential candidate in the 2016 Election.

Granted, his son's other other son did catch herpes from East Asian sex-workers. But his son's other other son was a black sheep.

And if you were the relative of the person whose body was robbed, you'd have a good chance of being mired in poverty. You'd have a good chance of starving and struggling with alcoholism on a reservation administered by the country that stole your land.

But don't worry.

We live in the best of all possible worlds!

J. KARACEHENNEM was turning from 22nd Street onto Valencia. He was thinking about his father Mehmet Karacehennem.

Mehmet Karacehennem was an alcoholic.

Unlike Adeline's mother Suzanne, Mehmet had been sober for seven years.

This sobriety coincided with his departure from America. He moved back to İzmir, Turkey, the city in which he was born and raised. He gave up drinking.

BEFORE HE WENT BACK HOME, Mehmet had lived in America for over twenty-five years. He'd worked in the jewelry factories of Southeastern New England. His co-workers had taught him the intricacies and pleasures of swearing in both English and Spanish.

No one needed to teach him about cursing in Turkish.

Other than monitoring the exchange rate between the US Dollar and the Turkish Lira, Mehmet's only real hobby was calling his son on the telephone and unleashing torrents of obscenities.

If J. Karacehennem did not answer when his father called, his father would unleash torrents of obscenity on J. Karacehennem's voicemail.

"Kid," he would say to the voicemail, "What the fuck is the problem? Are you a fucking *hain gavur* who doesn't call his fucking father? Why doesn't *hain gavur* call his fucking father? Are you trying to fucking antagonize me? You piece of fucking shit, I will murder you some day. *Küçük bok*. Don't be fucking *pislik*. Call your fucking father. Pick up the fucking phone, you garbage. Don't be *maricón*, kid. *Allah'ın belâsı!* Call your daddy."

WHEN *ZIAD* was published, J. Karacehennem sent his father a copy of the book.

As *ZIAD* was about Islamic themed religious fanaticism, J. Karacehennem was curious about the old man's thoughts.

Mehmet was quite simply the shittiest Muslim who'd ever lived.

This is not to say that Mehmet did not believe.

Belief in itself was not his problem. He believed in everything.

Mehmet believed in: (1) Ghostly Hauntings. (2) Time Travel. (3) Fairies. (4) Alien intervention in human destiny, by virtue of every major religious personage being an extraterrestrial in human form. (5) That the earth was a prison in which the worst souls of the universe were trapped until they had rehabilitated. (6) Witchcraft. (7) Satanism. (8) Demonology. (9) Telepathy. (10) Telekinesis. (11) ESP. (12) Alien abduction. (13) Bigfoot. (14) The Loch Ness Monster. (15) Indigo children. (16) Crystal healing. (17) Faked Moon Landing. (18) Biorhythms. (19) Reincarnation. (20) Metempsychosis. (21) Reiki. (22) The water words of Masaru Emoto.

And that list just scratches the surface.

That list doesn't say a word about the leprechauns.

BEFORE MEHMET READ *ZIAD,* his phone calls had centered on the problem of his son not being married.

After *ZIAD,* the phone calls became long digressive monologues during which Mehmet offered profane and obscene advice about the books that his son should write.

"Kid," said Mehmet, "Don't be a fucking dummy with fucking bullshit terrorism. Write some fucking sex in this shit, man. When I was young, we read books called *yakılacak kitaplar.* Books to be burned. That's what you call the book, kid, *A Book to Burn,* and make it all about sex. Don't be fucking stupid, kid. Make sure you don't say anything too explicit. You just say things like, 'I shook my branch at her ripe melons,' and 'Her peaches tasted sweet.'"

"Maybe I will," said J. Karacehennem.

"Everyone in America is fucking obsessed with sex, kid. They will love *yakılacak kitaplar.* Turkish people are obsessed with sex, too. Americans get married for love, but Turkish people get married so that they can get up to hanky-panky."

ONE TIME, Mehmet saw a televised news report about the runaway sales of *Fifty Shades of Grey*, a book by E.L. James that was a total piece of shit.

Like *Les 120 journées de Sodome*, it was a *graphic novel*. Like *Les 120 journées de Sodome*, it failed at being a novel. Unlike *Les 120 journées de Sodome*, it also failed at being graphic.

"Kid," he said, "Why the fuck don't you do something like this *Fifty Shades of Grey*?"

"Did they say what the book was about?" asked J. Karacehennem. "It's sadomasochism and bondage and domination. In the novel, there's a red room of pain where the guy practices all three on the woman."

"Kid," asked Mehmet, "Does it involve *The Agony and The Ecstasy*?"

THE AGONY AND THE ECSTASY was Mehmet Karacehennem's self-invented euphemism for anal sex.

Anal sex was a type of sex during which a male's penis penetrated the rectum and the anus of another human being. This could be painful. It could also be pleasurable.

Typically, both the rectum and the anus were used for the expulsion of solid human waste, so a certain *frisson* emerged from both the waste-factor and pain-factor of the rectum and the anus being penetrated by the male sexual organ.

Anal sex and its attendant *frisson* were given a great deal of value on the Internet.

MEHMET HAD INVENTED this euphemism for anal sex during one of J. Karacehennem's visits to İzmir.

One night in April of 2011, J. Karacehennem was woken at 4AM by the sounds of Mehmet's next door neighbor having sex with her boyfriend.

At first he mistook her wailing for a ghost because the wailing sounded like the real world representation of the ghostly wailing present in Floyd Gottfredson's classic Mickey Mouse newspaper serial *House of the Seven Haunts*, in which the ghosts made sounds like:

HOOHOOHOOHOOOHOOOOHOOO.

Then he remembered that he didn't believe in ghosts and that if ghosts did exist they probably wouldn't make sounds like the ghosts in Floyd Gottfredson's classic Mickey Mouse newspaper serial *House of the Seven Haunts.*

Then he remembered that in Floyd Gottfredson's classic Mickey Mouse newspaper serial *House of the Seven Haunts,* the ghosts had turned out to be fake.

Then he decided that the howling must be that of an owl.

Then he remembered that Turkey doesn't have owls.

Then he remembered that he had no idea whether or not Turkey had owls, but that if Turkey did have owls, they probably weren't in the urban environment of İzmir and they probably didn't sound like the ghosts in Floyd Gottfredson's classic Mickey Mouse newspaper serial *House of the Seven Haunts.*

Then he woke up a little more and realized that people were having sex on the other side of the wall next to his head.

J. KARACEHENNEM spoke to his father the next morning.

"Mehmet," he said, "she's so loud!"

"I know what is going on in there with *sürtük*, but I can't say it to you. She is doing a keetchy-keetchy special thing. She is having *The Agony and the Ecstasy.*"

"I thought this was a repressive country with restrictive sexual mores! I thought that you worshipped Allah and followed the religious strictures of the Prophet Muhammad (PBUH)! I've been sold a lot of lies!"

"Eh, kid," said Mehmet, "it's İzmir. *Sikişmiş* İzmir. We are a city of infidels. *Gavur* İzmir. What can you do?"

"ANYWAY," SAID J. Karacehennem to his father, "I'm not really sure I could do another *Fifty Shades of Grey.* I don't really know much about bondage or domination."

"Kid," a father asked his son, "Can't you learn?"

ANOTHER TIME, Mehmet suggested that his son write a book called *Stopped at the Top.*

"Kid," said Mehmet, "What you will do is this. You will go to Los Angeles and you will investigate what happened to all jurors in the O.J. Simpson trial. You will see where they are now and what kinds of houses they have bought. You will find out that they all got $5,000,000 each from the government to return a not guilty verdict. Kid, I know this because I saw it on the news that night. Bill Clinton went into the office next to the Oval Office and did a big sigh. Kid, they bought those jurors. Bill Clinton did it with secret money. If you write about it, oh, the books you will sell. Oh they will go fucking crazy for you, my boy."

J. KARACEHENNEM crossed Market Street at Church. He had just passed by Aardvark Books, the best used bookstore in the city. *Long may you live,* he thought. *Long may you thrive!*

He was going to 851 Haight Street, the venue at which he had agreed to do a literary reading.

851 Haight Street was on the third floor of an apartment building near Divisadero Street. The apartment was vacant. The apartment was in disrepair. It had been vacant for years. All the other apartments in the building were occupied.

A person called Janey Smith had come into possession of keys to the apartment.

Janey Smith had taken his name after the protagonist of Kathy Acker's great novel *Blood and Guts in High School.* Janey Smith said that he'd had sex with Kathy Acker back when he was 18. This was before Kathy Acker died of cancer, when Kathy Acker knew Kevin Killian.

Anyway, Janey Smith and his friend Mike Kitchell, neither of who had any eumelanin in the basale strata of the epidermises, decided that it might be interesting to host reading events in 851 Haight. The space was unused, so why not?

Both Mike Kitchell and Janey Smith wanted the readings to happen at night.

The apartment had no electricity. In fact, the apartment had no wiring and most of its walls were ripped open and half demolished. There was a thick layer of sawdust on everything. There were piles of unused doors and a half demolished bathtub.

As a result of the cheap candles which Janey Smith scattered around the apartment, the reading series was not only illegal but also offered the chance of everyone burning to death.

The first event was in December 2011. Subsequent events followed. Each attracted a bigger crowd, until it got to the point where 80 to 100 people would cram into the front room of the apartment.

DURING THE *ANNUS HORRIBILIS* of 2013, Janey Smith wrote an Internet post titled "Fuck List" on a website called HTMLGiant. "Fuck List" was a list of writers that Janey Smith wanted to fuck.

Another writer named peterBD asked Janey Smith if peterBD could make a book out of "Fuck List." The idea was that peterBD would take Janey Smith's original post and write short vignettes about Janey Smith having sex with the listed writers. Janey Smith said yes. peterBD would call this book *We're Fucked*.

This was a terrible idea.

By the Summer of 2014, *We're Fucked* was published. Janey Smith contributed the introduction.

The book's appearance coincided with much discussion on the Internet about several men in the Bay Area poetry scene. Basically, these discussions said: sexual predators are amongst us. Sexual assaults have occurred.

Five names were listed. Janey Smith was among them, although unlike several of the others, there were no clear accusations against Janey Smith.

Because the reading series at 851 Haight had some notoriety, Janey Smith was the highest profile of the named.

It did not escape notice that a person denounced on the Internet as a sexual predator was involved with a book containing a series of fictional vignettes about the denounced person having sex with a long list of writers. An equivalence was made between the accusations of being a sexual predator and the content of *We're Fucked*.

One of the people in both "Fuck List" and *We're Fucked* was a writer named Dianna Dragonetti. Diana Dragonetti wrote an interesting post for

HTMLGiant about Janey Smith, *We're Fucked*, the negation of consent, rape culture, the Patriarchy, and the fracas consuming the Bay Area poetry scene.

Like every other website on the Internet, HTMLGiant was about making money through adverts strategically placed around the content donated by its contributors.

When Dragonetti's essay appeared, its final paragraphs were followed by these advertisements:

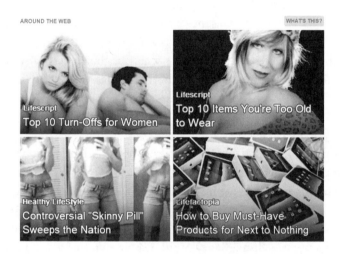

AS J. KARACEHENNEM walked up Steiner to Haight, he did not know that he was passing by Jeremy and Minerva's old apartment.

He was thinking about the iPhone.

J. KARACEHENNEM was thinking about both the iPhone and the iPad because he had been thinking about the *New York Times*, and its September 30, 1909 article asking whether or not J. Karacehennem was a White man.

Somewhere between its final piss-poor article about Weapons of Mass Destruction in Iraq and its first excellent article about Tartine, the *New York Times* had become the house organ of tech evangelism.

The *New York Times* published an awful lot of articles about Apple products. Many were about the impact of both the iPhone and the iPad.

The consensus, at the *New York Times* and elsewhere, was that the iPhone and iPad had *changed everything*.

AS J. KARACEHENNEM approached 851 Haight, he could see Adeline and Christine and a third person standing in front of the building. They were up the hill and a few blocks away.

The third person was Christine's boyfriend Bertrand.

J. Karacehennem was thinking about *apps* that he might develop. He'd heard there was a lot of money in *apps*.

The first app would be called *Jesty*.

This *app* would make people's iPhones unusable. *Jesty* would turn iPhones into bricks. *Jesty* would read the text of David Foster Wallace's *Infinite Jest* until the iPhone owner committed suicide from the sheer weight of pretension and boredom.

The second app didn't have a name.

It was based on a very popular *app* called Grindr.

Because the iPhone had *changed everything*, Grindr which was an *app* that alerted gay men to the presence of other gay men in the immediate area. Many Grindr meetings ended in furious sexual rutting. Which was a beautiful thing.

J. Karacehennem thought that since the iPhone had *changed everything*, surely the model of Grindr could be adapted to other situations.

He settled on the idea of an *app* catering to the emerging market of cross-Abrahamic relations in the Middle East.

He thought that he could build an *app* for Palestinians and Israelis looking to engage in consequence free violence. The *app* would tell a Palestinian about all the Israelis in the immediate area. The *app* would tell an Israeli about all the Palestinians in the immediate area.

Then Israelis and Palestinians could choose whom they wanted to meet without any messy introductions. They could choose upon whom they wanted to inflict massive, wounding violence.

The possibilities were endless. The iPhone had *changed everything*.

chapter twenty-two

Adeline and J. Karacehennem and Christine sat in a restaurant on Church Street called Sparky's.

Sparky's was one of the few restaurants open in San Francisco after 10PM. They hadn't gotten out of 851 Haight until 11pm.

"One of the very first things that Minerva told me about Sparky's is that it was instant diarrhea," said Adeline. "But I'm simply banned from Orphan Andy's, aren't I? There's nowhere else that we might go, is there?"

So they ended up in Sparky's.

J. KARACEHENNEM wasn't sure how his reading went. He'd read a poem that he'd written about North Beach.

It was titled, *"Rexroth Futurus!"*

The very best part of the poem was its end:

AND IF YOU'RE IN SAN FRANCISCO
COME AND FIND ME IN THE AFTERNOON
I'LL BE AT CAFFE TRIESTE

I'M THE ONE WITHOUT ANY HAIR
SITTING NEXT TO THE GIRL
WITH NO EYEBROWS

A FEW MONTHS earlier, J. Karacehennem had found an old hard drive which contained all the juvenilia he'd scribbled in his teenaged years.

He opened the files and discovered that the content of this juvenilia, mostly comprised of short stories, was universally disturbing.

They were hyperviolent and betrayed the sexual anxiety of the massively unfucked. They were some of the worst fiction in the history of the English language, the products of a mind deranged by puberty.

J. KARACEHENNEM'S TEENAGED SELF had done more than write these stories. His teenaged self had submitted them to a wide range of publications.

The old hard drive contained cover letters that he'd attached to these stories when he'd sent them to editors. They were funnier than the stories.

J. Karacehennem read the cover letters at 851 Haight.

Like the following:

February 24th, 1995

To Whom It May Concern:

Enclosed is my short story, entitled "FAT BOY", for your consideration. It is a tale of madness, plain and not-very-simple. I realize that there are parts of the text that do not seem to make sense, but again, this is a tale of madness, and there is a connecting plot.

The story itself is 3,043 words in length.

I was pleased to hear of your magazine over the Internet. I am a new writer, who is having a hard time convincing the major fiction (and secondary) markets that my fiction is of some value. Unfortunately, most of the places I have been submitting to are more concerned with big names than writing.

For your convenience, I have enclosed a SASE. You need not return the enclosed manuscript. I look forward to hearing your reply.

Like the following:

February 9th, 1995

Dear Mister Schweitzer,

Enclosed is my short story, "Poker was the ideal game". It is the somewhat convoluted tale of man and his love and what he does to win her back. It is a piece of good writing. I am not great and make no claims of being so. The story itself is 3,629 words in length.

I am submitting it to you, in hopes of publishing, and/or comments you might want to make. For your convenience, I have also enclosed a Self-Addressed, Stamped Envelope. The manuscript itself is not of any concern to me, and you may discard it if you deem it prudent.

A note added for you. This story has been rejected by many more mainstream fiction markets simply on the basis that it does NOT fit in with their themes. In submitting to you, I am hoping to avoid this initial prejudice.

Thank you for your time and consideration in this matter.

ADELINE AND CHRISTINE and J. Karacehennem were sitting in a booth by the back wall of Sparky's.

"Darlings," said Adeline, "Do you know that my *tweeting* has been rather successful? I'm up to 15,000 followers. All of these comic book fans and all the lovely young things are fascinated by the opinions of yours truly."

"What opinions can you even express in *tweets*?" asked J. Karacehennem. "Isn't the hard limit 140 characters?"

"You'd be stunned, sweet child," said Adeline. "For my larger exegeses, I've been going simply wild with the Facebook account that Jeremy set up. I've got about 2500 friends."

"You were a Luddite two months ago," said Christine.

"They put yours truly through the wringer," said Adeline. "I decided that if other people were using me to earn their filthy lucre, then I should at the very least try and sell some books."

"Have you affected sales?" asked Christine.

"It's rather shocking, darling. We've pushed the first volume of *Trill* into another printing and we've almost sold out of the omnibus. Do you know that even *Done Because We Are Too Menny* is getting a second printing?"

DONE BECAUSE WE ARE TOO MENNY was a solo project that Adeline published after the first inauguration of Barack Obama. She had published it with Image Comics.

The book reflected her deepening concern about *global warming* and *climate change* and the effects of *overpopulation* on the environment.

Overpopulation was a way of saying that the reproductive urges of the human species had spun out of control and that people could not stop creating babies.

The effect of *overpopulation* was to create a scarcity of resources and an economy in which selling low quality goods at high volumes was an acceptable business strategy rather than a source of shame.

Global warming and *climate change* were the methods by which the human species, plagued by guilt and unacknowledged depression, committed suicide.

The mechanisms of this suicide were eating too much beef, operating too many electronics and driving too many cars.

THE TITLE of *Done Because We Are Too Menny* was taken from *Jude the Obscure,* a Nineteenth Century novel by Thomas Hardy.

Jude the Obscure is about the misery which falls upon working class people if they ever make the mistake of hoping that they can achieve.

Jude the Obscure was written before the iPhone had *changed everything.* In the Twenty-First Century, after the iPad *changed everything,* the message of *Jude the Obscure* no longer resonated because all working class people listened to the music of Beyoncé on their Apple products.

They could achieve anything as long as they worked hard enough and believed in their dreams and followed their passions.

Anyway, in *Jude the Obscure,* one of Jude's children murders Jude's other children and then hangs himself. He leaves a suicide note that reads: "Done Because We Are Too Menny."

Adeline saw this as a perfect metaphor for climate change and overpopulation. So she created a plotless 64-page long comic book.

Done Because We Are Too Menny received nice reviews on the Internet, particularly from middle-aged men like Jeff Lester and Graeme McMillan.

It sold poorly.

GRAEME MCMILLAN AND JEFF LESTER were partners in an Internet *podcast* called *Wait, What?* Neither man had any eumelanin in the basale strata of their epidermises.

Jeff Lester's WaNks Index Score was 73.24857142857143.

Graeme McMillan's WaNks Index Score was 9.583211678832117.

The word *podcast* was a shitty neologism with the generalized meaning of an audio program distributed over the Internet. In the case of *Wait, What?* the program was two guys talking about comic books for two hour chunks of time.

This concept would appear to be terrible. Who wants to hear comic book guys talk to each other about comic books?

Yet in its execution, *Wait, What?* was fascinating.

Jeff Lester was a master in the art of rambling, a conversational shambler from the stars. Graeme McMillan was concise and insightful and tormented by having dedicated so much of his life to comic books.

The interplay was compelling.

Jeff Lester lived in San Francisco.

At the exact moment that Adeline, Christine and J. Karacehennem were talking in Sparky's, Jeff Lester was wandering around the city, doing something weird and incomprehensible. Possibly annoying his wife.

Anyway, it was Jeff Lester who came up with one of this bad novel's central ideas. It was Jeff Lester who realized that the American comic book industry is the key to the Twenty-First Century.

Here is Jeff Lester on the very topic:

"It's really hard to tell if the comic industry has changed for better or worse, in no small part because the comic industry more or less conquered the world. And I'm not just talking about the proliferation of superhero movies or whatever: I mean that the practices of the industry—dubious labor practices obscured by an endless supply of willing freelancers, the emphasis of brands over individuals (unless it's to celebrate how well an individual is serving a brand), the constant need for content—are now how so many other industries operate. All the talk we hear about the creative class, even as they've been turned into people on an assembly line, tasked with turning out so many listicles or reality TV shows in order to survive? Comics did that first and best."

"ADELINE SAYS you're a maniac about Google," said J. Karacehennem to Christine. "She says you got all kinds of crazy ideas."

"Don't make me regret introducing you, *hombre*. I never the once said her ideas are mad, did I? All I said is that Christine had gone into the realm of the *très outré*. Which any person would admit."

"It's okay," said Christine. "It is kind of crazy. It's worked so far. I'm still not evicted. My landlord hasn't converted the building."

"What's worked so far?" asked J. Karacehennem.

"I've started praying to Google," said Christine. "I offer obeisance to our masters."

"I've been in San Francisco too long," said J. Karacehennem.

CHRISTINE'S IDEA was simple. She had examined Ancient World mythologies and interpreted the divinities as symbolic and archetypal representations of universal human struggles.

The most applicable pantheon was that of the Ancient Greeks. The Greek Pantheon was the one where the gods were the most childish and thus the most like the brain trust of the Bay Area. Also, Christine respected the influence of the Greek Pantheon on present day Western thought.

Once Christine isolated the various archetypes, she began looking for analogues in the various personages associated with Google.

"THE MOST IMPORTANT THING to understand about Google," said Christine, "is that it's a company of liars. Their entire business model is lying. Advertising is the art of lying in such a way that everyone knows you're lying but no one will call you out on it, because you've disguised your lies behind money.

"If you want to know why the Bay Area is so messed up, it's simple. Other than Apple, the primary revenue stream of every other company is advertising. There is no way to make money off the Internet itself other than advertising. We are living in the biggest advertising economy that the world has ever seen, and no one will admit it."

"I have a theory," said J. Karacehennem, "That all money and technology is embedded with the ideology of its origin. You should Google 'packet switching.' It will explain everything. Advertising itself explains why everyone in the Bay Area is so full of shit and no one can tell the truth."

"Because they are advertisers," said Christine. "They can't say that they work in advertising. So they lie about what they do. Google wants us to believe that they're changing the world and offering a million services for free and that we're all part of the same team, but they're lying. All Google does is serve advertisements. Nothing else makes money.

"They are liars and I pray to liars."

CHRISTINE SAW ALL THE FOUNDERS and key players in Silicon Valley as new gods, like the New Gods created by Jack Kirby while he worked-for-hire at DC Comics, and Christine arranged them accordingly.

Larry Page, the CEO and co-founder of Google, was like Hephaestus because Hephaestus was the physically debilitated God of artisans and creators. Hephaestus was the out-classed God, like Larry Page was the outclassed CEO who wrested back control of the company in 2011 and forced it to start a social networking platform which everyone thought was terrible. Then Larry page bought Motorola, a maker of cellphones that was losing money and continued to bleed money. Christine didn't know it, but by 2014, Google would sell Motorola at a $12,000,000,000 loss. Just like Hephaestus had a sham marriage to Aphrodite that required keeping up appearances, Larry Page was considered a good CEO because Google's core business of advertising made so much money that no one noticed that Larry Page was bad at his job and operated off the principle that unexamined growth was a successful strategy for the future.

Sergey Brin, the other co-founder, was like Dionysius, the god of sex and drugs and revelry. Sergey Brin had rebranded himself as the head of Google X, Google's nonsense experimental lab which developed faddish technologies like wearable computers and cars that could drive themselves and dogs that didn't need to clean their genitals. These technologies would amount to nothing. They were banal visions of the future as imagined by the fans of Science Fiction. Google was an advertising company. Every time the company released a physical commodity, that commodity failed. Google X's real purpose was an advertisement for the mythical vision of Google as a company of innovation. Google X was Google lying about the company's actual function, using the methods of advertising to obfuscate its revenues derived from advertising. Google X was the pointless indulgence of one of the world's richest men. It was Sergey Brin's hobby. It was his awkward way of picking up chicks. It was the absolute heights of decadence. In any practical sense, Sergey Brin had left Google. He was a middle-aged party boy with weird mistresses and a habit of going to Burning Man every August. Burning Man was a big party in the desert where Sergey Brin would pretend like money didn't matter and that he wasn't a capitalist. He would surround himself with younger naked people who were high on drugs and dressed like low-rent circus performers and who were simply thrilled to be around someone famous.

Eric Schmidt, who Brin and Page made CEO of Google long enough to shepherd the company through its initial public offering, was like Zeus, the king of the gods. Eric Schmidt was the man behind the scenes, the unmoved mover, the guy who made deals with the government and the CIA and the NSA, the guy who worked on various Presidential commissions and had a hand in the company's Washington dealings. He loved that Google afforded him proximity to power. Like Zeus, he was weird and mysterious in a way that the others weren't. He was always there but you never knew what he was really like. And let's not get into his complicated romantic life, the servicing of which required a fuckpad on Manhattan island.

Susan Wojcicki was the sister of Anne Wojcicki, the wife of Sergey Brin, and she was the Senior Vice President of Advertising. She was like Demeter, the goddess of the harvest and the growing earth. It was Susan Wojcicki who let Sergey Brin and Larry Page start Google in her garage, and it was Susan Wojcicki who really ran the show, overseeing the advertising which was the source of all the money. Susan Wojcicki had wanted to be an artist and Susan Wojcicki was even more mysterious than Eric Schmidt. No one knew much about her, which reminded Christine of the Eleusinian Mysteries, shrouded in darkness.

And there was good ol' Steve Jobs, better known as Hades. And not just because he was dead and rotting in the dank recesses of the netherworld, doomed for an uncertain term to watch projected images of impoverished factories workers on the rocky walls of oblivion. Basically, Steve Jobs was Hades because Hades was a total unyielding dick. The defining aspect of Steve Jobs was the marriage of his innate dickishness with gauzy Bay Area entitlement. This blessed union birthed a blanket of darkness which settled over the Western world. Steve Jobs grew up reading *The Whole Earth Catalog*, a publication dedicated to the proposition that by spending your money in the *right way*, you could become the right kind of person. This was the mantra of the post-WWII economy, an unspoken ideology that cut across the social classes. But because *The Whole Earth Catalog* emerged from the Bay Area after the death of several utopian ideals, the stench of its message was masked by patchouli, incense and paperback editions of gruel-thin Eastern spirituality. It was a new kind of marketing, geared towards the insecure bourgeois aspirant. Steve Jobs sucked it in and shit it out and transformed himself into Hades. The one god that can't be escaped. His promise was simple: you have a choice. You can die ugly and unloved, or you can buy an overpriced computer or iPod and listen to early Bob Dylan and spin yourself off the wheel of Samsara. Your fundamental uncreativity will be masked by group membership. People will think you are interesting and beautiful and enlightened. One of us, one of us, one of us. Gooble gobble, gooble gobble. Nothing says individuality like 500 million consumer electronics built by slaves. Welcome to Hell.

Then there were the minor divinities.

Like Sheryl Sandberg, the billionaire who worked for Facebook and thought that the way women who weren't billionaires could get respect in the workplace was to act more like the men that disrespected them in the workplace. Before she was at Facebook, she was at Google, and Christine decided that Sheryl Sandberg was like Iris, the messenger of the Gods. It seemed like Sheryl Sandberg had spent her whole professional life doing nothing but delivering messages.

Like Ray Kurzweil, who Christine identified with Dolos, the Greek spirit of trickery and guile. Ray Kurzweil was the king of technological liberation theology. Or, in other words, he was king of the most intolerable of all intolerable bullshit. He believed in a future where computers would reach a moment of *technological singularity*. The *technological singularity* was a bullshit phrase invented by the Science Fiction writer Vernor Vinge. The *technological singularity* was the name for a theoretical moment in the future when computers would achieve a critical mass of artificial intelligence and wake up and change everything. The way that computers would change everything is by emerging into consciousness and telling people like Ray Kurzweil and Vernor Vinge that they were fucking awesome. The computers and Ray Kurzweil and Vernor Vinge would hang out and kick back and rule the universe forever. This is not an exaggeration. This is what Ray Kurzweil believed. This bullshit was reported by major American media outlets. This bullshit was taken as gospel by cub reporters who did not understand regular old intelligence, let alone intelligence crafted by man. So Ray Kurzweil was the god of lies. Who would deny the puissance of a man who thought that his computer was going to wake up and hang out with him and tell him he was awesome? Everyone in Silicon Valley loved Ray Kurzweil. He was their High Priest of Intolerable Bullshit. He was the Seer of Pseudoscience. He worked for Google. He was a director of engineering.

Like Marissa Mayer, who Christine identified with Elpis, the Greek goddess of hope. There was no way you could be Marissa Mayer without hope. When she worked at Google, she had at some point dated Larry Page while helping out on all kinds of projects that went nowhere, like Google Books, which she called, "Google's Moon Shot." Google Books was Google's attempt to steal the intellectual property of every writer in America by offering free copies of their work in an unusable system. Mayer had parlayed her experience with the unusable system of Google Books into being CEO and President of Yahoo!, which was a company that offered products which no one used. Yahoo! was a relic of the first tech boom. No one understood why Yahoo! still existed or what Marissa Mayer did at Yahoo! Yet there she was, making terrible billion dollar acquisitions and redesigning logos. There was no way you could be Marissa Mayer and not have any hope.

None of these divinities had any eumelanin in the basale strata of their epidermises.

THE MOST VISIBLE THING that Marissa Mayer did when she worked for Google was interview Lady Gaga for Musicians@Google.

Musicians@Google was part of the larger Talks@Google series.

Both Musicians@Google and Talks@Google were public presentations held in Google's various offices around the world.

The event with Lady Gaga was hosted at Google's headquarters. This was in Mountain View, California. Mountain View was part of Silicon Valley.

It was about forty minutes south of the city, depending on traffic. This is where the *Google buses* went.

GOOGLE WAS KNOWN for distributing t-shirts amongst it employees. These t-shirts were made for software milestones, company events and any other thing that struck the fancy of the company's emotionally bankrupt middle management.

Google made t-shirts for the Lady Gaga event. They read: GOOGLE GOES GAGA.

Marissa Mayer asked Lady Gaga questions like: "And also on the topic of style, you have tattoos. And one of the fans noticed that they're all on your left side. So TaylorMonster15 would like to know, why are all of your tattoos on the left side of your body?"

"WHAT'S REMARKABLE," said Adeline, "is that this ain't no gag. Christine prays to each of these gods in her various times of need."

"I believe it," said J. Karacehennem.

"How does one pray to the living?" asked Adeline, "What happens if you meet Larry Page?"

"The Greeks thought that the gods were living beings," said Christine. "Who personified certain aspects of existence. The Greeks also ran the risk of running into their gods. There's no difference."

"These aren't gods. These are dreary little people who've spent their lives advertising insurance."

"At a certain point of mass celebrity, people stop being people," said J. Karacehennem. "What is Madonna really? Madonna is a ray of light, an untouchable thing. It doesn't matter that once she was a pop star who released a book of pornography. She's become something else. You can never know Madonna because there is no Madonna. Even if you meet Madonna, you still wouldn't know Madonna. You'd be talking to a physical being that carries all the weight of Madonna but the physical being of Madonna would not be Madonna. Like Atlas in *Atlas Shrugged*. What would happen if Madonna shrugged?"

"I somehow doubt that either of you know this, but I've met Madonna," said Adeline. "Right after the premiere of Don Murphy's *Trill*, when there was a great delusion that the film might succeed. Madonna was as booooooring as you might imagine. She was most definitively not a ray of light. Somehow she knew that I had lived in the old New York. She asked if the Cubbyhole was still open. I said, 'Darling, I haven't stepped foot in the city in two years and even if I did, you may rest assured that I'd have the good taste to stay away from 12th Street.'"

"It's really no different than the Ancient Greeks and their gods," said Christine.

"Do you have an altar for these people?" asked J. Karacehennem.

"Darling," said Adeline. "Mine own eyes have rested upon it. It is fabulous."

"HERE'S MY PARANOID THOUGHT about the Bay Area," said J. Karacehennem. "A few years ago this artist and sex-worker named Sadie Lune held an insemination ritual on 16th Street. I wasn't there. I didn't know anything about it, but from what I've been told it was a big orgy with an audience. At the end, Sadie Lune's sperm donor, who was named Oberon, produced his sperm and it was inserted into Sadie Lune with the hopes of creating a child. Apparently it didn't work, but I wonder if maybe by accident they created a demonic being that's ruling over the city's gentrification. An ethereal being, a Moon Child. Maybe that Moon Child is the spirit of the current tech bubble in all its evil glory, dancing on the rocks of Corona Heights. Maybe that's the spirit of the age. Maybe it was created in an insemination ritual on 16th street.

"But who knows? Maybe the tech people are all just *Running to Mama*."

"RUNNING TO MAMA" was the title of a recent short story by Baby.

He'd written it a few months before Adeline's flame-out in Kevin Killian's classroom.

On the surface, everything in the story is identical to our world, but a few pages in and it becomes clear that, in this parallel world, the Internet is very different than our own.

After several creaky plot revelations that involve a woman addicted to Methamphetamine and obsessed with the 900 Theses of Pico della Mirandola, the reader discovers that the Internet on this parallel world is alive, a fully functioning intelligence, and that its primary purpose is not to enrich an oligarchy through a steady dose of celebrity gossip and destroyed lives, but rather to soothe and comfort its users by telling them that they're all right, and that everything is going to be okay, and that the source of their distress is just a terrible person who's jealous.

The effect of the Internet on the citizens of this parallel world is complete and total infantilization.

Whenever someone's feelings are hurt, they go and complain to the Internet, which they have taken to calling "Mama."

Using the Internet is called "Running to Mama." Hence the title.

ADELINE AND J. KARACEHENNEM were standing outside of Sparky's. Christine had disappeared into a taxi.

"I'm proud of you," said J. Karacehennem. "You made it through an entire evening without mentioning the cupcake or the pastry."

"A person may yet learn," said Adeline. "Tell me, how did you find Christine?"

"I don't judge anyone's religious beliefs because everyone's religious beliefs are equally ridiculous. Besides, what can I say, really? My father believes in leprechauns. I'm very sympathetic. In my heart, beneath it all, I am a pagan."

"What did you think of Bertrand?"

Bertrand was Christine's boyfriend. He'd been at the reading and left in the middle. He had to wake up early. He worked for an architect with an office near the Presidio.

"Are you asking because you think I didn't like him?"

"Honey child, I simply know that you didn't like him."

"How could you tell?"

"There was a point where you shied away, when he was distracted by that dreadful little creature reading poesy about Sarah Palin."

"He seemed okay," said J. Karacehennem. "It's only that he was too proud, really."

"Proud?"

"He kept talking about how his girlfriend was a girl like any other but that she just has a dick. He said it to me. I heard him say it to two other people. Word for word in his accent. 'My girlfriend is like any other, but my girlfriend has a dick.' You could hear it in his voice. All the pride."

chapter twenty-three

Time was passing. Summer arrived. J. Karacehennem had been chosen for a writer's residency in rural Denmark and disappeared into Scandinavia. Christine was busy with Bertrand.

Adeline had other friends. She saw some. She ignored others.

Most of her time was spent with Erik Willems.

Bromato was failing. The CEO was burning money at an unsustainable pace. There was a question about whether or not Bromato would make it to a Series C round of funding. They were not making money for HRH Mamduh bin Fatih bin Muhammad bin Abdulaziz al Saud, also known as Dennis.

MoriaMordor had given Bromato millions of dollars before its CEO and other co-founders had graduated college. They'd been attending Stanford University when they made their pitch.

Stanford University was yet another educational institution that wrapped a cloak of the humanities around its development of new weapons for future wars.

ADELINE AND ERIK were eating dinner at a restaurant on Valencia called Cafe Ethiopia.

Erik Willems had suggested eating at Local's Corner. Adeline turned him down.

"I think if I ate there, J. Karacehennem would simply murder me."

"Isn't he in Denmark?"

"If his emails are any indicator."

"How would he even know?"

"His girlfriend might see us, darling. I simply shan't take the risk."

Adeline liked Cafe Ethiopia because the food was both incomprehensible and delicious. The decor was spartan. She also liked that Cafe Ethiopia was next door to Borderlands Books, a specialty bookstore focusing on Science Fiction, Fantasy and Horror.

She loathed the three genres but she liked checking to see if they had Baby's full catalogue.

They always did. They had everything. Except for *Hot Mill Steam*.

Hot Mill Steam was out of print. So few copies had sold that it was difficult to find anywhere, even on the Internet, which was a wonderful resource for sexism, abusing the mentally ill, and libeling the dead.

ERIK WILLEMS was stuffing brown paste into his mouth.

"Darling," said Adeline. "I have two questions for you. You can answer in whatever order you so please. *Numero uno*. Why in the blurry blazes did you give millions of dollars to college undergraduates? *Numero dos*. Have you read *Hot Mill Steam*?"

Erik finished chewing.

"They came highly recommended. Some of their professors have steered us towards other investment opportunities that worked out. When they suggested we invest in Bromato, we ran the numbers and they made sense. That's the problem, isn't it? Numbers only tell you so much. You can't predict the variables of human failure. People's greed and emotion almost always get the best of them."

"Darling, aren't we speaky many big words about people who are, effectively, teenagers? Aren't they Emil's age? If you gave my progeny millions of your dollars, it'd be gone gone gone, Daddy-o."

"To answer your other question," said Erik, "I haven't read *Hot Mill Steam*. I couldn't find a copy and then I read the reviews online. It sounds terrible."

"There are clunky sections," said Adeline. "I'm not sure that Baby quite understands what it is that he's doing. Even with all of that, I think it's his best book. It's rather better than time travelers suffering from hyperintelligent gonorrhea."

BABY'S SECOND NOVEL, *Saving Anne Frank,* really did have a plot that included hyperintelligent gonorrhea.

In Baby's novel, the World Time Travel Authority infects all time travelers with a mutated strain of gonorrhea that pools in the back of the throat. The gonorrhea is hyperintelligent and capable of carrying on conversations with its host via shared control of the host's vocal cords.

Time travelers often experience isolation fatigue. So the gonorrhea keeps them company.

Unlike present day gonorrhea, the strain modified by The World Time Travel Authority has no negative physical effects and can not be transmitted through sexual contact.

THE PROTAGONIST of *Saving Anne Frank* is a man named Boaz ben-Haim. One of the quirks of the future is that all time travelers are Jewish. According to Baby's narrative, Jewish culture is the only culture with a realistic understanding of history.

The Ashkenazi handle recent history. The Mizrahim do the distant historical past. The Sephardim handle pre-history. At the time of writing, Baby was ignorant of Beta Israel so Beta Israel have no role in his novel.

Boaz ben-Haim is assigned to Nazi Germany during WWII. He experience produces a crisis of confidence. He decides that must save victims of the Holocaust, a course of action barred by the World Time Travel Authority.

He starts with Anne Frank.

BEFORE BOAZ BEN-HAIM can save anyone, he must rid himself of the gonorrhea.

Boaz ben-Haim believes the gonorrhea is more than an anti-isolation device. Boaz ben-Haim believes the gonorrhea is a spying mechanism. He believes the gonorrhea reads his thoughts and intends to report him to the World Time Travel Authority.

So he travels to the 1970s and gets some penicillin and kills the gonorrhea.

Usually when gonorrhea is removed from the throats of time travelers, it's done under sedation. Boaz ben-Haim can't sedate himself, which means that he hears the gonorrhea die in his throat, speaking words with his vocalcords.

In its last moments, the gonorrhea says: "help me, help me, help me. help. help. help. help."

Then it dies.

WHEN BABY WROTE *SAVING ANNE FRANK* in the mid-1990s, it was very hard to look at America and not feel like its unwitting citizens had been born into complex systems of unfathomable evil.

Americans were destroying the Earth and exploiting poor laborers in their own country and exploiting poor laborers in other countries and Americans were the beneficiaries of multiple genocides and economic horrors that stretched back to the country's founding.

There was no way out. The only escape was death.

Baby saw Boaz ben-Haim as an American stand-in, as someone who was in a situation that paralleled that of the American people.

Boaz ben-Haim worked for a world governmental body that refused to help people in the past for fear of what their deaths might wreak on the future. This was a terrible moral equivalence which suggested the lives of future people outweighed the lives of past people. By virtue of the past people being dead.

But they weren't dead. Not when you could travel in time and smell and hear and touch them. When you traveled in time, nothing ever really died. Not even gonorrhea.

ADELINE AND ERIK finished eating. They went outside.

It was 9pm on a Friday night. Valencia Street was packed with human bodies. People came in search of alcohol and food and the illusion that if you combined alcohol and food, they added up to meaning.

White lumbering *Google buses* drove past.

"I suppose anything is better than writing about gonorrhea," said Adeline.

"Pardon me?" asked Erik Willem.

"Oh, nothing, darling," she said. "Every time I see a *Google bus*, I concoct very strange thoughts."

"The symbolism is awkward," said Erik Willems. "I'd have figured out a less ostentatious way of handling the matter. That's me. I don't have billions of dollars. I don't think these buses belong to Google. I think they're either eBay or Apple."

"Do you know that sometimes I forget you still haven't cracked the big four zero," said Adeline.

"What should it matter?" asked Erik.

Many of Erik's coworkers knew that he was sleeping with a *MILF*. They never let him forget it.

How was last night? asked his co-workers. *Did the cougar's claws scratch her cub's back?*

What's it like tasting that stale cupcake and pastry? asked his co-workers. *Is the frosting bitter?*

"It shouldn't. It doesn't," said Adeline. "It's only that I was thinking yet again about how exhausting it is to get older. How miserable it is to see what happens to the lives of your friends. Not your favorite writer, darling. Don't worry your silly little head over that gunsel. Other than abandoning his early literary principles, our charming author has navigated the waters with rather heap big success. Minerva's doing dandy swell. So is Jeremy. But there are so many friends who've fallen by the wayside, victims of that creeeepy ol' middle-aged spiritual dissolution. Why, they start as strapping young things full of hopes and poetry and then the grind of life and jobs and spouses and children and mortgages and kids wears them down. Then they can't even say Bo to a goose. *C'est très cliché.* I prepared myself when I was younger, I said, 'Adeline, self, you simply must make certain that you don't become spiritually dissolute. If you catch the same blurry look as all of Mother's friends, you won't be able to spot your own peepers in the mirror, not for all the shame you'll see.' What yours truly didn't anticipate and for which I had no preparation is that the dissolution would creep upon the others. I was so self-obsessed that it never occurred to me the problem would be other people! Think of the compromises and strange choices. All the misery they've brought upon their selves. It's simply exhausting."

"I wouldn't know," said Erik. "My oldest friend is a Saudi prince with a media company and addiction issues."

"Ah yes," said Adeline. "My mysterious Arabian benefactor. Isn't it strange how small the world is? It's like a Russian novel. And I hate Russian novels."

"Did you meet Dennis?"

"*Nein*, darling, I stayed out of the process."

"I doubt you could have seen him, anyway," said Erik. "*Trill* was when he was doing another degree at the London School of Economics. Do you know who turned him on to that racket? Saif Gaddafi. Gaddafi's son!"

"YOU REMEMBER EMIL, don't you sweetheart? My son? Mine own flesh and blood? The one who'd flit away your filthy lucre in a flash? When we talk, sometimes I can't even hear his words. The only thing I hear is his youth. The eagerness for life. The innocence. I only want to tell him one thing. I simply want to say, *Good luck, kid! You're gonna need it!*

"Yet then I rebuke myself. I worry that the feeling is my own spiritual dissolution. But it can't be, can it? I still feel young. It's the others who've gotten old. Darling, what I wouldn't give for some friends as wild and maniacal as dear sweet Edward Snowden."

BABY WASN'T THE ONLY PERSON looking at America and feeling as if its unwitting citizens were born into complex and impossible systems of unfathomable evil.

The story of the season was about a eumelaninless guy named Edward Snowden, who contracted for an American intelligence agency called the National Security Agency.

The NSA was like the CIA, except the NSA didn't have field agents and hadn't funded the creation of American literary fiction.

Snowden had worked for the CIA before he worked for the NSA. But that was long after the CIA had stopped funding literary fiction.

You had to give the CIA credit. For an agency marked by a persistent tone deafness of cultural approach, they had realized literary fiction was completely pointless. No one cared about *good novels*.

The funding of *good novels* was based on an abandoned misapprehension that writers, being the apparent creators of culture, had some impact on contemporary international affairs.

This was, of course, insane.

The men who worked at the CIA were something of an aesthetic vanguard. They had learned a lesson in the mid-Twentieth Century that American writers still couldn't grasp in the early years of the Twenty-First.

The creators of culture had no impact on anything. The only thing writers were good for was sending messages across time.

The people who controlled mass production and the flow of meaningless information were the rulers of the modern world.

Now the CIA funded things that really mattered, like computer networks and systems of global surveillance.

When Snowden was working for the CIA, he had worked with their computer networks and systems of global surveillance.

AT THE NSA, Snowden was given access to a wide range of information about various programs instituted by the agency. Snowden found much of this disquieting.

He discovered that the NSA was funding elaborate computer networks which put all of the world's Internet communications under surveillance. The NSA could track everything that everyone did on their computers and cellphones.

Snowden was appalled.

THIS WAS A BIT NAÏVE. The Internet was a creation of the US Government's Department of Defense. It was built as a weapon against the Soviet Union.

To think that a government which had created a tool wouldn't use that tool to perform the basic task of every government, which is to say exert control over the lives of its citizens, was a bit strange. It was an expectation akin to running beneath Wernher von Braun's V2 rockets and hoping you'd be showered with flowers rather than death.

Snowden gathered up an unfathomable number of documents circulating inside the NSA. These documents bore evidence of the NSA's systems of global surveillance. These systems had been constructed with help from companies like Google, Facebook and Apple.

Snowden contacted several journalists and staged an elaborate leak of these documents to the world media. Much of this was orchestrated from a hotel room in Hong Kong, surrounded by media hacks who drooled over his every word.

SNOWDEN'S DOCUMENT DUMP was the public culmination of an anxiety about mass production and information technology. He wasn't the only person feeling this concern.

A great number of people in developed nations were very worried about the effects of a fully computerized society on *privacy*.

This discussion was happening primarily amongst the middle classes. The truly rich didn't care about *privacy*. They could buy their way out of anything. Poor people didn't care about *privacy* because poor people lived in social milieus where *privacy* did not exist.

The souls and bodies of the poor were property of the world's governments. They were the raw material burned in the fires of capitalism. Their private lives were subject to massive police and governmental intrusion. Thus it was and always would be.

The idea of *privacy* was rooted in the concept of individualism. As such, it was impossible to have *privacy* when the systems of control refused to see you as an individual.

Nowhere was this more true than in the lives of African-Americans. Their *privacy* was fucked from the beginning. There's no *privacy* when Ole Massa rapes your whole family. There's no *privacy* in the slave quarters. There's no such thing as *privacy* when the police systematically target you for every manner of abuse and stitch you up on bullshit drug charges. There's no such thing as *privacy* when every person on the street suspects you of anything.

Watching the media coverage of Snowden's revelations, it was hard not to feel like the world had been transformed.

It had become a place where the greatest concern was whether or not mass produced cellphones were turning White people into Black ones.

WHEN EDWARD SNOWDEN made his foray into the seedy world of hotel room revelations. he brought along some reading material. He had two books with him.

The first one was the hardcover edition of *Homeland* by Cory Doctorow. It was published by an imprint called Tor Teen.

The second book was a trade paperback of Baby's *Annie Zero*.

chapter twenty-four

A Buzzfeed contributor wrote an article about Adeline's twenty best *tweets*. Adeline was aware of Buzzfeed because Buzzfeed articles were the only things that people shared on Facebook.

These articles always appeared in the same format. These articles always appeared as lists.

Like: *25 Things That Get Harder After 25*.

Like: *35 Things You Will Never See Again In Your Life*

Like: *25 of Kanye West's Most Thought-Provoking Tweets*.

Like: *25 Things That Were Normal in 1999*.

Buzzfeed made money by serving content sponsored by its advertisers, which was a seamless way of mixing entertainment and product placement. It made other advertisements on the Internet look like total shit.

Most of the lists on Buzzfeed were built of material harvested from the Internet. The creators of the harvested material had very little say over Buzzfeed's harvesting. The creators of the material harvested were expected to eat whatever garbage the world served them.

The lists were accompanied by light commentary in simplified language. People had compared the writing style to book reports delivered by elementary school students.

Buzzfeed was one of the most popular sites on the Internet, which was a wonderful place for reading lists of tweets, learning about the construction of White Privilege, and critiquing Lady Gaga's bitchin' beach-bod.

20 Best Tweets from M. Abrahamovic Petrovitch

People know her as the artist of *Trill* with the name of a Russian man. After a video flame-out in a classroom, she started tweeting. Here's the twenty best examples of how she uses Twitter!

1. On becoming a Hindu.

> Given the predictable wrongness of crowds and the prevalence of #YOLO, I am forced to conclude in the factuality of reincarnation.

2. Disinterest in Catholicism.

> Pope Francis says that priests must work 'amid the muck of life.' I should be quite happy with a plumber amidst the muck of my bathroom.

3. Critiquing fellow artists.

> Saw more images of George W. Bush's paintings. Like peering into the shattered mind of a suicidal beagle that's lost depth perspective.

4. Harsh.

> Heard Kim Kardashian is 21st Century Jayne Mansfield. My hope is that it's a matching set and Allah sends both the Buick and the truck.

5. Let me guess. The other is Portland.

San Francisco, California: one of America's two cities where residency comes with an instruction manual for soy-free living.

6. Memories.

Remembered my first visit to SF. Cat-called a different way in each neighborhood and then the blessed silence of the Castro. #love

7. This is just hilarious.

Journalist phoned. Writing about comics. Asked about *Thrill*. Talked for hour about a literal emotional rollercoaster in an amusement park.

8. Troubles with parenting.

My son sent me an email. He's still embarrassed by my Twitter and again asked me to stop. Forgets I have baby pictures and am very proud.

9. Deep thoughts.

If art can be anything, then what's all that other stuff sitting at the bottom of my closet?

10. She has friends!

Message from J. Karacehennem: "Staying a week in Vienna, the world's most baroque monument to state oppression."

11. It kind of is...

Isn't it strange that @BretEastonEllis, an out gay man, is somehow a villain while everyone worships David Foster Wallace, a sexist jock?

12. Harsher.

Watching wedding video. Bride, groom, wedding party in choreographed song and dance numbers. Like tourism in Hell without any souvenirs.

13. What?

My great contribution to cinema scholarship: discovered Steeleye Span album *Commoner's Crown* in Florida bedroom scene of *The Shining*.

14. LOL. Too true!

Yes, please, mansplain why astrology is bullshit. No, darling, I've not heard this before.

15. Definitely.

Most inappropriate Comic Con costume? MAUS cosplay. #ithappened #2009

16. Um, okay.

You think that I couldn't possibly understand but I've been alive forever. I knew the people that used to be you and they were less boring.

17. Deeper thoughts.

Had a ride along the 101 today. Saw all the construction cranes hovering over the city, like elongated hammers waiting to strike.

18. Harshest.

Bay Area men + Eames lounge chairs. Simply can't fathom why tech ppl might want to look as if they're about to drop Napalm on Vietnam.

19. Don't we all have this friend?

Old friend married a professional photographer. Certain it's for inaccurate and well lit portrayal of her life on Facebook and Instagram.

20. They'll get right on that...

Advice to young men: for easy love, build a time machine, volunteer for first Obama campaign and bring a copy of *Everything is Illuminated*.

(the former)
chapter twenty-five

There used to be a chapter in this space. It wasn't very good.

The intention was a fine one.

But in the end, the chapter was terrible. So it's gone.

THE CHAPTER did contain a few things of note.

Like a description of Thanksgiving as a holiday in which America celebrated the genocide of its indigenous peoples through the gathering of extended families for a meal during which young people were made to feel awkward by their elders expressing thoughts of casual racism and homophobia.

Like an exploration of the word *homophobia,* and how it literally, in the Greek, meant the opposite of its intent.

There was also some discussion of how *homophobia* derived from the word *homosexual,* which was an awkward mishmash of Latin and Greek invented by an Austrian named Karl-Maria Kertbeny.

The joke was that if the Twentieth Century had taught the human race anything, it was to avoid words invented by Austrians.

There was also a discussion about the class-based distinctions between the sizeable number of Americans who'd sublimated their unfulfilled sexual urges into gluttony.

The people who'd sublimated their unfulfilled sexual urges and had money were called *foodies.* Everyone else was called a *fat fucking slob.*

There was the suggestion that Southeastern Massachusetts was a region which, in times of international crisis, ensured that the world would never be without someone to paint *FAGGOTS* on the side of a mosque.

There was a discussion of how Clarence Thomas, a Supreme Court Justice with a lot of eumelanin in the basale stratum of his epidermis, had been accused of *sexual harassment* by his underlings before his elevation to the court.

This discussion pivoted on the fact that Thomas was a devotee of Ayn Rand, and each year, his incoming crop of legal clerks came to his house, where he forced them to watch the film adaptation of Rand's *The Fountainhead.*

The *frisson* of this discussion derived from the juxtaposition of Thomas's history as a person known for practicing the art of *sexual harassment* and the presence, in both the mandatory film and the novel, of a rape scene.

Here's Ayn Rand in a letter dated June 5, 1946, describing the rape scene in a letter to Waldo Coleman: "But the fact is that Roark did not actually rape Dominique; she had asked for it, and he knew that she wanted it."

THE PROBLEM with removing the chapter is that it served as the ideological heart of the book. It was where everything tied together.

The whole thing revolved around Adeline's decision to tweet about a woman named Paula Deen, who, for a while in the Summer of 2013, was the scandal of the moment.

The reasons for the scandal were: (1) Paula Deen was famous and she didn't have any eumelanin in the basale stratum of her epidermis. (2) Paula Deen was deposed in a *sexual harassment* lawsuit, where she freely admitted her use of the word *%&$#?@.*

Paula Deen appeared on television, where she offered food-based pornography for *foodies* and *fat fucking slobs.* She was grotesque, but that wasn't unusual. Everyone on television was grotesque.

%&$#?@* was a word which encapsulated America's terrible history, and the country's brutal dealings with its minority populations. *%&$#?@ in particular carried the connotation of the raw deal and genocide that America had enacted on people like Jeremy Winterbloss and all of his relatives with eumelanin in the basale strata of their epidermises.

ANYWAY, IN THE DELETED CHAPTER, Adeline debates whether or not to tweet about *%&$#?@* and racism.

This is after the Buzzfeed article had doubled her followers on Twitter, lowering her WaNks Index Score to 0.73.

IN THE TWENTY-FIRST CENTURY, racism, like any formation of the human mind, was a useful product. Racism allowed for more advertisements.

The protesting of racism on social media was another formation of the human mind. It too was a useful product. It too allowed for more advertisements.

The system was perfect and self-contained. It was content neutral. It was designed to enhanced and induce inflamed human emotions.

On the Internet, you could be right. On the Internet, you could be wrong. You could love racism. You could hate racism. It didn't matter.

In the end, everything was just money.

THE SUM TOTAL EFFECT of Paula Deen admitting her use of the word *%&$#?@* was this: she made money for Google. She made money for Facebook.

She made money for Twitter. All of these companies were founded and run by White people.

THE CHAPTER also contained a list of characters in this book who harbored racist opinions and thoughts. It was a list of every character in this book. Welcome to America.

THERE WAS ALSO the suggestion that *%&$#?@* served as a helpful device amongst educated White people for distinguishing themselves from uneducated White people.

The idea, which was not stated with much clarity, was the saying of *%&$#?@* conveyed an impression that the speaker didn't believe that the goal of any civil society was the inclusion of all its members and the extension of opportunity all of its peoples.

Again, the chapter missed its mark by not extending the argument to its logical end-point.

It didn't suggest that most educated White people, by virtue of their interaction with consumer electronics built by slaves, demonstrated that they didn't believe in inclusion or fairness or justice. Fifty years ago, they had been ignorant in their unexamined racism and now they were ignorant in their unexamined anti-racism. They could switch back at any time. Expressing concern about racism was a new religion and focusing on language rather than political mechanics was an effortless, and meaningless, way of making sure one was seen in a front-row pew of the new church. They prayed not from any hard earned process of thought or genuine faith but because failing to bow and scrap before the shibboleths of the moneyed political Left might hurt their job prospects.

And poor job prospects meant less money to buy consumer electronics built by slaves.

THERE WAS ALSO SOME DISCUSSION about how people were still saying *%&$#?@* as much as ever, but now they employed a euphemism to indicated *%&$#?@*. This euphemism was *The N-Word*.

When the opposing attorney deponed Paula Deen, he didn't ask her if she had said *%&$#?@*.

He asked her if she had said *The N-Word*.

ANYWAY, THE CHAPTER'S FATAL FLAW was that it couldn't tie these ideas together. They were wispy threads of an unwoven tapestry.

ANOTHER FLAW OF EQUAL SIGNIFICANCE was that this chapter didn't link America's treatment of its minorities with the comic book industry's treatment of people like Jack Kirby, and finally, with the way that the Internet preyed on the gullible, asking them to create content based on inflamed emotion for the sake of serving advertisements.

Jeremy Winterbloss's ancestors were enslaved on the basis of their ability to provide free labor. The fruits of this labor were never shared with Jeremy's ancestors. His ancestors were property. Property can't own other property.

The American comic book industry had paid its employees for their labor but stole its fruits. Jack Kirby lost ownership of his creations, which were worth billions of dollars.

It was the greatest theft of intellectual property in history.

With the Internet, people produced reams of intellectual property over which they had no control. If you sent a message to someone on Facebook, Facebook owned that message for all time, and used it as the pretext for serving advertisements. Your expressions of outrage about Paula Deen and %&$#?@ made money for Mark Zuckerberg and his investors.

THE CURIOUS THING was that Facebook and Twitter and Tumblr and Blogspot, a media platform owned by Google, were the stomping grounds of self-styled intellectual and social radicals. It was where they were talking. It was where, they believed, the conversation was shifting.

They were typing morality lectures into devices built by slaves on platforms of expression owned by the Patriarchy, and they were making money for the Patriarchy. Somehow this was destroying the Patriarchy.

So there's always hope.

THE ILLUSION OF THE INTERNET was the idea that the opinions of powerless people, freely offered, had some impact on the world. This was, of course, total bullshit and based on a crazy idea of who ran the world.

The world was not run by its governments. The world was not run by its celebrities.

The world was run by its bankers. The world was run by its investor class. The world was run by its manufacturers. The history of human destiny was *money*, the men who controlled it, and nothing more.

Money, a measure of humiliation, was the only thing that mattered.

The illusion of opinions, freely offered, was encouraged because it made money for bankers. It made money for investors. It made money for manufacturers, who enslaved the citizens of far off nations to build the devices required for the free offering of opinions.

The one thing that freely offered opinions did not do, at all, was change the world. Opinions were only more words, only more shit that someone somewhere made up, and words were grease in the gears of capitalism.

Words were lubrication for a complex process that, every forty years, replaced one group of men who talked like they had paper assholes with another group of men who talked like they had paper assholes. Jarvis Cocker was right all along. Cunts really are still running the world.

WORDS WERE NOT POWER. Take it from a professional writer. The only place where words have power are scrawled on a bathroom wall.

The only effect of the words of powerless people on the Internet was to inflict misery on other powerless people.

When you need to defeat the hand, make the fingers attack each other. Divide and conquer.

ANYWAY, ADELINE DID IT.

She *tweeted* about *%&$#?@.*

At last, she had learned how to use the Internet.

chapter twenty-six

J. Karacehennem was in Denmark. He was a foreign writer in residence at Hald Hovedgaard, an old manor house built during the Eighteenth Century.

It was nice but boring. The other foreign writers were delightful. The Danish women writers were all lovely. None of the Danes had a hint of eumelanin in the basale strata of their epidermises.

The Danish male writers were horrible, except for Ole Tornbjerg, a crime writer who wrote books with his wife. Ole Tornbjerg was lovely.

Late in his visit, J. Karacehennem would meet Jussi Adler-Olsen, who had mastered the art of writing Scandinavian crime fiction, a subgenre in which squalid tales written by secular humanists reaffirm the Christian doctrine of original sin.

Jussi-Adler Olsen's crime novels were translated into countless languages and were huge sellers everywhere.

Jussi Adler-Olsen said that he'd sold 900,000 books in English.

J. KARACEHENNEM was waiting for a local bus. He was going to the nearby town of Viborg. Viborg was one of the oldest cities in Denmark. It was very boring but had an atmospheric medieval section and an excellent cathedral boasting some very gaudy frescoes.

THE BUS STOP was located across the street from the manor house in which J. Karacehennem was staying.

215

As J. Karacehennem waited for the bus, Brane Mozetič, a Slovene poet without much eumelanin in the basale stratum of his epidermis, walked out of the manor house. Brane Mozetič rushed over to the bus stop.

The bus pulled up.

J. Karacehennem and Brane Mozetič sat together.

They talked about the weather. They talked about Denmark.

Brane Mozetič said to J. Karacehennem, "Tell me, you are from California?"

"I used to live in Los Angeles," said J. Karacehennem, "I moved to San Francisco. So I guess I'm from San Francisco. Los Angeles feels more like home."

"San Francisco," said Brane Mozetič. "Do you know Kevin Killian?"

chapter twenty-seven

Adeline received a text from Jeremy Winterbloss. He was coming into the city. Adeline texted back.

She suggested that they meet at Coffee to the People.

Coffee to the People was in the Haight.

The Haight was one of the last places in the city with an actual mix of the social classes. There were rich people, there were middle class people, there were poor people.

All wandering half-dazed. Navigating crappy stores packed with hippie kitsch. Everything was covered in a layer of filth.

Coffee to the People was on Masonic. Adeline thought there might be some collectivist ideology embedded in the cafe. She wasn't sure. It could've been just a name.

She took the N-Judah over to Cole. She didn't pay her fare. She had lived in San Francisco for sixteen years and never paid, not once, for the N-Judah.

JEREMY WAS SITTING on a couch when Adeline arrived. The cafe had a few people but it was quiet. It was always quiet.

"Darling, are we staying or should we go for a walk?" asked Adeline.

"Let's stay," said Jeremy.

"Have you ordered?"

"Not yet," said Jeremy.

ADELINE AND JEREMY stood in line behind an old hippie. The old hippie took his time. The old hippie asked questions and pontificated about his lactose intolerance and his almond allergy.

Adeline examined the display cases with all of the baked goods.

"Look, darling," said Adeline to Jeremy, "They have both a cupcake and a pastry."

Jeremy ignored her.

"NOW, MISTER J.W. BLOSS, why ever have you visited our fair city?" asked Adeline as they sat down. "I do believe that when last I gazed upon your grim visage, you stated sans ambiguity that you found the general airs of this particular environment to be an intense toxicity."

"I'm here because of you," said Jeremy.

"Moi?"

"You've got to stop *tweeting*."

"'Swounds! Strewth! What sayest thou, sirrah? Dost thou forget t'was on thine very own recommendation that I adopted the fine art of *tweeting*?"

"You can't just go around *tweeting* about the word %&$#?@."

"Darling, did I give offense?"

THERE WAS ADELINE. Her son was the child of a Persian father. Her son with eumelanin in the basale stratum of his epidermis, marking him as something other than a member of the social construct of the White race. Her son whom she has witnessed struggle with his racial identity.

She was *tweeting* the word %&$#?@.

She knew that people on Twitter would freak out. She knew that people on the Internet would freak out. That's the whole purpose of the Internet. Freaking out and making money for other people. Why not Adeline?

She never imagined that Jeremy would care. She hadn't even given it a thought.

Adeline was from the 1990s, when confrontational aesthetics were all the rage.

Many artists had become very interested in confronting racism, and, in particular, a subset of eumelaninless artists used the word *%&$#?@* in their confrontations of the social order.

The problem is that the aesthetics of the 1990s weren't only confronting the oppressors of the Patriarchy. They were also confronting people who had, in their day-to-day lives, been called *%&$#?@*.

And many of those people didn't have a lot of interest in the difference between a *peckerwood* in the back of a pick up truck and a pointed critique from SoHo.

"THAT BULLSHIT has been part of my life for years before I met you and it'll be around until the day that I'm dead and gone," said Jeremy. "That's not the problem."

"What ever then is the problem?"

"When you go around *tweeting* about the word *%&$#?@*, people think of me. I'm the one who gets the emails from Scholastic. People come and find me. Everyone knows we're friends. We've worked together for decades. They want to hear what I have to say, and my interest in being your Negro Spokesman is less than zero, Adeline. Negative balance. I've got much better things to do. I'm exhausted. I'm tired. I want to live my life without cleaning up your mess."

Jeremy reached into his pocket. He took out his phone. His phone was an iPhone. The iPhone had *changed everything*.

He stroked the glass of his iPhone and opened up GMail, Google's free e-mail service that served targeted advertisements based on the content of individual user's messages.

"Look," he said, passing the phone to Adeline.

Every email was from a journalist asking about Adeline.

JEREMY REALLY DID have better things. He was busy.

He was freelance writing for a few video game companies and he was still working in comics, doing work for DC on a reboot of *Wild Dog*.

WILD DOG was a comic book property created by Max Allen Collins and Terry Beatty in the 1980s, when Adeline and Jeremy both lived in New York City.

There was a crack cocaine epidemic linked to a meteoric rise in crime. The CIA, which had funded the *good novel,* had also funded the crack cocaine epidemic and the meteoric rise in crime, both causing unfathomable suffering for people with eumelanin in the basale strata of their epidermises.

The comics industry responded to the rise in crime by creating anti-hero vigilantes. These anti-hero vigilantes were different than Spider-Man, a property created by Steve Ditko, or Superman, a property created by Jerry Siegel and Joe Shuster. The new anti-hero vigilantes had no superpowers beyond indignant Whiteness and a willingness to murder.

Almost all of these anti-hero vigilantes had suffered family trauma at the hands of criminals. Dead wives and dead children were very common.

Wild Dog was good with guns, he was ex-military, he wore a hockey mask and a sports jersey that featured an angry cartoon dog.

The mafia had killed his fiancée. Now he walked the streets of the Quad Cities, waging his one man war on crime. Killing domestic terrorists was his business. And business was good.

Jeremy presumed he'd gotten the gig because of a perceived linguistic similarity between the titles of *Wild Dog* and *Trill.*

He was working a post-economic crash angle with an al-Qaeda overlay.

WHEN HE WASN'T WORKING, Jeremy had developed an interest in early recorded American music. He was also in the process of reading all the books by a writer named Anna Kavan.

Jeremy liked Anna Kavan because he thought that her best work was the most exact representation of heroin's psychoactive effects.

Characters in books by Anna Kavan went out on the nod, experiencing elaborate psychoactive fantasies that spiraled out from the moment when they nodded off.

Anna Kavan was fierce. Her prose was ferocious. She was Gothic at a time when no one wanted Gothic fiction. She was the greatest.

AND JEREMY HAD a very active sex life. This active sex life occurred with both his wife Minerva and other partners. Jeremy and Minerva were a Bay Area couple. They had adopted a non-traditional sexual lifestyle.

Which made sense, really, when one considered that they'd met back in 1989, when they were both in their early twenties.

THEY'D NEVER ADOPTED any of the ideological terms that developed in the Twentieth Century to describe arrangements which had existed since the dawn of marriage.

They had never called themselves *polyamorous*, which was another stupid word like *homosexual* with a Greek prefix and a Latin root.

They had never said they were in an open marriage. One time Minerva had suggested they make up their own word and self-apply it.

"What word?" Jeremy asked his wife.

"Winterbloss," said his wife, "Why not *fuckmasters*?"

For obvious reasons, they didn't call themselves *fuckmasters*. They did fool around with other people. Sometimes together.

POLYAMOROUS WAS A WORD made up by a witch named Morning Glory Zell-Ravenheart. The word first appeared in her 1990 article entitled, "A Bouquet of Lovers."

Like Jeremy and Minerva, Morning Glory Zell-Ravenheart had lived in Marin County.

Unlike Jeremy and Minerva, Morning Glory Zell-Ravenheart had filled much of her life in Marin County with the systematic torture of goats.

Morning Glory Zell-Ravenheart and her husband Oberon Zell-Ravenheart had tortured goats by surgically altering the beasts' horn buds to ensure the growth of a single horn centered in the middle of the skull.

The Zell-Ravenhearts wanted to create living approximations of *unicorns*, which were mythical creatures akin to universal health care, gender pay equity, and the democratic acceptance of dissenting opinions.

In 1985, four of the goats tortured by Morning Glory Zell-Ravenheart went on tour with the Ringling Brothers and Barnum & Bailey Circus. The most famous of these goats was named Lancelot.

The circus said Lancelot was a *unicorn*.

But Lancelot wasn't a *unicorn*. Lancelot was a goat that had been tortured by the person who would later invent the word *polyamorous*.

This is 100% true.

NEITHER MINERVA NOR JEREMY liked threesomes. Threesomes required an awful lot of negotiation. You had to work with the feelings of the other person in the marriage and with the feelings of the third party. There was an unfathomable amount of checking-in and touching base.

Talk before the sex, talk during the sex, talk after the sex.

There was the twosome sex after the threesomes, with Jeremy and Minerva making sure that the original equilibrium wasn't disrupted.

Then there was dealing with the inevitable development of better chemistry between the third person and either Jeremy or Minerva.

They gave up on threesomes and started seeing other people on an individual basis.

JEREMY MET WOMEN through a website called OKCupid.

OKCupid asked Jeremy banal questions about his hobbies and religious beliefs. Then the website compared Jeremy's answers with the answers of its female userbase. The website calculated a percentage of shared banality.

Jeremy would send messages to attractive women with whom he shared a high percentage of banality. Or the women would message him.

If the messaging worked out, Jeremy would meet the women in person.

If he met a woman in person and the interpersonal interaction worked out, Jeremy and the woman might have sex.

If Jeremy and the woman had sex, then they would be sharing a new banality beyond their original shared banality.

They would be sharing the futility of the orgasm and its pursuit.

MOST OF THE WOMEN on OKCupid were not interested in having sex with a married man whose wife knew that her husband was having sex beyond the marital bed.

Still, Jeremy learned that if he was upfront and told women about the situation, a sizeable amount would be intrigued and interested. A subsection of that sizeable amount would have sex with him.

THE ARRANGEMENT worked, despite its shaky moments, because Jeremy and Minerva had developed a fairly realistic assessment of human biology and the nature of relationships.

They had been having sex with each other for almost thirty years.

MANY OF THE PEOPLE with whom they slept did not have a realistic assessment of human biology or the nature of relationships.

Lots of Minerva's sexual partners, by-and-large men, were almost psychotic in their need.

Some became jealous of Jeremy. This would happen when a new sexual partner had known Minerva for, at most, a few weeks.

The situation with Jeremy's partners was different. There was a sizeable number of White women who were interested in having sex with a Black man for very unpleasant reasons. These women were to be avoided.

Some of the women he dated had eumelanin in the basale strata of their epidermises. These were Black women and some of them found themselves unhappy about being in a situation where they were having sex with a Black man who had a White wife.

The whole society was idiotic and had created an enormous amount of madness around people from one social construct having sex with people from other social constructs.

This is because American society had an extraordinarily warped idea of beauty that tended to exclude and marginalize women of color.

Especially Black women. Which was manifestly fucking nuts.

EVEN WITHOUT Adeline's ill-fated excursion as an online race commentator, Blackness had been on Jeremy's mind. More than usual. And race was always on Jeremy's mind.

In addition to *Wild Dog*, he was working on a new creator owned comic.

There wasn't a title but Jeremy had written a few scripts.

It was going to be a comic without any supernatural or supranatural or crime elements. It was going to be a realistic depiction of a middle class African-American family.

He'd thought about asking Adeline if she wanted to do the art.

Now that her WaNks Index Score was so low, he was having second thoughts.

DESPITE THE THOUSANDS AND THOUSANDS and thousands of titles published each year, despite almost a century of the comic book, Jeremy's idea was new to the medium.

Comic books were as valid a medium of expression as any other and thus could encompass the simple joys and mistake of a family. Regardless of race.

But it was 2013 and it still hadn't happened.

JEREMY GREW UP as the youngest child of two parents who had attended Howard University.

Much to their later discomfort, Jeremy's parents had met at a *brown paper bag party*, a campus event where the only individuals in attendance were people whose skin color was lighter in shade than a brown paper bag.

Anyway, because of the eumelanin distribution in the basale strata of their epidermises, and because they had earned degrees from an elite institution of higher education, Jeremy's parents had entered the Black middle class and moved to a White neighborhood in Virginia, near Washington, D.C.

They were the only family in the neighborhood with eumelanin in the basale strata of the epidermises.

When Jeremy met Nash Mac, the two men bonded over the fact that their childhood homes were less than forty miles apart.

JEREMY WAS RAISED with access to money. The money had fostered a love for junk media like comic books and Science Fiction.

At his private high school, Jeremy's interest in junk media helped carve out a protective niche.

He was part of a group of kids who sat around and talked about the shifting loyalties of Raistlin Majere, a chaotic-neutral mage, and the seemingly doomed love between Tanis Half-Elven and Lauralanthalasa Kanan, a princess of the Qualinesti elves.

Students at Jeremy's high school hated and feared him because he was Black, but everyone found the situation more socially acceptable if the kids who hated Jeremy pretended that their hatred emerged from his interest in the novels of Tracy Hickman and Margaret Weis.

On the face of things, Jeremy was not a target of victimization and bullying because of his race. He was a target of victimization and bullying because of his *Red Sonja* t-shirt.

WHEN JEREMY went to work for Marvel Comics, he wasn't particularly surprised by racism in the comic book industry.

With the exception of Larry Hama and Jim Owsley, both of who had eumelanin in the basale stratum of their epidermises, the employees at Marvel were adult versions of the people from his high school clique.

And despite a superior attitude derived from their dogged adherence to corporate owned intellectual properties, the kids in Jeremy's high school social clique had been clueless about race. Jeremy had suffered some awful shit at the hands of his friends.

People touching his hair without permission. People who talked about their parents marching with Martin Luther King at Selma and then remarking about how Jeremy acted so White. People calling Jeremy their "Negro High Bard of Endor." People asking him if John M. Ford's *The Dragon Waiting* was a popular novel in the ghetto. People telling him that Octavia Butler's *Kindred* was *okay,* for what it was. People asking him if Samuel Delaney was his favorite author.

JEREMY'S INSPIRATION for his new comic was "My Black Mama," a 78 record by Son House.

Son House was a blues musician from the Mississippi Delta. Son House recorded for the Paramount record label of Grafton, Wisconsin in 1930. He had tons of eumelanin in the basal stratum of his epidermis.

A 78 release was a vinyl disc with enough space for one short song on each of its two sides. In the case of "My Black Mama," the vinyl record contained "My Black Mama, Part I" and "My Black Mama, Part II."

The album was meant for an African-American audience but it was released at a time of economic catastrophe. Its sales were worse than the sales of *Hot Mill Steam.*

Decades later, there arose a general belief amongst record collectors without much eumelanin in the basale strata of their epidermises that musicians like Son House offered an authenticity which rebuked the increasing commercialization of American culture.

There was a general belief that Son House was a primitive with a direct line to pickaninny suffering, an ancientness rural goodness that existed beyond the modern world.

This was, of course, intolerable bullshit.

Son House was a modernist master. He was a genius. Both sides of "My Black Mama" were profound works.

Part II of the 78 release of "My Black Mama" was famous. It became Son House's signature song in later years when White record collectors found him living in Rochester, NY.

Part II is about the singer learning that the girl he loves is dead. He takes off down the road and finds his good ol' gal in a morgue. She's laying on a cooling board.

Basically, it's a reworking of "St. James Infirmary," which in turn was a reworking of "The Unfortunate Rake." When Son House performed Part II in later decades, after he was found by White record collectors, he used the title "Death Letter Blues."

It became a *classic.* It was covered by hundreds of musicians. By and large, the great percentage of musicians who covered "Death Letter Blues" did not have eumelanin in the basal strata of the epidermises.

No one talked about Part I, which was a song about the singer's preference for a woman with a heavier distribution of eumelanin in the basale stratum of her epidermis over a woman with less eumelanin in the basale stratum of her epidermis. It expressed an ideology in exact opposition to that of the *brown paper bag parties* attended by Jeremy's parents.

The focus on Part II fell into very common receptions of African-Americans and their culture. Everyone wanted to hear about Black people dying and being sad. Everyone wanted a Black woman dead on a cooling board.

Part I was a song about how the singer lusted for his black mama, regardless of the consequences, worldly or spiritual.

Jeremy liked the conjunction of the following verses:

You take a brown-skinned woman will make a rabbit move to town
Say but a jet Black woman will make a mule kick his stable down
Oh brown skinned woman will make a rabbit move to town
Oh but a real Black woman will make a mule kick his stable down

There taint no Heaven, there ain't no burning Hell
Said where I'm going when I die, can't nobody tell
Lord, ain't no Heaven now, ain't no burning Hell
Oh, where I'm going when I die, can't nobody tell

Jeremy recognized the humor. It was the humor of his family. Not his nuclear family. His parents and sisters were uptight.

But his extended family.

His uncles and aunts and cousins and grandparents.

Part I was the humor of normal people in normal houses trying to keep on keeping on. It was a humor that did not emasculate the African-American male. It was a humor that had always been there but ignored in favor of good ol' gals on a cooling board.

IT WOULD BE DIFFICULT to launch a new book about an African-American family. It might be possible to go with a traditional publisher and have distribution in regular book stores.

But Jeremy had grown up in the direct market. He had worked for Marvel. *Trill* had succeeded on the strength of the comic book store.

The mentally backwards who made up the comics market were his people. He wanted to do a book that would help bring them to the light and might attract new customers to the stores.

He wanted to do a comic for the Twenty-First Century versions of Jeremy Winterbloss, for the kids who were experiencing the peculiar loneliness of being young and Black and a reader of J.R.R. Tolkien.

NONE OF THIS would be any easier if Adeline kept using the Internet. Nothing about her *tweeting* made Jeremy's life any less stressful.

"Haven't I increased our sales?" asked Adeline.

"You have," said Jeremy.

"Then here's what I shall do," she said. "I shall stay away from the race issue as much as I find possible. I can't promise you the Moon, darling, but I shall do my damndest. I shall not *tweet* about the word *%&$#?@*."

"I wish you'd quit," said Jeremy. "Go cold turkey."

"Darling," said Adeline, "Who told me to use Twitter? Who made me a Facebook account?"

"Me," said Jeremy.

"I'm only trying to make us some money. If I'm going to help Google earn out its filthy lucre then I might as well embrace the future. We all must serve somebody. And ain't that the God's honest, *mon oncle*?"

THEY LEFT COFFEE TO THE PEOPLE and walked to Buena Vista Park.

Buena Vista Park was one of the city's treasures, a sprawling verdant mass built on a hill and filled with ancient trees. Entering it was like passing through a veil into another world.

"Do you remember," asked Jeremy, "when we went to the Grant Morrison signing at Comic Relief?"

"Only vaguely," said Adeline.

GRANT MORRISON was a comic book writer without eumelanin in the basale stratum of his epidermis. Other than the oodles of quality which seeped from his work, Morrison's principle distinguishing feature was that he had the bad luck of being a comic book writer at the same time as Alan Moore.

To paraphrase the preeminent comics critic Andrew Hickey, who had no eumelanin in the basale stratum of his epidermis, if Alan Moore had not existed, Grant Morrison would have been considered the single greatest writer in the history of the medium.

But Alan Moore did exist.

He had no eumelanin in the basale stratum of his epidermis.

And he really was the single greatest writer in the history of the medium. There was Alan Moore and then there was everyone else.

Grant Morrison was doomed to play Number Two.

Life was cruel.

THE SIGNING IN QUESTION happened back in 1993. Grant Morrison was on tour with Vertigo, the more experimentally inclined imprint of DC Comics.

The modern incarnation of DC Comics was distinguished, principally, by having fucked over Alan Moore. They stole his most valuable intellectual property, *Watchmen*.

Having committed this theft, the company cheapened *Watchmen* in the typical fashion: (1) Terrible merchandise. (2) A terrible film. (3) Terrible, creator-unauthorized prequels.

This theft and cheapening was achieved through a series of complex contractual gymnastics which occurred in 1985 between a multinational corporation and someone who had grown up without indoor plumbing.

COMIC RELIEF WAS A COMIC BOOK STORE that had been located on Haight Street. After the store closed, a great number of other establishments had occupied its former address.

In that moment, as Jeremy and Adeline ambled through Buena Vista Park, the storefront was occupied by an establishment called BEHIND CLOSED DOORS.

It sold sex toys and lingerie.

"WHAT I CAN'T GET OVER these days," said Jeremy, "is that the world seems obsessed with everything that I really cared about when I was fifteen years old. Comic books. Geek media. It's all so mainstream. I used to get more shit than you can imagine because of my *Red Sonja* t-shirt."

"Darling," said Adeline, "What if you're a bellwether? What if all American culture is on a thirty year time-delay from your interests at any given moment?"

"Maybe it's been passed on to you. What if it's your interests, right now, that'll determine the tastes of the future?"

"I sincerely hope not," said Adeline, "Or else I've doomed our planet to a terrible dystopia comprised entirely of Krautrock, antique postcards of St. Augustine, and enema porn."

ADELINE WAS ONLY KIDDING. She was using *irony*.

No one with a social life cared about Krautrock.

"EVERYTHING CHANGES," said Jeremy, looking at the ancient trees. "I remember when you lived on our couch. I told you not come in here at night."

"Why ever was that?"

"It was dangerous. There was a lot of violence. They would find bodies."

"Do you know," said Adeline, "I am quite convinced that it's much better to live in cities of our present moment. We no longer face the threat of death on every block. But emotionally, I wish we were back in those bad old days. It kept the scum out. It was terribly frightening, darling, but wasn't it fun?"

"Beats me," said Jeremy. "Why do you think I live in the suburbs? I hate cities. I hated them then, I hate them now."

THEY CLIMBED towards the top of the park.

Adeline challenged Jeremy to a game. She asked him to think of the worst possible way that the tech industry could ruin Buena Vista Park.

"You're the writer, darling," she said, "I should hope that you'll best me at my own contest."

"Give me a second," he said. "I'll think of something."

chapter twenty-eight

"Those assholes," said J. Karacehennem, "fucked with the wrong person."

THOSE ASSHOLES were the nineteen terrorists who hijacked airplanes on September 11, 2001 with the intent of crashing them into the World Trade Center, the Pentagon and the United States Capitol.

Those assholes had managed to crash their hijacked airplanes into the two buildings of the World Trade Center and the Pentagon. The airplane piloted by Ziad Jarrah did not crash into the United States Capitol. The airplane piloted by Ziad Jarrah had crashed in a field in Pennsylvania after its passengers used a food cart as a battering ram and stormed the cabin.

Ziad Jarrah was the subject of *ZIAD*. There'd been a moderate amount of eumelanin in the basale stratum of his epidermis.

J. KARACEHENNEM was walking with Adeline in Chinatown. He had returned from Europe about a week earlier.

This was the first time that he had seen Adeline since his return. He convinced her to go to Caffe Trieste in North Beach.

Adeline met J. Karacehennem at the Powell BART stop. She found him leaning against the railing by the Cable Car, standing with one foot atop a brown box.

"Whatever do you have in the box, darling?" asked Adeline.

"It's the Spanish translation of *ZIAD*. I haven't opened it yet. I opened the original box of *ZIAD* in Caffe Trieste. I figured I'd do it again with the translation."

They walked up Powell to Union Station and over to Grant Street and then up through the Chinatown gates.

"How do you feel about the book being translated?" asked Adeline.

Which is when he said: "Those assholes fucked with the wrong person."

Then he added: "They really fucked with the wrong neurotic. They thought they could bomb the living fucking shit out of America but they didn't realize that twelve years later I'd be making fun of them in Spanish."

JUST THEN, J. Karacehennem bumped into a middle-aged immigrant. The middle-aged immigrant was smoking a cigarette. The middle-aged immigrant had some eumelanin in the basal stratum of his epidermis.

The middle-aged immigrant looked at J. Karacehennem.

"I'm terribly sorry," said J. Karacehennem.

The middle-aged immigrant spit on the sidewalk, threw his cigarette at J. Karacehennem's feet and shouted, "*Gwai lo!*"

"WHAT DID HE CALL YOU?" asked Adeline.

"He called me a *gwai lo*," said J. Karacehennem. "It's Cantonese. It means something like 'white boy' or 'foreign devil.' I used to do Ving Tsun in New York with this kung fu master named Moy Yat. He always was calling us *gwai lo*."

"How charming," said Adeline.

CAFFE TRIESTE was empty except for its regulars. J. Karacehennem had come here for years and had yet to know any of the regulars beyond simple observation.

The regulars were crazed relics of San Francisco from the era before the Internet economy exploded into the collective consciousness.

Radicals and poets and free thinkers. They were all, at the very least, middle-aged. Almost all of them lacked eumelanin in the basal layers of their epidermis.

HE OPENED THE BOX. The cover showed an airplane crashing in the cedars of Lebanon. Ziad was from Lebanon. Adeline and J. Karacehennem fondled the books and drank coffee.

"I simply can not remember," said Adeline. "Did I inform you about Christine?"

"What about her?"

"She's marrying Bertrand. In February."

"Some people move fast," said J. Karacehennem.

CHRISTINE HAD ASKED Adeline to be a bridesmaid.

Adeline was touched but declined.

She'd been in too many weddings, she said, and couldn't stand another. She hated how the wedding party was always on display.

ONE OF THE REGULARS came into Caffe Trieste. His name was Roy. He suffered an unspecified mental illness. He had no eumelanin in the basale stratum of his epidermis.

Roy's mental illness caused him to shout at all of Caffe Trieste's customers. He did this every day.

Roy was also one of the best dressed men in San Francisco. He clothes were always immaculate.

Roy shouted at some tourists.

"Whatever did he say?" asked Adeline. "All I could make out was something about Sicilian bastards."

"I've heard him yell at a million people," said J. Karacehennem, "I can never understand him. He is a perfect example of why Caffe Trieste is the greatest place in the city. Did I tell you about election night last year?"

IN 2012, President Barack Obama ran for re-election against Mitt Romney, the former Governor of Massachusetts, who didn't have any eumelanin in the basale stratum of his epidermis.

It was the usual bargain for J. Karacehennem and other people of the Loony Left.

You supported a person whose policies you agreed with, sort of, but who you felt was too beholden to corporate interests and whose foreign policy made you sick.

If you didn't support this person, the alternative was something even worse. Voting was little more than triage.

J. KARACEHENNEM went to Caffe Trieste and watched the election results. The anxiety fell away very soon. It was obvious that Obama had won re-election.

The night was punctuated by the unexpected appearance of the great and neglected poet Jack Hirschman.

Hirschman was the oldest of the old school. Hirschman was enough of a throwback that he was still an active, believing Marxist. Hirschman had edited the *Artaud Anthology*, a book published by City Lights which Karacehennem had admired as a teenager.

Hirschman stormed in with his great walrus moustache and his long stringy hair dangling beneath a black cowboy hat, a red scarf thrown over his shoulder.

Hirschman waved his arm at the television and started shouting, "HERE IS YOUR DEMOCRACY FOR YOU! HERE IS YOUR DEMOCRACY FOR YOU! HERE IS YOUR DEMOCRACY FOR YOU!"

J. Karacehennem knew that he himself loved San Francisco.

NOW HE WAS SITTING in the same seat, talking to Adeline, and he knew that he hated San Francisco.

"I'm moving," he said. "After *WTF* comes out and I do the events."

WTF was his new book. It was being published in the small press.

"Why now?" asked Adeline.

"This morning," he said. "I woke up to a 400 people protesting outside of my door."

J. KARACEHENNEM really had woken up to 400 people protesting on the other side of his door.

Oh Christ, he thought when he heard the sounds of the crowd, *they've come at last. Why did I write a book about Islamic terrorists?*

The protestors weren't protesting J. Karacehennem.

They were protesting Local's Corner.

THE HOUSING SITUATION in San Francisco was bad enough that people were regularly staging protests against the effects of the tech industry on the rental market.

People were being evicted at a rapid clip.

The cost of living was skyrocketing.

A protest was planned on 24th Street. It started between York and Hampshire and moved towards Mission. As the procession reached Bryant, a decision was made to divert the hundreds of protestors down to 23rd Street.

23rd & Bryant was the intersection that hosted Local's Corner.

J. Karacehennem lived a few doors down.

J. KARACEHENNEM and The Hangman's Beautiful Daughter woke to the sounds of people cheering. And the sounds of people banging drums. And the sounds of a flatbed truck with a PA system parked in the intersection. And the sounds of people yelling at Local's Corner through the PA system.

J. Karacehennem and The Hangman's Beautiful Daughter went outside. They looked at the flatbed truck.

Sandra Cuadra was speaking through the PA system. She was telling the story of how Local's Corner denied her service.

Here is some of what she said: "So another person that was with us said, 'Hey, you know what, let's go to this Local's Corner on 23rd and Bryant. I want to try it out.' I said, 'Yeah, I want to try it out too. It's a new place.' So we walked over here. It was six of us. Two of them were my niece and nephew.

One was 14 and the other one was 12, and we came here to come eat. And it was two people on the outside table and there was I think two other people inside the restaurant. So I walked into the door and I asked the lady, 'Six people.' There was a lady on the ground, kind of cleaning something, and she kind of looked up with the deer in headlights. So she looked at the guy behind the counter, and she kind of looked at him, didn't say anything, she's like 'Uh, uh.' He's like, 'Can I help you?' I go, 'Yeah, there's six of us.' And then he says, 'We can't accommodate you.' And at first I didn't trip, I thought maybe he had to move tables. So we're like, okay, we'll wait a minute. Right, so we're kind of waiting. And then he says, 'No, we can't accommodate you.' I go, 'What do you mean, you have tables inside, right?' And then he goes, 'Uh, uh, uh, we kinda can't.' Right, kind of stuttering, kind of like shocked, he didn't know what to do. So you know, we're like, 'Well, you know, we can move tables together.' We didn't mind eating separately because I have a big family we're used to doing lots of tables. He just kept saying they couldn't accommodate us. And then, you know, kind of wait, pause a moment and he goes, 'You can go to our restaurant over there on 24th Street.'"

SANDRA CUADRA stopped speaking. The protest continued for another ten minutes before moving back up Bryant. People stood outside of the restaurant banging on its windows and beating drums.

J. Karacehennem said to The Hangman's Beautiful Daughter, "We have to move. We can't live like this."

The Hangman's Beautiful Daughter agreed.

"WHEN WE MOVE, we're leaving San Francisco," said J. Karacehennem to Adeline. "I want to leave the city. I hate San Francisco. Or at least whatever the hell it's become. But it's not like we have any choice. There's no way we can find an apartment even remotely comparable for the same rent that we're paying."

"Where ever will you go?" asked Adeline.

"I've got a few events set up for *WTF*. One of them is in Los Angeles. Another is in Portland. I guess we'll look at both cities."

"Portland is so dreary," said Adeline. "It's like San Francisco but even worse. Do you think that your constitution could truly handle a return to Los Angeles?"

"I'm more inclined towards Los Angeles," said J. Karacehennem. "It's still the only place that ever felt like home."

ADELINE DIDN'T SAY ANYTHING but she worried that if J. Karacehennem and The Hangman's Beautiful Daughter dropped out, then it was only a matter of time before everyone else dropped out too.

Adeline herself was fine. Her family was rich. She owned her apartment as part of a tenancy-in-common. But she felt loss around the margins. The slow disappearance of her friends.

For a moment, things had hung in perfect balance.

But all things end.

Adeline learned that on the day her brother killed himself. Nothing lasted. The whole world was on a script of loss and people only received their pages moments before they read their lines.

Adeline lifted up a copy of the Spanish translation of *ZIAD*. She flipped through.

"How is the translation?" she asked.

"*Lo siento,*" said J. Karacehennem. "*¡No habla Español!*"

"Do you feel anything?" she asked. "I remember when mine eyes espied the first translation of *Trill*. It was into that barbaric language of German. I hoped that it would mean something. In the end it meant nothing."

"I guess it makes it real," said J. Karacehennem. "It's too bad, there's another book that I'd love to do. I can't. I just can't. If I do one more book about terrorism, then I'm just that guy. I'm just the terrorism guy."

"What's the book?" asked Adeline.

"I want to do a book about the really hot terrorists and freedom fight-ers from the 1960s and 1970s. People don't remember, but there was this amazing moment when terrorism was high fashion. When you didn't have to be an ugly little man from the middle of nowhere with an overwhelming fear of sex. Terrorists and freedom fighters used to be really hot. Don't you remember Leila Khaled? Leila Khaled was one of the most beautiful women who ever lived! Or Djamila Bouhired? Holy shit, Djamila Bouhired! Don't forget Dolours Price! Fuck, even Gudrun Ensslin or Patty Hearst. It'd be a book about closing doors on a wide variety of semi-valid political expressions. It'd be about the death of romance in modern life. Why are all of today's terrorists so bland and so drab? I'd call it *Death in a Miniskirt.*"

chapter twenty-nine

Ellen Flitcraft of Truth and Consequences, New Mexico was visiting San Francisco. She was crashing with her friend, Hilary, who Ellen knew from UCLA. Hilary didn't have any eumelanin in the basale stratum of her epidermis.

Hilary and Ellen had been freshmen year roommates. They'd lived together at Hendrick Hall, in the close quarters endemic to Third World countries and the student housing of American public universities.

SIX MONTHS HAD PASSED since Ashley Nelson uploaded pictures of Ellen performing oral sex on Maximiliano Rojas.

Ellen'd been fired, she'd been shamed, she'd sunk into a state of anxiety followed by a long depression. She had self-medicated with processed foods. She'd gained weight.

The latter helped, a little. The weight gain made Ellen somewhat unrecognizable to the men of T or C.

Being a woman in a society that hated women, Ellen had spent her post-pubescent life tormented by the unwanted attention of men. After Ashley uploaded the photographs, a personal element had entered the rictus grins of the world's men.

A few men had stopped Ellen and asked about the photographs. These conversations tended to start with opening questions like: "Haven't I seen you somewhere before?"

The questions were rhetorical. Everyone in Truth or Consequences had seen Ellen.

Even Ashley Nelson had approached Ellen. This occurred in the parking lot of the Shell gas station. Ashley more or less admitted that she had uploaded the photographs.

"Everyone's heard that you got yourself into some trouble," said Ashley Nelson. "I don't know if you deserved it, but you always did think you were better than everyone else. It just shows what can happen."

ELLEN WAS STILL taking care of her grandmother. She'd managed to get another job, also in insurance, from an office manager who'd heard about the situation and taken pity.

"The only thing," said the office manager, "and I hate to admit it, but your name is mud. I'm going to need you to work under a new one."

So Ellen Flitcraft, for the sake of business, had become Ellen Pierce.

WHEN THE PHOTOS leaked, Ellen deleted her social media accounts. Months later, she opened new accounts on Facebook and Twitter, using the name Ellen Pierce.

There were no pictures attached to the accounts. Ellen was judicious about whom she allowed to be her Facebook friends and Twitter *followers*. Her WaNks Index Score was 5.

In early August, Hilary sent Ellen a message on Facebook. She suggested that Ellen visit San Francisco, where Hilary was working at a startup called Bromato.

"lol," wrote Ellen in her reply, "what the hell is a bromato?"

"the answer is 2 complicated," wrote Hilary.

Ellen agreed to visit San Francisco. Hilary offered to pay for the plane ticket.

Ellen's vacation took some wrangling with her office manager and her grandmother's neighbor. The neighbor, who burned with the meanness of a Pentecostal Christian, viewed Ellen with a great deal of suspicion but agreed to take care of Ellen's grandmother.

i hate the internet

HILARY LIVED IN A 3BR APARTMENT near the corner of Fillmore and California. She had five roommates. Hilary was being overpaid by Bromato. She was the only person in the apartment with her own room.

She put a spare futon mattress on the floor.

Ellen slept on the mattress.

"The neighborhood isn't that interesting," said Hilary. "I wanted to, like, live in the Mission but this was the only place I could find."

"How much do you pay?" asked Ellen.

"Sixteen hundred dollars," said Hilary.

"A month? That's more than double my grandmother's mortgage. For a room."

"Who wants to live in Truth or Consequences?"

WHILE HILARY WAS BUSY at work, Ellen wandered alone through the streets of San Francisco. She did all the usual tourist crap like seeing the Golden Gate Bridge and taking a boat out to Alcatraz and riding the Cable Cars and going to City Lights, where she bought a copy of *Howl*, which was a poem about men performing oral sex on each other in mental hospitals.

She was amazed by San Francisco's public transportation. Never before had she experienced the sheer pleasure of not driving. Never before had she experienced the wonder of city walking.

On her second day in the city, a young man asked Ellen if she liked getting fucked from behind. She'd been in San Francisco for less than forty-eight hours. This was the ninth man to sexually harass her.

Ellen didn't make eye contact with the young man who asked if she liked getting fucked from behind. She walked away. When she neared the Hilton on Kearny Street, Ellen let herself breathe.

Nine instances of sexual harassment in less than forty-eight hours. It was like being in Truth or Consequences, but at least in San Francisco no one was sexually harassing her for photographs uploaded to the Internet.

Her life had become so baroque that this felt like a relief.

She started walking. A man in a suit asked Ellen to smile.

Ellen walked to Washington Square Park. She sat on a park bench in Washington Square. She started to cry.

The sound drew the attention of another man. He said that Ellen looked too pretty to be so sad.

IN THE EVENINGS, Hilary took Ellen to bars in the Mission, where they met up with Hilary's friends and co-workers. Ellen had resisted the idea at first, saying, "The last time I went to a bar, things didn't end so great."

One night, as they were headed home from a bar called Doc's Clock, Hilary said, "It's been wonderful, like, having you here. No one here fucking cares about any of that shit. Why don't you, just, you know, move here?"

"With what money?" asked Ellen.

"I could totally get you a job at Bromato," said Hilary. "It's not like we have any standards. You should see some of the idiots at work."

"I can't leave my grandmother," said Ellen. "Otherwise, I'd be out of New Mexico in a heartbeat."

ON HER LAST DAY in San Francisco, Ellen's flight back to New Mexico was scheduled to depart at 3 pm. Ellen decided to rise early and walk through the city for a final time.

She woke up Hilary. It was a work day. They said their goodbyes.

"Come back any time you want," said Hilary. "My door is always, like, open."

"I might," said Ellen. "I really might."

She showered and left Hilary's apartment.

ELLEN WALKED TO FISHERMAN'S WHARF, a place that she had avoided on the advice of Hilary's friends. One of these friends, who worked for Facebook, had said, "The only people who hang around Fisherman's Wharf are frat assholes and tourists. It sucks."

But Fisherman's Wharf was the one tourist destination that Ellen hadn't seen. She had no idea if she'd ever come back. So why not?

When she got to Fisherman's Wharf, almost no one was on the streets. Most of the stores were closed. Hilary's friend was right. It did look like a place for frat assholes.

Ellen walked west. She sat down on the small beach of Aquatic Cove, watching the shallow waves lap up against the sand. Back in Los Angeles, she'd always liked the beach.

Not sun bathing. By the time she was thirteen, New Mexico had drained away the sun's pleasure. But there was something about the repetition of the sound of the Pacific.

It was the same thing with Aquatic Cove. Peace washed over her. She felt herself dissolving into the cosmos.

She looked at her phone. She was losing time. There was a plane to catch. She started the walk back to Hilary's apartment.

ELLEN WAITED for the traffic signal to change at the corner of Van Ness and Broadway. The light turned green. Ellen stepped off of the sidewalk.

There were more people on the street than when she'd left Hilary's apartment. They were going to pointless jobs where they would earn meaningless money to buy ugly shit which they thought might alleviate their garden variety misery.

When Ellen was almost halfway across the street, she heard a slight, high-pitched sound.

She felt the blast of wind. She turned. She saw the grey blur of an electric car, less than two inches from her body. She didn't see the driver's face.

The car went through the red light.

Ellen looked to the other side of the intersection. A young woman, about Ellen's age, was rushing across the street.

The electric car smashed into the young woman's body. The young woman flew back four feet and crumpled against the pavement.

ELLEN WAS ONE OF MANY PEOPLE who rushed to the woman. Some were on their cellphones. They were calling the police. The thought hadn't occurred to Ellen.

One man, who had some eumelanin in the basale stratum of his epidermis, took charge of the situation, yelling at everyone to stay back.

"Don't move her," he yelled. "Don't touch her!"

The woman's face was covered in blood. Her breathing was shallow. The gore obscured the woman's features.

That could have been me, though Ellen, *I could be the one on the ground, bleeding and broken, dying amongst strangers.*

The broken body. Van Ness. Broadway. The old church. The faces. The cellphones. A billboard above an apartment building advertising *Man of Steel*.

But there were no men of steel nor women neither.

Ellen walked back towards Hilary's apartment. She had come so close to death. She had almost died and she'd spent the last six months worried about the opinions of people who lived in Truth or Consequences.

She had almost died and she'd spent the last six months tormented over shit from high school. She had almost died and she'd spent the last six months acting as if her life was preordained for failure.

But life wasn't preordained. Life was an electric car just out of the Broadway tunnel, speeding through a red light at Van Ness. Life was a young woman crushed in blood, gathering a crowd of people on their cellphones.

I can't keep living like this, thought Ellen. *I've got to do something else. I can do anything in my life. I can do anything I want.*

MAN OF STEEL was a film adaptation of Superman, a comic book intellectual property.

Superman was worth billions of dollars. Its creators, Jerry Siegel and Joe Schuster, signed over the rights to their intellectual property for $130.

They were both 24 years old. They were from Cleveland. It was 1938.

A BLOCK LATER, as her thoughts cleared, Ellen realized that she had no money and was returning to Truth or Consequences to care for an elderly woman. Life wasn't an either/or proposition. Life was both random death and decades of suffering. Life was a trickle of days that dripped away with no meaning and no purpose.

She had been raised to think that her identity was hers and hers alone. But Ashley Nelson had taught Ellen a lesson.

A person's identity wasn't just about what they wanted or how they lived or the choices they made. Life wasn't made of self-determination. Life was the Chinese wage slave manacled to a factory line, building iPhones. Life was a $130 cheque in 1938. Life was about trying to salve the wounds inflicted by other people, fixing the damage done by strangers and friends.

And thanks to the corporations headquartered in, around and near San Francisco, the capacity for that damage was infinite.

chapter thirty

Christine was out with her friend Denise. Denise was one of Christine's bridesmaids.

Denise and Christine were having drinks at The Two Sisters, a literary themed bar on Hayes Street. They avoided the specialty cocktails. They both ordered vodka sodas.

They talked about the wedding. Christine and Bertrand had come up with a way to minimize the misery of planning.

They decided to get married at City Hall.

"We'll be just like Marilyn Monroe and Joe DiMaggio," said Christine. "Plus, it's cheap. It's only a couple thousand."

JOE DIMAGGIO was a native of San Francisco who played baseball for the New York Yankees from 1936 until 1951, punctuated by a four year break for World War Two. He didn't have any eumelanin in the basale stratum of his epidermis.

Baseball was a *sport,* which meant that it was a formalized system of control. Baseball involved moving balls around a constricted space in an attempt to create the illusion of meaning.

Joe DiMaggio's time with the New York Yankees had created enough illusion that he ended up as ill-conceived metaphorical bullshit in Ernest Hemingway's short novel *The Old Man and the Sea.*

The Old Man and The Sea was a book about how a senior citizen demonstrates the continued potency of his testosterone reserves by killing a dumb animal before being outwitted by other dumb animals.

MARILYN MONROE was the world's most famous actress until an allergic reaction to celebrity forced her to swallow a bottle's worth of Nembutal. She didn't have any eumelanin in the basale stratum of his epidermis.

She married Joe DiMaggio at San Francisco City Hall.

The marriage ended in tears.

Then she swallowed a bottle's worth of Nembutal.

When Christine said that she and Bertrand would be like Marilyn Monroe and Joe DiMaggio, she didn't mean that her marriage to Bertrand would end in tears and then Christine would swallow a bottle of Nembutal.

She just meant they'd have a nice wedding.

CHRISTINE AND DENISE left the Two Sisters. Denise walked towards Market Street. Christine walked towards her apartment. She stopped at a Thai restaurant on Haight Street.

She ate some green curry chicken and then walked home.

About ten minutes from her apartment, she felt very strange. It was as if she'd drunk six vodka sodas instead of two.

SHE STUMBLED into her apartment. Her head was spinning. She couldn't do anything but she didn't want to sleep. She decided to watch something on Netflix, so she watched Béla Tarr's *The Turin Horse*.

Netflix was a streaming video service. Christine paid Netflix $7.99 a month and in turn Netflix gave her access to a wide range of films and television programs.

THE SCREEN WAS BLACK.

The title appeared in white text: *A TORINÓI LÓ*.

Narration began over the black screen.

The narration was about the German philosopher Friedrich Nietzsche and a horse he encountered in the streets of Turin.

Christine's eyes rolled back up into her head. She knew that she was going to be sick. She wasn't sure how but she knew that she had been poisoned.

She ran to her bathroom. She flung open her toilet.

She vomited and vomited and vomited.

When there was nothing left in her stomach, she felt sober.

"Can I blame Béla Tarr's for this?" she asked the empty air. Then she said a prayer to Ray Kurzweil.

But, really, Béla Tarr hadn't poisoned Christine. Neither had the alcohol. It was the green curry chicken from Haight Street. The meat was bad.

Do yourself a favor. Stop eating chicken.

THE NEXT AFTERNOON, Christine still felt wobbly. She couldn't go out. She invited Adeline over to her apartment.

Adeline was happy to come over. She liked Christine's apartment and she liked Christine's cat. Christine's cat was a fat old Maine Coon named Beard.

Back in New York, back in the 1980s, Adeline and Baby had co-owned a Maine Coon. They had named him Captain Jenckes of the Horse Marines.

They'd found the name in a book about Maine Coons. The first Maine Coon that appears in the historical record was named Captain Jenckes of the Horse Marine.

"Captain Jenckes of the Horse Marines" was a mouthful. So Adeline and Baby called their cat The Captain.

Beard reminded Adeline of the Captain.

ADELINE AND CHRISTINE were sitting in Christine's living room. They were talking about the wedding.

"I'm sorry to keep going on," said Christine. "Ever since I said yes, I feel like I can't talk about anything except getting married."

"Have you and your beau decided upon the ceremony?"

"Bertrand is a failed Catholic," said Christine. "We can't be married in the Church. For obvious reasons. I think we're going with a justice of the peace," said Christine. "It's easiest for everyone. Me included. You have no idea about how stressful this is until you've gone through it."

"Which is one reason," said Adeline, "that I have long eschewed the diabolical art. Not that I stand in judgment on your decisions."

"I didn't think you were," said Christine.

"Have you arranged matters with your families?" asked Adeline.

"It's complicated," said Christine.

THE COMPLICATIONS emerged from Christine's decision to outwardly conform as a woman. She had been always been a woman but she was born with the reproductive biology of a male. She had lived the majority of her life outwardly conforming as a man.

Some members of her family continued to insist that Christine was a man. They did not take seriously the schism between gender and sex. They believed that Christine would grow out of it and return to being a man.

Christine had never been a man. She was always a woman.

Her brother had come around. Her mother was tolerant. Her father wouldn't speak to her. This says nothing of the extended family.

When Christine was still called Christian, she lived as a gay man. Her extended family practiced a benign tolerance towards Christian being a gay man. They disapproved but didn't exclude.

Christine as a woman proved too much.

It was possible that Christine would only have two family members at her wedding.

BERTRAND'S FAMILY was no easier.

Christine had warned him that he should approach the topic of her pre-transitioned life with caution. She had told him, flat out, that she didn't mind if he never told his family.

"I don't care if a bunch of people in Belgium know about my personal history," said Christine. "I have my own problems here in America."

Bertrand insisted on telling his parents and his siblings. He said that if they loved him then they too would love the person that he loved.

This was before he had proposed marriage.

"Be careful," warned Christine. "Nothing is ever as simple as you think."

Bertrand hadn't listened. He did a very poor job preparing his family for the news.

He called his parents and told them flat out. He did the same with his siblings. The same with his aunts and uncles and cousins.

It went worse than when Christine had told her family that she was no longer Christian.

Other than one cousin who was an artist and lived in Berlin, none of Bertrand's family was coming to the wedding.

And his cousin could only make the wedding if Bertrand paid for her airfare and found her a place to crash.

"IF THERE'S ANYTHING I'm glad about," said Christine, "It's that gay marriage is legal in California again."

"Darling, you aren't gay," said Adeline.

"It's a little sad but I never legally changed my gender. It's so much paperwork. Now there's not enough time."

ADELINE TOLD CHRISTINE that Adeline was working on a new comic called *The Blind Washerwoman of Moorfields*.

"Have you done much work on it?"

"Only the first few pages. The Blind Washerwoman makes her way through the familiar town of her birth. She thinks of her old father and how cruel it is that death takes us all."

CHRISTINE WENT INTO HER BEDROOM and came back. She was holding a magazine.

"Have you seen this?" she asked.

She gave Adeline the magazine, which appeared as it does on the next page.

The Iran Opportunity By Fareed Zakaria / E-Cigarettes / $20K Homes

TIME

CAN

Google

SOLVE

DEATH?

The search giant is launching a venture
to extend the human life span.

That would be crazy—if it weren't Google
By Harry McCracken and Lev Grossman

FAREED ZAKARIA was one of the many best selling authors and *public intellectuals* who supported George Bush II's War in Iraq. He had a decent amount of eumelanin in the basale stratum of his epidermis.

Back during the War in Iraq, Fareed Zakaria had believed that bringing something like Jeffersonian Democracy to a country with no history of participatory politics would be a net good. He believed it would stabilize the Middle East.

This opinion had been very popular with *public intellectuals* in the run-up to the War.

Most *private intellectuals,* who were people without best selling books or prominent media positions, had opposed the War.

IF YOU WERE FROM CALIFORNIA and the year was 2013, and you were discussing the consensus amongst *public intellectuals* who supported the War in Iraq, you might say, "It was, like, so *ironic,* because, you know, like, all of America's, like, *public intellectuals* supported a total, you know, disaster of a war and, like, thought, that there could be, like, you know, democracy in Iraq."

You'd be wrong.

There was nothing *ironic* in the wrongness of a bunch of dumb assholes who offer bogus opinions for money.

Dumb assholes who offer bogus opinions for money don't need to be right. They only need to be loud.

"I WAS VERY MUCH CAPTIVATED," said Adeline, "by news of Sergey Brin's affair."

Sergey Brin was one of the co-founders of Google. He was married to Anne Wojcicki.

Over the summer, news had broken that Sergey Brin was having an affair with an underling at Google X.

Google X was an experimental lab that developed products like driverless cars, dogs that don't need to lick their own genitals, and *Google Glass.*

Google Glass was a wearable computer built into a pair of ugly eyeglasses. *Google Glass* allowed its wearers to act out their social inadequacies. They could record videos with *Google Glass* and alienate everyone in their surrounding vicinity.

Sergey Brin's sexual dalliance was with the Marketing Manager for *Google Glass.* He had internalized his company's business model.

"I told you," said Christine. "Google X is just picking up chicks."

ADELINE DECIDED TO GO HOME. Christine saw Adeline to the door.

Adeline was in the hallway.

"There's something I need to tell you," said Christine.

"Yes, darling?" asked Adeline. "It's not about Google, is it? Whatever will they solve next? Gravity?"

"Bertrand and I have been talking," said Christine. "I think I'm giving notice on this place. After the wedding. I think we're moving to the East Bay. There's enough money to buy a house. You know, in case we ever want to start a family."

"Good luck, kid. You're gonna need it," said Adeline. "I shall miss you."

chapter thirty-one

In September, Adeline asked Minerva to help with a project. Minerva agreed. If for no other reason than to escape San Venetia and the hospital.

"Sure thing, bright girl," said Minerva. "When do you want me?"

"Tomorrow afternoon," said Adeline.

WHEN ADELINE VISITED SAN FRANCISCO in 1993, she stayed on Jeremy and Minerva's couch on Steiner off of Haight Street.

By the time of Adeline's arrival, Minerva had whittled away a year as the lead vocalist and guitarist in an almost all-girl punk band called Daddy Was in KGB.

Daddy Was in KGB had a gimmick. None of its members had eumelanin in the basale strata of their epidermises. Other than the drummer, all of its members were women and former citizens of The Union of Soviet Socialist Republics.

Which was also known as the USSR. Which was also known as the CCCP. Which was also known as The Russians.

The Russians were the people who caused the CIA to fund literary fiction. There was the idea that literary endeavors could open up a valid front in the information war.

KGB stood for Комитет государственной безопасности, which translated into English as The Committee for State Security. The *KGB* were the Russian equivalent of the CIA.

The *KGB* didn't fund literary fiction.

Mostly, the KGB just kicked the shit out of Russian writers.

jarett kobek

MINERVA MET THE OTHER MEMBERS of her band at Night Break, a now-defunct music venue on Haight. Night Break hosted Sunday events called *Sushi Sundays.*

During *Sushi Sundays,* local bands performed on Night Break's stage while a sushi chef served spicy tuna rolls to punk rockers, metalheads, heroin addicts and tweakers.

ANYWAY, THE BAND'S FEMALE MEMBERS met on a *Sushi Sunday.* There was Minerva and there was Vasilisa and there was Galina.

They spoke Russian and discovered a shared love of three chord punk. They discovered a mutual desire to be in a band.

Minerva could sing, sort of. She had a guitar that she could play, sort of. Galina could play guitar, too. Sort of.

Vasilisa's roommate had a bass guitar. Vasilisa couldn't play bass but that didn't matter. Bass guitar was punk's least important instrument.

Most people ignored it.

MINERVA, WHO HAD ATTENDED the Parsons School of Design, designed a flyer stating that the band was in search of a drummer.

She took the flyer to a copy shop. She was friends with one the employees. She ran off about 300 copies of the flyer. The employee hated his boss. He didn't charge Minerva.

The flyer was taped to lampposts across the city.

A HANDFUL OF PEOPLE RESPONDED.

The only decent applicant had four serious defects: (1) He was 16 years old. (2) He wasn't a woman. (3) He was American. (4) He lived in San Rafael.

But Minerva liked the kid. His drum sound was primitive and crude.

She convinced her fellow ex-Soviets by saying, "What is problem? Making music with pubescent is perfect punk rock. He is dissonant note in symphony of disaster."

DADDY WAS IN KGB lasted a few years. They recorded a demo and released two 7" vinyl records.

Then the drummer made a pass at Galina, which was rebuffed, and then he went to college.

Then Vasilisa got pregnant after a one night stand with the guitarist from another band called DRUNK PEOPLE R LOUD.

And that was weird because Vasilisa was a lesbian.

But whatever. People are complicated.

The band broke up.

MINERVA COULDN'T REMEMBER who suggested it, but someone said that she should look into nursing. Which she did. It turned out that she loved it.

She believed that the confrontational aesthetics of Daddy Was in KGB were not about offending or hurting people but about healing them from their personal and social traumas.

Now she was healing bodies from physical trauma.

It was all the same thing, really. It depended on your point of view.

MINERVA PICKED UP ADELINE.

"What do you need, bright girl? Why do you need car?"

"Darling," said Adeline, "I can't fathom whether or not you've made the acquaintance of my friend Christine, but I have simply accepted her crackpot theory that the Bay Area is nothing but a very great monstrosity of advertising. What I want to do is drive out to the airport, and then as you drive back, I will photograph every billboard as we approach the city. Perhaps we can know San Francisco's unconscious thoughts."

"Sure thing, bright girl," said Minerva.

AS THEY DROVE TO THE AIRPORT, Adeline told Minerva about the latest Twitter scandal.

A journalist named Caroline Criado-Perez had started a campaign to get Jane Austen on the ten pound British note. Thousands of people signed up and supported the effort. Caroline Criado-Perez's WaNks Index Score was 2.577861406696081.

Jane Austen was a writer from the Nineteenth Century who had written books about marriage and money.

The Bank of England acquiesced. The Bank of England announced that Jane Austen would appear on the ten pound British note.

After the Bank of England announced that Jane Austen would appear on the ten pound British note, certain users of Twitter were outraged.

They were furious. They were frothing at the mouths. They were dumb assholes. Nothing is more odious in a society that hates women than a woman who expresses an opinion.

The more that people *tweeted* about Caroline Criado-Perez, the more that Twitter could serve advertisements. Nothing made people *tweet* like outrage.

So Twitter made money off of rape and death threats sent to Caroline Criado-Perez.

Adeline watched with fascination.

"Darling," she said to Minerva, "If I keep on, I am rather sure I am going to receive my own threats of rape and death."

"Fuck all bullshit men," said Minerva. "Fuck them until they die. You say what you want. Fuck them all."

MINERVA ARRIVED at San Francisco International Airport. She turned off the 101 South and then merged on to the 101 North. She drove all the way to Market Street.

Adeline was in the passenger seat with her camera. Her camera used actual 35mm film. She made Minerva drive in the right lane at 45 miles per hour.

Adeline took pictures of every billboard along the highway. These advertisements were the first thing which travelers saw upon entering the city. They were premium messages of the moment.

THIS IS WHAT SAN FRANCISCO was saying in September 2013. This was the message of the streets, if only it could be deciphered and interpreted. These were the pieces of a puzzle:

i hate the internet

(1) Giant Sweep

This billboard advertised a public service campaign spearheaded by the city of San Francisco and the San Francisco Giants. The San Francisco Giants were a baseball team which generated the illusion of meaning by winning the 2010 and 2012 World Series. *Giant Sweep* was a campaign dedicated to keeping San Francisco clean by guilting its citizens into performing services that should have been financed through taxes on the obscene wealth of its residents.

(2) iPad

This billboard advertised the iPad. The iPad had *changed everything.*

(3) Distributors Run NetSuite

This billboard advertised business management software, which was a tool for middle management boors. It allowed them to craft the illusion that their jobs had purpose in large, bureaucratic institutions. NetSuite was co-founded by a billionaire named Larry Ellison.

(4) Corporate mobile data will double this year. Are you in control?

This billboard advertised a company named Druva, which offered secure data integration across computers, tablets and mobile phones. Druva had raised funding from the venture capital firm Sequoia Capital.

(5) Oracle Open World, Sept 22 - 26, San Francisco, #OOW13

This billboard advertised a conference dedicated to the products of Oracle, a company that sold database management software to other companies. Oracle was co-founded by a billionaire named Larry Ellison.

(6) NetApp is the world's #1 storage OS? Yes, NetApp.

This billboard advertised NetApp, which was a company that offered remote data storage to other companies. Back in the 1990s, NetApp had raised funding from the venture capital firm Sequoia Capital.

(7) #1 for a Reason

This billboard advertised Trend Micro Inc, a Japanese company that sold consumer and enterprise level security software and services.

(8) IMAGINE 30 YEARS OR MORE OF DOING WHAT YOU LOVE. Let's get ready for a longer retirement.

This billboard advertised retirement and money management services with Prudential Insurance Company of America.

(9) iPad

This billboard advertised the iPad. The iPad had *changed everything.*

(10) New Homes at Candlestick Cove With 2-Car Garages

This billboard advertised condos for sale in the low $700,000s.

(11) puppetconf 2013

This billboard advertised PuppetConf 2013, a conference organized by puppet labs. puppet labs was a company that had raised capital from Google's venture capital firm Google Ventures. puppet labs offered software that automated routine tasks performed by systems administrators, leading to a market environment in which automation had rendered most systems administrators inept and moved them ever closer towards obsolescence.

(12) Join the Learning Revolution

This billboard advertised a product called Litmos, offered by CallidusCloud. Litmos allowed companies to create videos and training materials that worked along the moronic and ill-conceived principles of *e-learning*, which was an ephemeral system of pedagogy designed by people who hated teachers and formal education.

(13) RingCentral. Many locations. One cloud phone system.

This billboard advertised RingCentral, which was a company that offered cloud-based phone systems. RingCentral had raised funding from the venture capital firm Sequoia Capital.

(14) TAKE A BREAK FROM HAVING IT ALL TO ENJOY IT ALL.

This billboard advertised the Bay Club, a chain of private fitness clubs and spas located throughout the Bay Area.

(15) TechCrunch DISRUPT SF 2013

This billboard advertised the TechCrunch DISRUPT 2013 San Francisco conference. TechCrunch was a website that provided biased, pro-industry pseudojournalism about developments in imaginary technologies. DISRUPT was the name of TechCrunch's many conferences, after *disruptive innovation,* a popular Silicon Valley concept developed by a Mormon who believed, literally, that he was in verbal communication with God.

(16) The All New Droid

This billboard advertised the Motorola Droid, which was a smartphone. Motorola was a company owned by Google. The brandname *Droid* was a trademark of LucasFilm and licensed to Motorola. LucasFilm was owned by Disney.

(17) #1 for a Reason

This billboard advertised Trend Micro Inc, a Japanese company that sold consumer level and enterprise level security software and services.

(18) iPad

This billboard advertised the iPad. The iPad had *changed everything.*

chapter thirty-two

It came to pass that J. Karacehennem and The Hangman's Beautiful Daughter had packed up their lives. The movers had come and taken everything away.

Their apartment was empty. They were moving tomorrow.

J. KARACEHENNEM spent his last night hanging out with Adeline. The Hangman's Beautiful Daughter didn't mind.

She had her own plans. She was going to a dinner party full of people for whom she didn't particularly care.

"It's your last night in the city," said J. Karacehennem. "Why would you spend it with people you can't stand?"

"I agreed months ago," she said. "Before we knew we were moving. I can't just cancel."

"Sure you can," said J. Karacehennem. "Just don't show."

"That's not how I am," said The Hangman's Beautiful Daughter.

So she sat around eating mediocre vegan food while listening to the inane babblings of people for whom she didn't particularly care.

The topic of discussion was Miley Cyrus.

MILEY CYRUS was a pop star.

You could say MILEY to almost anyone anywhere in the industrialized world and conjure a vague neurological image of Miley Cyrus.

Her songs were about the same six subjects of all songs by all pop stars: love, celebrity, fucking, heartbreak, money and buying ugly shit.

PEOPLE WERE TALKING about Miley Cyrus because she'd spent the summer changing her image.

Miley Cyrus's career had started as a teenaged actress on the Disney Channel, a cable network owned by the company founded by Walt Disney.

Miley Cyrus produced a great deal of intellectual property for Disney. All of this intellectual property was targeted towards children. It dripped with sugar and tasted of bubblegum.

By the Summer of 2013, Miley Cyrus had grown into a young woman and adopted a public image resting on conspicuous consumption, drug use and open sexuality.

It was hard to remember, but there'd been a time when the Political Left had considered drug use and open sexuality as tools of liberation.

Then it turned out that Republicans liked to fuck and shoot smack, too.

ANYWAY, MILEY CYRUS appeared at MTV's Video Music Awards with an unmemorable pop singer named Robin Thicke, who had no eumelanin in the basale stratum of his epidermis.

Robin Thicke had stirred some controversy over the summer with his hit pop song, "Blurred Lines."

Social activists on Twitter, Tumblr and Facebook had taken issue with the song's lyrical content, which they believed promoted rape.

The song's promotional video featured a gaggle of half-naked female models sporting glazed expressions and an inability to dance on beat. The models looked, basically, like they were full of heroin.

Social activists wrote many long screeds and *tweeted* heavily about Robin Thicke's "Blurred Lines." They were challenging the prevailing social trends that they found mirrored in the content of the song.

Their social activism occurred on mechanisms owned by the Patriarchy. Their social activism occurred on platforms designed for the sole purpose of advertising.

So all they did was advertise for Robin Thicke. The sum total effect of the protest was to make Robin Thicke richer.

THERE WAS MILEY CYRUS at the Video Music Awards. She was on stage with Robin Thicke. She was engaged in a form of dance known as *twerking*.

Twerking was characterized by the *twerker* squatting low while thrusting their hips back and forth. This thrusting caused the *twerker's* buttocks to shake in a manner that many moral scolds considered sexual but actually just looked goofy.

Twerking had been a traditionally African-American and Afro-Caribbean dance, meaning that it originated and was performed by people with eumelanin in the basale stratum of their epidermises.

Miley Cyrus didn't have eumelanin in her epidermis.

SO THAT WAS THE SUBJECT of the dinner party's inane babbling. A group of middle-aged White people sat around discussing Miley Cyrus's cultural appropriation of *twerking*.

The Hangman's Beautiful Daughter suffered the evening.

MEANWHILE, J. KARACEHENNEM picked up Adeline in a rental car. He had rented the car for the next day, when he and The Hangman's Beautiful Daughter would drive to Los Angeles.

"Darling," said Adeline as she climbed into the car, "do you want to eat first or must we indulge your madness?"

"It has to be at 8PM," he said. "I don't think we have time for food before then."

J. KARACEHENNEM had told Adeline that what he wanted to do on his last night in the city was drive to the top of Twin Peaks and scream at San Francisco.

Twin Peaks were a pair of hills near the center of the city. They were marked by a giant television antenna called Sutro Tower. The tower was visible from almost anywhere in the city. From Twin Peaks, you could see every neighborhood with any importance to J. Karacehennem.

You could see the Haight. You could see the Richmond. You could see the Sunset. You could see the Financial District. You could see Hayes Valley. You could see Corona Heights. You could see North Beach. You could see, sort of, Fisherman's Wharf. You could see the Presidio.

"It's madness," said Adeline. "*C'est fou!* I shall accompany you if you insist."

"What else is there to do?" he asked. "I want my John Galt moment."

"Who is John Galt?" asked Adeline.

"That's the question, isn't it?" said J. Karacehennem.

JOHN GALT was the central personage of Ayn Rand's *Atlas Shrugged*. It is John Galt who organizes a strike of the world's richest people. It's John Galt who gives a 60 page speech about how poor people are worthless trash that should die in the gutter.

J. KARACEHENNEM drove to the top of Twin Peaks. There was fog over the city. Neither J. Karacehennem nor Adeline expected the park to be very busy.

As they got out of the car, Adeline noticed that it was very cold. She assumed that the weather was too frigid for anyone to deliver a speech. She also noticed that the cold hadn't stopped the tourists. A large number appeared to be from China. They were taking pictures of the city, even though much of it was obscured by fog.

"Darling," Adeline said to J. Karacehennem, "if you're going to do it, then now's your moment. Otherwise let's go and eat."

THE HAND OF THE CLOCK reached the dot of 8.00.

"Ladies and gentlemen," said the voice of J. Karacehennem, "Mr. Thompson will not speak to you tonight. I've taken over. You wanted to hear a report on the world crisis but instead you will hear me babble like a maniac for an ungracious amount of time."

The tourists turned to look at J. Karacehennem. He had done many book events. He had learned how to project his voice. He could be very loud indeed.

Adeline tried not to feel mortified.

"For twelve years, you have been asking: who is J. Karacehennem? This is J. Karacehennem speaking. I am the man who is sick of San Francisco. I am the man who has come to shout impotently at a city from a hillside scenic overlook. If you wish to hear the babblings of an incoherent lunatic, then I am the man for you."

The tourists moved in closer.

Oh great God almighty, thought Adeline, *What if he starts screaming about Falun Gong and UFOs?* After all, he was his father's son.

"San Francisco," continued J. Karacehennem, "You are the worst place on earth! You have taken the dream of a bohemian enclave for misfits and morons and you have transformed it into a Disneyland for the nouveau riche. You have replaced your artists and your independent movie theaters with locally sourced restaurants! You have taken an enormous shit on the independent value of culture. You have made it exponentially harder for freaks to find peace! San Francisco, though you may not believe it, I am here to inform you that your shit stinks!

"You have given shelter to the worst people imaginable. You have elevated annoying nerds to minor celebrities. You have made us suffer beneath the terrible lash of Mark Zuckerberg. You have bequeathed to us a vision of the billionaire in a hooded sweatshirt and you have created an environment in which no one will acknowledge the idiotic theater of a billionaire in a hooded sweatshirt!

"You have taken the last true good thing, the initial utopian vision of the Internet, and you have perverted it into a series of interlocking fiefdoms with no purpose other than serving advertisements. Listen, San Francisco, I was there. I know what the Internet was like before people used it to make money. I am the only literary writer in America with a serious tech background! I am the only literary writer in America who ran Slackware 1.0 on his 386sx! I am the only literary writer in the world who coded his own BBS software in badly indented C++! I am the only literary writer in America who can use the ncurses library!

"The Internet is in my blood. I am of the Internet. I know that everything on the Internet which we take as inevitable was engineered by nerds with a fondness for shitty novels. The reason why people harass teenagers into suicide is because a bunch of White dudes with no sense of the human experience decided that they would build anonymity into the Internet as a feature rather than a bug! You nerds have blood on your hands!

"Fuck Steve Jobs and fuck your worship of Steve Jobs. Steve Jobs was no more than nothing! His only distinction was that, unlike every other awful CEO in tech, he had a mild sense of design. His jeans were rubbish! His turtle necks were awful! He owed seven percent of Disney! Apple was a company run by a bully surrounded by cultists so indoctrinated that they didn't realize they were being bullied. In the end, all the sycophancy killed their god! The man's death was the most public suicide since Marilyn Monroe or maybe Jesus Christ! I know, I know, I know. I know that my criticism is without merit because I know that the iPad *changed everything!*

"San Francisco, you are the most beautiful city in America and you are full of America's most annoying people! You were annoying before the tech people arrived! You created a half-baked gauzy ideology of narcissism disguised as self-empowerment and now you have spread your filth across the world! Philip K. Dick saw you for what you are! That's why he wrote *The Transmigration of Timothy Archer.* You are nothing more than a city of people who thought they could brute force their way to enlightenment by buying a Beatles LP! You haven't changed!

"Fuck anyone who believes it is their duty to lecture poor people about the appropriate terminology! You bags of shit put forth your commentary on platform technologies owned by your enemies! You are making money for rich White dudes! Every critique of the racist cisgender homophobic misogynistic patriarchy that you post on Tumblr just makes money for Tumblr! All you're doing is advertising for the very people and companies that perpetuate the economic system of injustice which you are supposedly challenging!

"Fuck your unbelievable ability to pick on the powerless. Fuck all the crocodile tears that you shed every time a mentally backwards idiot calls some Turk a towelhead camelfucker! I don't give a fuck about the opinions of illiterate gas station attendants in Dubuque! It's so easy to demonstrate your own righteousness and it's so easy to challenge the social order when all you're doing is picking on idiots who are better off ignored and left to wither in the stench of their own lives! You have transformed activism into high school politics! You are no better than nothing! To Hell with all language police!

"You are buried beneath your own celebrity gossip! Buried beneath *tweets* about how awful it is that drunken Republican Congresspersons from the South hold opinions you don't like! You are a city and a nation of bullies and you are very selective in your targets! Maybe it's not the fault of the people who use these elaborate mechanisms of the Internet! Maybe it's the fault of the people who engineered these systems to prey on the worst instincts of the human race because preying on the worst instincts of people is a much better way to generate advertising revenue than appeals to the angels of our better nature!

"Fuck your insipid and limp vision of multiculturalism which has nothing to do with the lives of the people outside of your hidey-holes! I have no fucking idea what you're talking about! Come to Hollywood Boulevard on a Saturday night and reconcile your racial and gender politics with the club scene! Please, save me from my ignorance! Please, tell me more about Pussy Riot!

"Down with your literary people, San Francisco! Down with all literary people! Book people are the only people who had the natural resources to resist the Internet's misery! Book people are the only people who have a half-way interesting argument to make against the Internet! Instead, book people rolled over like dogs at the kitchen table! The very first time that they saw a website! Begging their master for a scratch of the stomach! Publishing evolves and consolidates and rots from the inside but no technology can ever overwhelm Charlotte Brontë! Nothing can deal with *Villette!* Nothing ever changes, the world is the same as it was in 79AD! The empire never ended! The only defense is William MAKEPEACE Thackeray and Gloria Naylor! Now all writers are on Twitter, pretending they can't spell in pathetic attempts to win a larger audience! Fuck all of you! Fuck all of you except for Kevin Killian! Kevin Killian is the only one amongst you who's worth a damn! And Dodie Bellamy too!

"Fuck every teenager who talks with his or her parents! Your parents are the fucking enemy! They love having you on the Internet! They can monitor you! You must throw down the tools of your oppressors! You must rebel against *tweeting* about television and you must cast down your iPad, even though it has *changed everything*. You must hold vinyl records close to your heart and listen to them while you read paperback books and stop taking the drugs your parents' doctors have prescribed for you! If you must do drugs, teenagers of America, have the decency to buy street drugs from actual dealers! Make sure your gay sex is perverse! Stop having cute gay sex! Straight people are your enemy! They only want you for a pet!

"San Francisco, fuck your ethnic cleansing! Fuck the massive decrease in your African-American population! Fuck your gentrification! Fuck your working class, too, for being so deluded by the shiny baubles of consumerism that their every protest only comes too late, when the die is cast and the deed is done! Fuck everyone who thought that the newest business would improve the neighborhood only to discover two years later that they couldn't afford their rent!

"San Francisco, your future is a vast ethnic ghetto! The Mark Zuckerbergs of the world are working on immigration reform. They don't give a fuck about Latinos but they love using Latinos as a disguise for their agenda! Their goal is to replace their existing workforce with workers from Asian countries. Because tech workers from Asia will work for one-third the salary! All the low level cogs in the tech industry are so fucked up their own asses that while they were hosting public mournings for net neutrality, they failed to get anything like a political education! They have no idea what's happening to them! They can't conceive of the natural path of business! They can't believe that all companies which create a middle class then systematically dismantle it!

"All of your luxury condo developments will be the slums of the future! You will have tens of people crammed into every 2BR shithole and none of the new residents will care about your granite counter tops with full backsplash or your handset ceramic tile entries or your European hinges or your melamine interiors! You will be a dystopian slum like in the shitty novels that all the tech idiots read back in the 1980s, except nothing will be fun and the hackers won't be cool! There is no cypherpunk future! The cypherpunk future is cancelled! The future will be like the past! Boring and full of shitty jobs! Poor people bussed to and fro, working on the latest rollout of the PageRank algorithm!

"Fuck you, San Francisco! I'm moving back to Los Angeles where the rich people are honest in their deceits! I am moving back to Los Angeles where all of the bullshit is transparent because everyone is a total idiot! I am moving back to Los Angeles where I can watch SpongeBob SquarePants sexually harass teenagers on Hollywood Boulevard! I am moving back to Los Angeles where gentrification barely works because everything is a hideous strip mall and there is nothing worth destroying!

"San Francisco, true change is possible! All you need to do is install adblockers on every web browser! It can all change tomorrow if you spend the three minutes on Google learning how to dismantle Google! Do it! Freedom is yours!

"A short term solution! The fundamental problem is that every technology embeds the ideologies of its creators! Who made the Internet? The military! The Internet is the product of the Defense Advanced Research Projects Agency! We call it DARPA for short! Who worked for DARPA? DARPA was a bunch of men! Not a single woman worked on the underlying technologies that fuel our digital universe! Men are the shit of the world and all of our political systems and philosophies were created and devised without the input of women! Half of the world's population lives beneath systems of government and technological innovation into which their gender had zero input! Democracy is a bullshit ideology that a bunch of slaveholding Greek men constructed between rounds of beating their wives! All the presumed ideologies of men were taken for inescapable actualities and designed into the Internet! Packet switching is an incredible evil!

"The Internet is the last stand of the Patriarchy. It was designed by warmongering men to systematically dehumanize women! The whole thing is fucked! It's where straight men are hosting their final battle! They've discovered the grim truth of their own obsolescence! They lost control of the complex systems we call society, so they created a new one! A new one where they could play by their own rules! Rules devised according to the tepid pseudo-philosophical thought of Ayn Rand and junk science fiction! Women, you can't win! Not if you play on their terms! Not if you use the Internet!

"Women must develop their own Internet! They must group together and engineer a new, gynocentric Internet and they must exclude all the stupid assumptions of men in its implementation and design! They must not repeat its mistakes! No bullshit about freedom of speech, no bullshit about individual liberties, no bullshit reimagining of juvenile literature! No IPv4! No packet switching! Packet switching is the root of all evil! When women have finished engineering their own Internet, they must ban men from it! For at least ten years until the bugs are worked out!"

J. Karacehennem stopped talking.

"That's all I've got," he said.

"How do you feel?"

"It didn't really do much. I guess it was worth trying."

ONE OF THE TOURISTS walked up to J. Karacehennem. She was a young woman, maybe twenty-two years old.

Her father was a powerful man who had made a great deal of money enslaving his countrymen and making them build consumer electronics like the *iPad* and the *iPhone*.

She had not come to Twin Peaks to hear the towelheaded son of a Turkish camelfucker holler into nothingness.

She stared at him. He stared back.

Then she said, "Diu nei puk gai gwai lo."

This is what it meant: *Fuck you till you fall down in the street, foreign devil.*

chapter thirty-three

Then it was New Year's Eve.

Adeline was invited to a soirée at Mike Kitchell's apartment. Mike Kitchell's apartment was on 26th Street near Mission.

Mike Kitchell was best friends with J. Karacehennem. Adeline suspected that her invitation derived from the simple fact that J. Karacehennem had fled San Francisco and Mike Kitchell felt a little lonely.

THE TRANSITION from 2013 to 2014 came in Mike Kitchell's kitchen, with everyone looking through Mike Kitchell's windows. Fireworks were exploding over the Mission.

Adeline even smoked a few of Mike Kitchell's cigarettes. Mike Kitchell smoked Marlboro Menthol Lights 100s. Cigarette smoking was a vice that Adeline did not enjoy or indulge. But she was slightly drunk and it was 2014. So she lit up.

Mike Kitchell's boyfriend Dean Smith was there. Dean Smith was an excellent artist with too small of a reputation.

Mike Kitchell was *tweeting* about New Year's Eve. His WaNks Index Score was 8.374449339207048.

Konrad Steiner was there. So was Tatiana Luboviski-Acosta. So was a friend of Tatiana Luboviski-Acosta, but Adeline failed to catch the friend's name.

A few days earlier, Tatiana Luboviski-Acosta's apartment had burned down. Tatiana Luboviski-Acosta had been out of town.

J. Karacehennem, Mike Kitchell, Dean Smith and The Hangman's Beautiful Daughter spent Christmas morning rescuing the cat.

The cat was fine. The apartment was destroyed.

Everyone agreed that 2013 had been, without question, the worst year that they could remember.

Only Tatiana Luboviski-Acosta had a moderate amount of eumelanin in the basale stratum of her epidermis.

ERIK WILLEMS was not there. Adeline thought about inviting him but he was busy.

His Royal Highness Mamduh bin Fatih bin Muhammad bin Abdulaziz al Saud, also known as Dennis, was in town.

Dennis was having a housewarming party. He'd just closed on the top floor condo of a building on Alabama Street.

Dennis's new condo featured custom LED-lit soffits and built-out niches, an EcoSmart fireplace with white oak surround, radiant heat floors with zone nested controls, a Siedle video intercom entry and alarm system, automatic sun shades, ebony stained rift-cut white oak floors, a private elevator to every level of the home including the panoramic view roof terrace, a poured concrete gas fire pit, a Calcutta marble kitchen with custom German designed Leicht cabinetry, Axor and Hans Grohe bathroom fixtures, two Carrara marble bathrooms with Toto low flush toilets, CAT-5 wiring for phone and data, and shielded CAT-6 for media.

"Maybe we'll make one another's acquaintance later," said Adeline. "I will be *tres enchantée*, darling."

AROUND 12:30AM on January 1st, 2014, Adeline left Mike Kitchell's apartment. She walked over to South Van Ness and headed north.

At the corner of 25th Street, she stood beside a bar called the Phone Booth. The Phone Booth was a relic from an earlier era, named for the giant Telco building across 25th Street at Capp.

The Phone Booth had been a gay bar for the phone company's gay employees. A lot of the gay people were gone but the bar still felt queer.

Until New Year's Day, 2013, the Phone Booth had allowed its patrons to smoke on its premises.

This had been illegal since 1998. No one really cared.

But San Francisco was changing. The patrons of the Phone Booth could no longer smoke indoors.

Anyway, Adeline was outside of the Phone Booth. Someone from inside called her name.

Adeline looked inside and saw Minerva sitting at a round table by the door.

MINERVA WAS DRINKING with a man named Salaam, which was one of the Arabic words that meant *peace*. Salaam wasn't an Arab like Dennis. He didn't speak Arabic.

He was called Salaam because his parents were hippies from Berkeley. Salaam's hippie parents had a startling lack of eumelanin in the strata basale of their epidermises.

Minerva and Salaam were sleeping together. He was one of Minerva's extra-marital sexual partners. Minerva had extra-marital sexual partners because she was a *fuckmaster*.

Adeline sat down. Though she knew of the *arrangement,* she had never met any of the extra-marital sexual partners of either Jeremy or Minerva.

Adeline avoided Marin County, which was the seat of Jeremy and Minerva's copious fucking.

Adeline didn't avoid Marin County because it was the seat of Jeremy and Minerva's copious fucking. She avoided Marin County because it was full of rich assholes like George Lucas. She avoided Marin County because it was the kind of place where words like *polyamorous* were invented following sessions of goat torture.

It felt odd to see Minerva with another man. It'd been decades of her and Winterbloss.

Adeline couldn't see the appeal. Salaam seemed a bit of a bore. He kept talking about Arcade Fire.

ARCADE FIRE was a Canadian band which experienced minor popularity in the early 2000s before transforming into a market commodity that aging parents used as a theoretical common reference point with their Internet addicted children.

Adeline could never imagine liking Arcade Fire, let alone talking to Emil about Arcade Fire.

Poor Emil. He was emailing with increased regularity. Most of the messages asked Adeline to quit Twitter.

SALAAM OFFERED to buy Adeline a drink. Adeline asked for a vodka soda. Salaam stood and went to the bar.

"What is new, pussycat?" asked Minerva.

"Image Comics has agreed to publish *The Blind Washerwoman of Moorfields* as an on-going."

"Wonderful. Did you tell Winterbloss?"

"I only received the news but a few hours past," said Adeline. "I owe it all to Jeremy. We've come a long way from the days of Marvel rodgering Jack Kirby. But, darling, should we speak of Jeremy before your little friend?"

"Life is strange," said Minerva. "Salaam is decent. Excellent bedman."

"If it makes you happy, dear," said Adeline, "then who can say anything?"

Salaam came back and pushed a drink at Adeline.

She took a sip. It was astoundingly powerful.

"I suspect this evening will end poorly."

ADELINE WATCHED PEOPLE on the makeshift dance floor. The pool table had been turned sideways and was being used as a DJ booth. The empty space was filled with writhing bodies.

Someone had left a pair of novelty glasses on the table beside Adeline.

The novelty of the glasses was that the glasses celebrated the New Year by arranging the numerals 2-0-1-4 around the human face.

A person wearing the glasses would be demonstrating her affinity for the year 2014 through its constituent numerals being arranged on her visage.

Adeline picked up the glasses and put them on her face. She wore the year over her eyes.

"THIS PLACE is really full of *hipsters*," said Salaam.

Hipster was a popular word on the Internet. Back in the previous century, *hipster* had an actual meaning. Now it was just a way for a speaker to indicate his or her dislike of someone whose disinterest in the speaker left the speaker feeling intimidated.

One of the *hipsters* came up to Adeline.

"Don't I recognize you from somewhere?" asked the *hipster,* who wasn't a day over twenty-two.

"Darling," said Adeline. "I'm the artist. Marina Abramović. The artist is present! Perhaps you do not recognize me because I wear the year on my face."

"No, you're lying to me," said the *hipster.* "You're not Marina Abramović."

"Darling," said Adeline, "I am."

"You are not Marina," said the *hipster.* "My parents are friends with Marina. I've spent time with Marina. I've totally been to Marina's loft."

"So, what you're saying, dearie," said Adeline, "is that you come from serious money."

ADELINE BID A FOND ADIEU to Minerva and Salaam.

She was back on South Van Ness. She texted Erik Willems.

He texted her back. It turned out that he was on 24th Street, eating a vegetarian burrito at Taqueria Vallarta.

He told Adeline to meet him at the corner of South Van Ness and 24th.

SHE MET ERIK WILLEMS at the corner of South Van Ness and 24th Street. They embraced. Adeline stuck her tongue in Erik Willems's mouth. She suggested that they go to her apartment.

"We can do that, but let's walk down a few blocks. There's a party that I should pop into and say hello."

"Darling," said Adeline, "Must we?"

"It won't take long," said Erik Willems. "It's for work. Someone texted me. Ron Conway is there, and he's wearing a lampshide on his head."

"Fine," said Adeline.

THEY WALKED for a few blocks. Adeline was drunk.

"What I find so fascinating," she said, "is that you consider yourself an Objectivist, don't you? Isn't it true that you adhere to the pseudophilosophical tenants of Ayn Rand?"

"We've talked about this before," said Erik Willems. "I'm not a strict Randian, but yes, I think there's something to be said for Objectivism."

"Which means that you believe that A = A. You believe that there are objective facts the observer can know through rational thinking?"

"Yes," said Erik. "I've told you before. Yes."

"Darling," said Adeline, "Please, tell me again, how can an Objectivist like you also believe in the floating value of the cupcake and the pastry? How can the ass be both the cupcake and the pastry if A = A and A ≠ B? I think I may have rather identified a logical inconsistency in your system of thought."

"I'm so tired of hearing you talk about the cupcake and the pastry."

"Oh, dear," said Adeline. "Is that not a problem for thee, sirrah? Surely for thine own self to tire of the cupcake of the pastry is a betrayal of your sweet whole life, is it not? Isn't every little thing that you speaky, in the end, all the opinions of you Internet lost boys, all the precious thoughts that you cast into the wind, all the vertical integration and decisioning and disruption and incubation and innovation and cross-function collaboration, all of these little kisses that you scatter across Never Never Land, isn't it all just someone in a *Star Wars* t-shirt talking about the cupcake and the pastry?"

ERIK WILLEMS left Adeline standing at the corner of South Van Ness and 17th Street.

She wondered if he'd come back or if he was gone. She wondered if he'd left temporarily or if this was for forever.

In the past, Adeline had walked away from men on the street. In the past, other men had walked away from Adeline.

She was a *MILF*. She was kind of famous. She was rich. She was using the Internet.

She didn't care. She decided to walk home.

ADELINE HADN'T GOTTEN FARTHER than a block before she heard the sounds of a crowd. She looked across the street.

It was a large number of Latino youth. They were drunk and they were stoned and they were screaming. They were celebrating 2014.

She heard a bus pulling up opposite her.

It was a *Google bus*.

THE DOOR of the *Google bus* opened. A team of twenty engineers emerged.

They all sported *Google Glass*, a wearable computer built into eyeglasses. The principle virtue of *Google Glass* was that it allowed its wearers to record videos and thus act out their social inadequacies by alienating everyone around them.

Adeline made a clucking noise about the team of engineers wearing *Google Glass*. She thought that they looked simply absurd.

Then Adeline remembered she was still wearing 2014 on her face.

The engineers all wore matching t-shirts which read: GOOGLE GOES GAGA.

They were lead by a diminutive little man who wore black vinyl pants from the 1990s.

The little man pointed at the Latino youths.

The little man screamed.

This is what the little man screamed: "There stands a shaika of cheap stinking chip oils, O my droogies, let us meet them on battle field with chain and nozh and britva. Come up and tolchok these globby moodges and let spill their krovvy keeshkas!"

THE LEAD ENGINEER was speaking *Nadsat*. *Nadsat* was an imaginary dialect invented by Anthony Burgess for his dystopian Science Fiction novel *A Clockwork Orange*. This novel had been turned into one of the greatest films ever made.

In *A Clockwork Orange*, both the film and the book, teenagers speak *Nadsat*, a kind of criminal slang polyglot influenced by the penetration of subliminal Russian propaganda into popular culture.

Youth gangs in *A Clockwork Orange* speak *Nadsat* whilst they are rampaging in the streets.

The youth gangs go on the prowl in a search of the old *ultraviolence*.

THE LEAD ENGINEER screamed.

This is what he screamed: "Come on, you filthy rotting groodies. Come and get one in the yarbles, if you have any yarbles, you eunuch jelly thous!"

The Latino youths rushed towards the employees of Google.

The employees of Google rushed towards the Latino youths.

ABOVE THE DIN AND CLAMOR, just before the violence, Adeline's cellphone vibrated.

Comes now a message someone sent her on Twitter.

This is what it said: "Drp slut... hope u get gang rape.... bi bunch, uv siphilis elegial aliens............"

Comes now another message someone sent Adeline on Twitter.

This is what it said: "Bitch... im cumin 2 kill u... in San Francisco..."